HE SAT UP STRAIGHT AND STIFF. "Don't you have to study or something? Go home. And—"

"Keep my mouth shut? Yeah, I got it."

"Now, Nick." He stood, held the restaurant door open.

I stomped by him, mad as hell. A car on the far side of the nearly empty lot backfired, its moaning transmission wailing its departure. I thought nothing of the raggedy beater as I snatched up my bike to ride home.

That little oversight would come back to haunt me later.

LAMAR GILES

Amistad
An Imprint of HarperCollinsPublishers

Amistad is an imprint of HarperCollins Publishers.

Fake ID
Copyright © 2014 by Lamar Giles
All rights reserved. Printed in the United States of America.
No part of this book may be used or reproduced in any manner whatsoever without written
permission except in the case of brief quotations embodied in critical articles and reviews.
For information address HarperCollins Children's Books, a division of HarperCollins
Publishers, 195 Broadway, New York, NY 10007
www.epicreads.com

Library of Congress Cataloging-in-Publication Data
Giles, Lamar R.
 Fake ID / L. R. Giles. — First edition.
  pages cm
 Summary: "An African-American teen in the Witness Protection Program moves to a
new town and finds himself trying to solve a murder mystery when his first friend is found
dead"— Provided by publisher.
 ISBN 978-0-06-212185-1
  [1. Mystery and detective stories. 2. Conspiracies—Fiction. 3. Witness protection
programs—Fiction. 4. African Americans—Fiction.] I. Title.
PZ7.G39235 Fak 2014   2013032149
[Fic]—dc23   CIP
                                                                                      AC

Typography by Megan Stitt
  20   PC/LSCH   20 19 18 17 16 15 14 13 12
❖
First paperback edition, 2015

For Adrienne, if only I could write something as great as you.

FAKE ID

CHAPTER 1

THIS IS HOW YOU GET YOUR ass kicked.

Bump into the wrong girl. Or have her bump into you. Whatever.

It was my first day at a new school, so I didn't *know* she was the wrong girl. In the moment, the way we met seemed as right as right could get. Considering how things have been for me and my family the last few years, I should've known better.

How right can things ever be when you're running for your life?

First-period gym. The worst class scheduling scenario ever. You either sweat and stink all day or indulge in a group shower where the water's never hot. I was hating Stepton High already.

As the new guy I got a pass on jumping jacks and squat thrusts while Coach Peyton dug through endless cardboard cartons for a crimson-and-gold uniform that might fit me. Before handing over the clothes, he laid them flat on his desk and wrote my name beneath the school's crest with a Sharpie: *N. Pearson*. My name . . . here.

He shoved the shirt, tiny shorts, and a combination lock in my arms, then jerked his head in the general direction of the boys' locker room.

Outside his office the gym had an old feel, like in those historical sports movies where the team plays a championship game against racism or something. I could tell by the bleachers. They were wooden with that weird gloss from years of staining. The bottom row had handholds, to extend them manually.

My last school had new bleachers made of tough plastic that deployed with a button push. The school before that had a sports complex with three different, interchangeable areas. The one before *that* shared a stadium with the local college teams because they were good at everything and drew large crowds.

Stepton High's gym, with its regional and district championship banners—no state—most more than a decade old, told me they weren't good at anything. No big deal. I was used to downgrading.

Coach Peyton knocked on his window and made this exaggerated pointing gesture toward his watch, then toward the locker room again. I moved on.

Sneakers squeaked like mice on the hardwood. My new classmates were engaged in a volleyball game. At the far end of the floor girls clapped and stepped in sync before one exploded into back handsprings. Jocks and cheerleaders. I could've been watching kids on TV.

A loose group of student invalids sat consigned to the bleachers with crutches, casts protecting mending bones, and suspiciously large asthma pumps. The PE usual suspects.

Except for the one Latino kid.

Despite some conservative glasses, he seemed physically able and wasn't sucking down chest medicine. It wasn't him I noticed as much as the camera hanging from his neck. The thing looked like it weighed fifty pounds, but I would've spotted him even if he'd been sneaking snapshots with his iPhone. It's what I'd been taught to look for . . . and avoid.

You won't find a yearbook picture of me at any of my old schools.

My stomach sank when he lifted his big camera with its big lens, aimed at me, and fired. I heard the shutter click in my head even though he was halfway across the gym.

Maybe I should postpone the locker room, I thought. *See what the hell his problem—*

Her forehead smacked my chest.

It didn't hurt. I was half a foot taller than her, had her by at least thirty pounds. She bounced backward, her footing off. Falling.

Reflex took over. I dropped my uniform and lock, snaked an arm around her waist, and bent my knees slightly so we didn't both go down. At the same time she looped an arm around my neck to catch herself. We looked like (bad) dancers.

"*Mira donde vas*," she said, wincing from the accidental head butt.

Spanish. I didn't speak the language.

It must've shown. She rephrased. "Walk much?"

"Sorry." I shifted my weight and put her back on her feet. "I didn't mean to get in your way."

Behind her, a couple of giggling girls gave me an up-and-down look, ran away.

The girl I'd bumped steadied herself, said, "It's okay. I'll live."

I barely heard her, though. Too busy *seeing* her.

You know how in the movies when a gorgeous girl enters the scene there's music, and slow motion, and fans blowing her hair? None of that happened or anything, but for the first time, the concept didn't seem stupid. She made a gym uniform look *good*.

She was Latina, thus the Spanish. About five five and athletic, black hair with brown highlights, and sun-darkened skin despite the cool weather. You couldn't *not* notice this girl.

She retrieved a pink lip-gloss tin from her pocket. When she popped the top, the scent of candy watermelon overwhelmed. With her index finger, she smeared a thin coat of pink gel on lips that didn't need the help. I watched like it was a spectator sport.

"Are you okay?" she asked, noticing my stalker stare.

I looked away, my heart beating like I'd run a mile. "I wanted to make sure you're not hurt."

"I'm not."

"And that you're not mad at me."

A knowing smile. She was used to attention, to the vibe I was throwing off. "I don't know you well enough to get mad at you."

"Yet."

She moved onto the court. I couldn't let her go that easy. "What's your name?"

Without breaking stride, she turned, walking backward and stretching her shirttail so I could read the faded ink below the school's crest: *R. Cruz.*

"What's the *R* stand for?"

Another smile. "Guess you've got a mystery to solve."

She skipped to the cheerleaders at the end of the volleyball court while I gathered my uniform and lock. Watching her go, the corners of my mouth turned up. A mystery. I was happy to take the case.

That's where I messed up. I was so happy that I forgot about the guy with the camera.

So happy I didn't notice the squeaky sneakers were silent, the volleyball game over.

So happy I didn't see the four guys following me into the deserted locker room.

Happy has a short battery life in my world.

I was deep in the locker maze, seeking an unoccupied unit, when they jumped me.

Quick, padding footsteps and huffing breaths were the only warning. They'd done this before, a pack of wolves cornering that day's deer.

I'm no f'n deer.

The chubby kid bear-hugged me from behind. I dropped my shoulder and hooked his arm, sheer reflex. I spun him—*SMACK*—into a wall of lockers. In the same motion, I slung my backpack off my shoulder so there wasn't much for the guy to grab on to. Wasn't him I had to worry about.

His *clone* came in low from my other side and scooped my legs. He lifted me, then reversed direction; grimy floor tiles rushed up at me. He pinned me before two more guys joined in.

I swung, but on my back with no leverage, I barely clipped his chin. He drew back his fat fist to show me a better punch.

"Not the face," one of them said. "Not yet."

The fat kid nodded. The *other* fat kid—his twin, not his clone—helped him wrestle me up. They looked chunky but had some muscle happening. Not tough guys though. Not taking orders the way they were. They were clowns. Dee and Dum.

The third guy was shorter than me, and slim. He seemed a little too Boy Band for this kind of thing. He stood off to the side, leaning on a locker like someone was about to take his picture.

The last guy—the Leader—looked built for this. He had me by a few inches, with a bull neck and shoulders stuck midshrug. His eyes flickered, giving me a millisecond to tense my abdomen before he swung.

It felt like he hit my spine from the front. I squeezed my eyes shut against the pain and he hit me again before I could open them. I sagged, but Dee and Dum kept me upright.

"I seen you checking out my girl, dude. Didn't you see him, Russ?"

Boy Band Russ said, "Yep. I saw him."

Leader looked to Dee and Dum. "Did y'all see him?"

They nodded in unison.

He said, "You want her, you little puss?"

If I had the breath to sigh, I would've. His girl. I could still smell her watermelon lip gloss.

"You ain't pretty enough." Another gut punch. "Not yet." And another. "We can work on that."

Balling my shirt collar in one fist, he cocked the other to start improving my looks.

Then a nuke exploded.

That's how bright the flash seemed.

"Eli," Leader said, "I know you didn't."

"I did."

Leader stomped away. Dee and Dum let me collapse so they could follow their master like loyal dogs. Russ peeled himself off the locker he was holding up and strutted along, too. They'd all lost interest in me. Thanks to Eli, whoever he was.

I expected someone the size of the Rock. Not the scrawny kid with the camera who'd been staring me down from the bleachers. He stood there as casual as the guys busting me up, nudging those black-framed glasses high on his nose.

Leader approached the little guy. "Eli, what are you going to do with that picture?"

"Depends."

Leader huffed, "On?"

"Photoshop. I'm not sure how twisted I can make it look before I post it on the net."

"Whatever. Like I care about that web-prank crap."

"I bet you'll care if I email this directly to your coach. Last I heard you've been walking a thin line."

Leader loomed over Eli, a redwood and a sapling. "You don't like breathing much."

"Zach, if you *could* kill me, you would've done it by now."

Leader—*Zach*—clenched and unclenched his fists, then, "Come on, fellas. Enough fun for one day."

He shot me a final, hateful glance, then rolled. Russ, Dee, and Dum on his heels. A quiet moment passed after they left. Air hummed through the vents overhead.

Eli reviewed the camera's digital display. "I didn't even get a clear shot." He approached me and offered a hand. "Lucky for you they didn't know that."

"Tell me about it," I gasped, and got my feet under me.

I hobbled into the bathroom area, turned on the cold water. It ran rusty at first, and I waited for it to clear. That didn't ever happen, so I shut it off and dry patted my checks until I felt halfway normal again. I checked my face in the mirror, then lifted my shirt and looked for bruises. None yet.

I said, "Who was that guy?"

"Zach Lynch."

"Lynch? For real?" Somewhere my civil-rights-era ancestors were shaking their heads.

"He's an all-star athlete and all-world dumb ass. Let me guess, you breathed in the same vicinity as Reya."

Reya. What the *R* stood for.

Eli snapped his fingers an inch from my nose. "Hey, hey. That spacey look in your eye, I hope it's not for her. She's trouble in a training bra."

If I remembered correctly, she wasn't in training. But, point taken.

"What's your name?" he asked.

The question surprised me despite all my coaching. Too busy thinking about the girl, a classic downfall. Five names—one real, four manufactured—scrolled through my mind. I came to the most recent and said it as naturally as I could. "Nick. Nick Pearson."

"I'm Eli, but I guess you know that already." He extended his hand. "Glad I found you."

I bristled. *Glad I found you.*

Not *glad to meet you.*

More coaching came to mind. I heard Deputy Marshal Bertram's voice: *If anything seems suspicious, don't downplay it. You have instincts for a reason.*

"You were watching me from the bleachers." I prepared to punch him in the throat. I wouldn't be caught off guard again.

"Yeah. I'm your student guide. All new kids get assigned one. I saw you go in the locker room, and I saw Zach follow you."

I relaxed. A little. He seemed to be telling the truth, none of the tics or tells I'd learned to look for (and hide) over the years. Something else bothered me, though. "You saw them following me, but you didn't jump in until a minute ago. Why wait so long if you were going to help at all?"

"Well, my job is to get you oriented. To tell you how things are. But I think Zach and his crew taught you everything you need to know. Welcome to Stepton High. Stay—"

"—low-key."

"Wow," Eli said, "a mind reader."

Not quite. That's just another of Bertram's maxims. *Stay low-key.*

Great job so far, Nick.

Eli looked away. "Are you pissed? That I didn't help sooner, I mean?"

"No." He came when it counted. And I'd taken beatings before at other schools.

Eli smiled. "Sweet. Time for the rest of the tour."

"What about gym class?"

He pulled two blue laminates from his jacket. Hall passes. "I have significant influence around here, Nick."

I laughed. He didn't even sound like *he* believed that, but scoring the passes was a plus. I grabbed my stuff, jammed my gym uniform and lock in my bag, and left the locker room, realizing Eli was a decent guy to save my ass at all.

I took his tour. Didn't see anything wrong with it at the time.

I might've reconsidered if I'd known he'd be dead in a month.

CHAPTER 2

ELI WALKED FAST, AND DIDN'T POINT out anything of interest. His tour kind of sucked.

I said, "I've never heard of a student guide before. What's that about?"

"We get a lot of new kids," Eli said as we made what felt like a random turn. "There's an army base between us and the next city. Whenever new soldiers get stationed there, their kids will either go to Portside High or here. It happens so much the school started assigning people to show the transfers around. You an army brat?"

"Naw," I said. It was all I said.

We stopped at a solitary door on a hallway where the ceiling lights flickered more than they actually lit. Eli said, "Here it is."

"Here *what* is?"

"The most important room in the school."

"Unless this is a secret entrance to the girls' locker room, I call BS."

He frowned, produced a key ring, and granted us entrance.

I wrinkled my nose. "The most important room in the school smells like mildew."

"That is the smell of current events. Welcome to the J-Room."

He paused, waiting for my reaction. No, he didn't have to explain what the *J* stood for. I said, "Journalism."

My student guide was a newspaper nerd.

The J-Room was the size of a large walk-in closet. Maybe. Enough space for one window, a couple of desks—the biggest propped up by two books because the front legs were too short—an ancient Apple computer, and a dot matrix printer. There wasn't room for a bookshelf so all the reference volumes were arranged along the far wall in teetering stacks, some as high as my belt buckle.

Eli said, "I know it's not much. But we're doing some powerful things."

"We? You have a staff?"

"Not exactly." He rounded the largest desk, set his camera aside, and unlocked the bottom drawer, retrieving a laptop. Sci-fi decals—*Star Wars* and *Legend of Korra* and *Fringe*—adorned it, along with a large, blue crown decal that I assumed was his Lord of the Rings battle crest or something equally geeky.

He continued, "The *Rebel Yell* is more of a solo operation at the moment."

"The what?"

"We're the Stepton Rebels—our mascot. The paper is the *Rebel Yell*."

"Like, from the Civil War?" I didn't remember a lot of history, but I did remember that little skirmish. First a beat down from Zach Lynch, now a newspaper in the tradition of the Confederacy. We'd probably eat lunch in the Ku Klux Kafé.

"I know. Not very PC. I've lobbied to change the name, but you know how they are about their traditions here in the South."

They. Not we. At least he recognized that the rebels his paper was named after probably wouldn't have much more love for a Latino kid than they would for me.

"I've been recruiting new talent," he said, not casually, while waiting for his machine to boot.

I bit. "How's that going?"

"You tell me."

That's what this tour and the "I'm a man with significant influence" stuff was about.

I ran my finger across the old Macintosh and took off about eight years of dust. "I don't know if this is really my thing."

He got twitchy. "Sure. Okay."

I probably should've left then. It would've been better for me in the long run. But where was I supposed to go? My next class? Next fight? Or the next town? I'd been doing that for three years. I was sick of next. "Let me think about it. I'm still getting used to things around here."

Eli's expression didn't brighten, but shifted to an I've-heard-that-one-before kind of bland.

"It's cool, man." His focus shifted to his glowing laptop screen. "I've got some important stuff to work on, so . . ."

I looked over his shoulder and caught a glimpse of the document header. "What's Whispertown?"

Eli snapped the laptop shut. "That's staff business."

"Of which I'm not a part."

"I just mean it's boring. Really boring."

"It's not a good idea to tell your recruits how dull the work is."

"Fine, not boring."

"Let me see." I moved in closer.

Eli leaned forward, curling his arm around the computer the way smart kids hunch over test papers to ward off cheaters.

"Bro, chill. I'm not going to take your stuff."

He relaxed. Or tried to look like he was relaxing. "I know, I just . . . I lied, okay?"

"Depends on what you lied about."

"Whispertown isn't boring at all. It's pretty big-time."

Sure it was. The prom theme, or the title of the school musical. "So if I sign up as part of your staff, then I get full access. Is that how it is?"

"Don't take it the wrong way. I can't show Whispertown to anyone until I'm absolutely sure. I'm almost there, too. I just need to confirm some things. Okay?"

He'd misunderstood my last question, at least the feelings behind it. I wasn't mad. Who understood secrets better than me? But he really didn't want me to walk away from this newspaper thing. I saw an opportunity. "The whole secret-story angle . . . that's how you sell a job. Makes it sound cool."

"So you're in?"

I raised my hand. "Didn't say that."

"Oh."

"Do I get to play with any of the equipment? Like this camera?"

I reached for it hesitantly, gauging his reaction. He looked horrified, like I was reaching for his thigh, but fought his reluctance. "Sure," he said, too loudly. "It's really the school's anyway. I just keep it most of the time."

I picked it up, even though I knew he didn't want me touching it. After his heart attack over his precious story, I figured he wouldn't risk scaring me off over the camera, too. I'd been counting on it.

"This is sweet." Pretending to scan the room, I stopped with the lens on Eli. "Don't move."

"Oh, I get it. Revenge for the shot I took in the gym."

Not exactly.

The camera was in review mode. I clicked through the last few images. Me in a fight. Me walking into the locker room. Me talking to that girl. I paused on that for half a second too long.

"Do you know how to work it?" Eli asked.

"I got it." I deleted all the pictures of me before taking a quick shot of him. Bertram applauded in my head.

Eli asked, "How's it look?"

I turned the camera off. "I don't think I'll be shooting models in the Caribbean anytime soon."

The bell rang, signaling the end of the period.

Eli gathered his laptop and camera as I stepped into the hall.

"You sure you aren't mad about Whispertown?" he asked.

I couldn't have cared less about Whispertown. Not at the time. "I'm sure."

"As far as joining the paper . . . ? I could really use the help."

"I'll think about it. Seriously."

Students trickled into, then flooded, the corridor beyond the lonely hall where the J-Room was located. Eli said some more stuff about the paper but I didn't hear because I spotted Reya walking with friends, laughing, her hair bouncing like in those shampoo commercials. Again, I thought of those movies with the slo-mo and cheesy music.

It *was insane*. Bumping into that girl had copped me a beating during my first hour at Stepton High. Yet I was still drinking the Kool-Aid.

She stopped laughing when she looked my way. I smiled. Smooth. She grimaced, raised her fist, and extended her middle finger slowly.

Ever see somebody—like actually caught them in the moment—when they planted one foot into a steaming pile of fresh dog crap? Then you might be able to picture the look on Reya's face.

Tiny, hot needles pricked my cheeks and forehead. I was glad Eli's hall was deserted. I couldn't tell if my embarrassment was noticeable or not. At least here, he'd be the only one to see, and he'd already seen me look worse.

When I turned from Reya, I found Eli flipping double birds in her direction.

He waved both middle fingers in a rhythmic taunt. I looked to Reya, then back to Eli, then back to Reya, and understood her obscene gesture was never meant for me.

Reya flicked her palm in a talk-to-the-hand motion before she proceeded to the next class.

Eli shrugged, double-checked the J-Room lock, then said, "The office gave me a copy of your schedule. I can show you where your next class is."

"Dude, what was that?"

He shrugged. "Just how me and my sister say XOXO."

CHAPTER 3

HE MAY HAVE BEEN THE NEWSPAPER nerd, but I felt like the reporter the way I chased him down with a hundred questions. "'Trouble in a training bra' is your *sister*?"

"I didn't tell you that?"

"No, you didn't tell me that. Is she older or younger?"

"Physically, she's older by ten months—my parents were *freaks*—but mentally she's still in diapers." He stopped at a classroom where a couple of students sprinted in just as the bell rang. "This is you. Don't worry about being late. You've got your hall pass. It's good all day."

"Yeah, thanks."

"Come by the J-Room after school?"

"Yeah," I said. Then, "I mean no." Mom wanted me home right after school for some kind of, I don't know, *conference call*. Attendance mandatory.

Shadows crossed Eli's face. That same twitchiness from before.

I said, "I'll come by tomorrow. For sure."

He nodded, two quick, jerky motions. "Okay."

It would have to be. Maybe I owed him for the locker room save, but I wasn't about to piss off Mom.

When she's mad, Zach Lynch and his crew had nothing on her.

Rest of the day = status quo.

"We have a new student, class. Would you like to stand up and tell us about yourself?" some teacher would say, like I had a choice.

This was my favorite part of the new school experience, because it gave all your classmates a chance to size you up and decide how much of a threat you were. Totally fun. In Opposite World.

The first couple of times I had to do it, I was still in middle school, so the backlash was minimal. There's very little at stake with seventh and eighth graders.

Last year was my first high school experience as the New Kid in Idaho. The cliques had been established, the social hierarchy set. In comes me, fresh off a growth spurt, too skinny to threaten the farm boy football players, but an instant enemy of the garbage varsity basketball team. Obviously, the tall black guy had come to take somebody's starting spot.

In all fairness to their stereotype, I probably could've.

What they didn't realize was being a b-ball star went against the whole "stay low-key" thing. I never planned to try out. Not that it mattered once their girlfriends noticed me.

Like I said, this was the varsity team. Juniors and seniors. I was a freshman, but still of instant interest to their women. The New Kid always is as long as he's not butt ugly. No ego or anything.

Things went south fast for me in Boise. Not first-day fast like here, though.

I introduced myself as Nick Pearson, gave my cover, hit the replay button. While the reception wasn't exactly warm—my history teacher dozed off while I was talking—there was no further violence that day. Final bell rang at two thirty. One hour until the call.

I learned to avoid buses a few years back, after an altercation in San Diego. So I rode a Huffy ten-speed to school. If I stepped on it, I could make it home in five minutes. I didn't do that. I wasn't going to be late— Mom's wrath and all—but there was no point in being early. There'd still be plenty of boxes to unpack and tension to ignore whenever I got there.

My house was east of Stepton High. I went west, tried to pretend I was riding for the fresh air like I did in Texas, but couldn't pull it off. There was a chemical plant on the edge of town, its thick stacks sticking up over the trees like a giant chain-smoker's cigarettes. They pumped storm clouds and gave the air a scent you could taste. I kept thinking I now knew what it'd be like to lick a matchbook.

I turned onto streets without checking signs, and tailed cars that had interesting license plates through a business district that I should've called something else. Half the establishments had soapy windows with faded For Lease signs wedged in the frames. Veering into residential territory, I came across a lot of lawns gone wild where rusted chain-link fences had the task of keeping the vegetation contained to the deserted properties.

In the occupied homes, more than a few yards were brown, the grass dying beneath tireless cars and sagging, rain-filled wading pools. As I coasted down one street, a front door burst open, rattling against the home's outer wall. An oily-haired woman exited with a baby on her hip and a toddler by the hand. She cursed into the doorway while backing into the yard.

A dirtier man in a yellowed T-shirt staggered into the daylight carrying a half-empty forty-ounce beer. He cursed back, threw the bottle. It thudded off the grassless lawn but didn't break, missing her legs just barely.

My new cell vibrated in my back pocket. I grabbed it, checked the caller ID even though I knew it could be only one of two people.

I held my handlebars with one hand as I pedaled by the angry couple. A police cruiser rounded the corner with its flashers on, stopping near the title fight. From the corner of my eye, I saw the dirty man jump off the porch, retrieve his forty, then smash it on the hood of the cop's car, still not breaking the invincible bottle. What the hell?

Then the whole scene was gone. Or I was, cruising east.

My phone kept shaking. For the briefest moment, I thought, *Don't answer, keep riding.*

Of course it was stupid. A kid on a bike. Thirty bucks in his pocket. No contacts. That would last about as long as it took to eat two pizzas and a value meal. It was *still* tempting. I hit Talk.

"You forget the time?" said the man who had me contemplating how far I could make my short money stretch. The man responsible for getting us stuck in this crappy town where drunk a-holes threw bottles at women, children, and cops. The man who'd ruined the lives of his family in a way that was almost awe inspiring.

Through gritted teeth, I said, "I'm on my way, Dad."

CHAPTER 4

I DROPPED MY BIKE IN THE front yard and entered the modest, two-story home of the Pearsons. It was a cottage-style house, sky blue, and looked like every other house in the neighborhood, as if it was trying harder to blend than we were.

The front door swung open. My mom waited at the threshold, the lines in her forehead and around her mouth cutting deep. "I wasn't sure you'd make it, Steven."

"*Nick*, Mom. Steven was the last name."

She blinked rapidly and brought a hand to her forehead. "God, you're right."

I kissed her on the cheek. "It's a lot to keep track of."

"Too much."

I peeled off my jacket in the foyer, my eyes watering from a chemical smell stronger than the Stepton air. Bleach. My nose burned from the scent as I scoped the den, where boxes were stacked high this morning. Now, no cardboard. Only dust-free furniture and shiny wood floors.

"All this today?"

Mom brushed past me. "It's not like I had anything more pressing to do."

"My room, too?" I asked, hopeful.

"Hardly. You'll be busy tonight."

I followed her into the kitchen. "What's the deal with this phone call?"

"I don't know, but we're going to be late."

The microwave clock said 3:29. Heavy footfalls thudded over my head, then on the stairs.

Mom said, "Here he comes."

Dad strolled in, a half-eaten apple in one hand and a slip of paper in the other. Casual. He didn't act like a man whose life and the lives of his family hung in the balance. He never did. That was the problem.

He paused for a second and locked gazes with Mom. Her eyes narrowed to near slits and I recognized the aftermath of some epic argument. So she hadn't spent the *whole* day cleaning.

Three thirty. I snatched the slip from Dad's hand, interrupting the stare down. He turned his anger vision on me, his watch-yourself-boy look.

The paper held a special toll-free number and passcode. Mom activated the speakerphone and I dialed. A series of beeps sounded while we were connected. The microwave clock stared at us: 3:31.

Dad finished his apple and began digging through the fridge with all the concern of someone calling to check movie times.

The line went silent until a familiar voice broke in. "A bit late, aren't we?"

No one said anything. Mom and Dad were back in their staring contest.

I said, "What's up, Bertram."

"Nicholas."

Ugh. Really? "Nick's fine."

"Deputy Marshal," Mom said, relenting as Dad went shoulder deep into the fridge again, "what's this call about? I thought we were supposed to avoid contact unless it's an emergency."

"That's kind of what this is, I'm afraid. After all the chances your family has been given, and blown, I need to stress that this is the last relocation we're offering. One more slipup, and you'll be expelled from the Program. No more federal protection. Considering the enemies you've made, I think that's a worst-case scenario. Am I wrong?"

He wasn't.

For us, home is not where we decide to hang our hats. It's where WitSec *tells* us to hang our hats.

WitSec, short for the Witness Security Program. More commonly known as Witness Protection. Our federal sponsors for the last four years.

Bertram said, "James, do you hear me?"

Dad emerged from the fridge with a slice of roast beef and provolone cheese folded together. He bit into his snack, made a show of not responding to his newly assigned government name. A "slave name," he liked to say.

"James, are you there?" Bertram asked, a strained note in his voice. "Nicholas, is your father there? Everyone should be present for this call."

"He's here."

Dad kept right on chewing slowly, with a lot of lip, like a camel. Mom hugged herself and shook her head, too used to his stubbornness. When he finished, he reached for the fridge again. I rammed the door with my shoulder as he cracked the seal, rocking the appliance.

Dad rolled his eyes, spoke. "This is Robert Bordeaux."

"Not anymore," countered Bertram. "You haven't been that man for a long time. Let's see, you were Stuart Petrie of Boise, Idaho, until you started a gambling parlor in your garage, garnering the attention of the local news. You were Jerry Epps of Addison, Texas, until an identity theft scam was traced back to you. And"—papers shuffled on Bertram's side—"ah, this is my favorite. You were Randall Bell of San Diego, California, until you attempted to extort 'protection' money from the neighborhood trash collectors. Quite the résumé, huh, *James*?"

Dad's jaw flexed. Criminals don't like hearing lists of their past transgressions. Particularly the ones that got them caught. "I'm here, Bertram. What do you want?"

"It's not about what I want. It's about what the government wants—what you promised but have yet to deliver. Testimony that can put your old boss, Kreso, away."

Kreso Maric, the gangster who used to pay Dad to count his dirty money. Until Dad snitched, and Kreso pulled a vanishing act. Now Bertram treated Kreso like the boogeyman, invoking his name whenever he wanted to scare Dad into submission. It might work one day.

Dad said, "I can't testify if you can't catch him. It's not my fault he fell off the face of the earth."

"The government has spent a lot of money protecting you and your family over the last four years, James. We'd like to see a return on that investment. *But* we are willing to cut our losses if you continue to be a problem. I could read you some information on what life is like for an unprotected federal witness. It's a short paragraph."

Dad's face twitched like something was alive and burrowing under his skin. His mouth opened to say something most likely stupid, but snapped shut like for once he knew better than to push.

Bertram continued, "Supervision will be more stringent this time. We'll be doing a call like this once a week so I can gauge your acclimation."

"Once a week?" Mom said. "We don't have a say in that? We've always been told minimal contact is best."

She was right. We were supposed to be normal. Calling your U.S. Marshal didn't sound like the average "family night."

Bertram said, "I need to determine if this arrangement is working. If it isn't, you will not be allowed to suckle on the teat of Joe and Mary Taxpayer any longer."

Teat?

"Nicholas, you first. Tell me about your day at school."

I told him. I told him how great it was and how I made lots of friends. My mom went next with a too-cheery voice, recapping a day of joy and wonder. Then Dad. A family of liars doing what we do best.

After the call, I left my parents to get on to Round 2. I wasn't halfway up the stairs before Mom struck, a blame jab. "We have to check in once a week like little kids at camp. Are you satisfied?"

"I felt like something was missing until you started nagging. Now I'm content." Dad landed a sarcasm uppercut, his stock in trade.

I closed my door, maneuvered around unpacked junk, and lay on my unmade bed. Earbuds in, iPod cranked, I stayed there until the sun went down, then fell asleep with a rapper shouting at me.

At least his yelling had a good beat.

CHAPTER 5

THE NEXT DAY, I GRABBED A roll of quarters from one of the open boxes in my room. When I walked into the gym, I formed a fist around the coins, anticipating another run-in with Zach Lynch. Coach Peyton stopped me before I made it to the locker room.

"Schedule change, Pearson."

He handed me a warm sheet of paper fresh off the printer. All my classes had been switched around. I was now due in English this period.

"Why?" I said.

Peyton gave me a look that made me feel like I was coated in slime. "Better for everyone. Now get."

He went into his office and closed the door. Kids exited the locker room in their tight uniforms, ready to stretch and jump. Even though I still wore my street clothes, I felt more exposed than them, and tried to spot a familiar face. Eli. Or Reya. Or even Zach. Someone who might make eye contact, nod, and let me know that totally random schedule changes were the norm at Stepton High. I didn't see any of them.

The warning bell rang, and I didn't have a hall pass today. I got going, slipping the roll of quarters I'd been planning to bash Zach's face with in my pocket. I'd use the money to get a soda or some candy from one of the vending machines.

Maybe this change *was* better for everyone.

The rest of the week felt like starting over at a completely different school. I didn't see any of the people I'd met on my first day. No more photo ops or student guides. No one tried to beat me up. All of my day-one drama faded like every other school experience I'd had.

Homework piled. I did most of it and managed to unpack the boxes in my room, a good distraction between the alternating fights and prolonged silences from my parents.

At the start of the weekend, I left school contemplating a very serious question: What do people do on Fridays in Stepton? I got home, found Mom staring through the living room window, almost trancelike, and new questions came to mind.

"Mom?"

She spoke without looking at me. "What direction do you think that is?"

"South," I said, having memorized much of the town's topography. "Why?"

"I bet Florida is nice this time of year. Remember when we all went to Disney for the first time?"

No, I didn't. I was like four. I sniffed and detected the smell of dinner in the oven, only slightly stronger than the scent of fresh bleach. "Did you spend all day cleaning again?"

"Just the morning."

I asked my real question. "Mom, are you going crazy?"

She smiled. "Going? I think we all arrived at that destination a while ago."

Maybe she had a point. On many days I felt like I was on the far side of sane. The constant game of make-believe got to you after a while. When you're in the Program, you got what's called a legend. It sounds epic, like that Will Smith movie with the zombie vampires, but it's not. Trust.

Every new identity needs a backstory. You can't just move to a town and start stuttering when your neighbor asks where you're from and what brought you to the area. Thus the legend, a detailed history of everyone in the family.

The Pearsons were the victims of an auto industry layoff in Detroit. We moved to Virginia because the cost of living was cheaper than up north. Dad, he's good with numbers, so they got him a job at a local accounting office. Mom worked as a Realtor at our last assignment, but they made her a housewife here. Me? My legend says I'm an average teen who likes to play lacrosse, is an overachiever when it comes to science, and enjoys hip music.

Really, that's what it says: "enjoys hip music."

They told us they factored in aspects of our true selves, but after four do-overs, I imagined the guys in the legend department playing Wheel of Personalities and assigning us whatever the needle stopped on. Mom caught a bad spin this time.

She'd always had a job before. Busy. Gone all day. Ever since we got to Stepton, she'd been stuck in the house, alone, nothing to do but think and clean. Clean and th—

A booming sound echoed through the house. A sound like gongs.

Mom and I locked eyes. I felt like we were rabbits in the forest, and that noise was incoming bulldozers.

"What is that?" I said. It happened again. *Dong-DONG-dong-DONG.*

Mom bent her knees like she was about to dive behind the couch. "Is that—?"

She didn't finish because she didn't have to. I knew what it was. Yes, *that.*

The doorbell.

We crouched by the windowsill, peeking through the blinds. An unexpected visitor? We'd barely had any during our time in the Program, and they were always a source of anxiety. In the event my family's enemies showed up to kill us, we had an emergency procedure . . . provided you weren't, you know, already dead. It involved evacuation. Making sure you weren't being followed. Getting to a safe house. In the panic moment, it occurred to me that assassins might not be nice enough to ring.

"Who is it?" Mom asked.

"I don't know." I did know. The person stepped away from the door like they might leave, giving us a better view. I recognized the blue crown emblem stitched into his bag. "Eli."

Mom said, "Who?"

"What's that wonderful smell, Mrs. Pearson? Meat loaf?"

I grabbed Eli's backpack strap and dragged him toward the stairs. "Don't worry about it. You aren't staying long."

"Nick," Mom said, "you're being rude."

I ignored her, pulling Eli along.

He said, "It was a pleasure to meet you, Mrs. Pearson."

In my room, with the door closed, I turned on him. "WTF, dude?"

"I could ask you the same thing." He dropped the exaggerated pleasantries. "You never came back."

"What are you—?" I flashed on my first day and the J-Room. God, it felt like it happened last year. "Oh, right. My schedule got changed."

"I know. That only accounts for school hours, though. I waited until like five on Tuesday."

"Sorry, I forgot. My bad."

"It is."

What was this? I felt like my parents when they argue. "You know this is weird, right?"

Eli wasn't shy about checking out my room, touching things on my desk, eyeballing my posters. Violating my personal space. Now I knew how he felt when I grabbed his camera in the J-Room. "Eli, how did you know where I live?"

"Small town. I barely had to ask." He examined the disks stacked next to my game system. "Mostly sports. No shooters?"

He had a twinge of disgust in his voice. A challenge I met with enthusiasm. I grabbed a plastic GameStop bag I'd unpacked the night before and pulled the shrink-wrapped disk from it. "I got the new *Modern Battlefield* last week, haven't had a chance to play yet."

He reached for a controller. "That's too bad, since I've been playing all *this* week. I sense a brutal defeat in your future."

Eli made himself at home, taking a seat in my desk chair. Kicked off his shoes. Deputy Marshal Bertram droned in my mind, buzzing all kinds of warnings about being alert, and being suspicious of people I don't know.

I ignored the voice. This guy was in my room, talking trash. I needed to shoot him with a rocket launcher. "Load it up."

Two hours later, Eli was up six death matches to four, but I was mounting a comeback. Empty plates stained with meat loaf gravy and mashed potato remnants rested at our feet. Crumpled orange soda cans crested the lip of my trash bin. Old-school rap bumped through my iPod dock. Eli was a fan, which made the trouncing he was giving me forgivable.

I never found out what the *average* Steptonian did on a Friday night, but we were doing fine.

We stopped around seven o'clock at a 10–10 tie, mostly due to finger cramps. We agreed to a tiebreaker when we'd had a chance to rest, so we could bring our A games.

Eli powered down the system and rubbed fatigue from his eyes. "Your schedule got changed because of what happened with Zach."

"What?"

"Russ was running his mouth about what they did to you. It got back to Coach Peyton. He wants to keep Zach eligible for football, so they decided to remove anything that might trigger his poor impulse control."

That marinated a moment. "*I'm* the problem?"

"That's the way they see it. Welcome to Stepton, where the innocent are the guiltiest."

"And you know this, how?"

He gave me a sideways look. Right. He's got a lot of influence in Stepton High. He said, "You coming to the J-Room on Monday?"

"You'd make a great car salesman."

With an eyebrow arched, "Well?"

"Promise not to come by here without shooting me a text first. My parents are funny about that sort of thing."

"Your mom didn't seem to mind."

"She's not my only parent. Text me."

"I promise. So, J-Room?"

"I'll come by Monday."

"Good, because I'm expecting you to get invited to a Dust Off fairly soon, and I want to prep you."

"Invited to a what?"

He handed me his cell. "Put your number in."

I took it and two versions of Bertram got into a shouting match in my head like the devil and the angel in cartoons. One screamed about acting normal, and the other yelled about being careful. It might look weird if I didn't give up the digits, so I went with normal, despite some concerns. I entered my number. "What is a 'Dust Off,' Eli?"

"A Dust Off—a party. Don't worry, we'll go over everything next week."

He took back his phone with my number entered and pressed Send, and my cell buzzed in my pocket. "Okay," he said. "You should have my number now. If anything comes up over the weekend I'll be in touch. Otherwise, Monday."

Eli tried to leave. I grabbed his shoulder, stopping him. "What just happened?"

"I spared you a weekend of fixating on my victory."

"No, I mean this party thing. What's that about?"

He smirked and gave me what I'd come to think of as general Eli weirdness. "Patience. We're forming Voltron: Defender of the Universe. Just wait."

Was he speaking English?

His phone rang. "I gotta take this. Monday, don't be late or I'm coming by for dinner *and* a movie next time." He took the stairs and shouted, "See you later, Mrs. Pearson."

The front door slammed and he was gone. Mom met me on the first-floor landing. "I'm glad you're making friends, sweetie. He seems nice. And hungry."

I stared at the door like I could still see Eli through it. "I'm not exactly sure he is a friend. Not yet."

"At least he left before your father came home. Whatever that boy is, we don't want him to get a bad impression of us, do we?"

Before I could answer she returned to a mop and bucket in the kitchen.

Eli could've stayed an hour—or four—later and still maintained a good impression of us. Dad didn't get home until almost eleven o'clock, kicking off Friday Night Fights at the Pearsons'. Mom was asking what my strip-mall-accountant father was doing so late on a Friday. So was I. History tells us he probably wasn't feeding the homeless.

Of course, he didn't give a straight answer, or any answer. Unless you counted grunts and attitude. I tried not to make too much of it. We'd only been in town a week. That's a short time to stir up any serious trouble, even for Dad. Still . . .

I stayed up practicing *Modern Battlefield*—and contemplating Dad's tardiness—while police sirens wailed low somewhere in town.

CHAPTER 6

ON MONDAY, I LEARNED OF THE phenomenon known as the Dust Off. Not from Eli but from the organizer himself, during lunch.

I searched for an isolated seat where I could force-gag a rectangular slice of pizza down my throat. A crowded table in the middle of the cafeteria generated most of the noise in the room, a murmuring roar. Pretty girls and bulky guys packed in so tight some didn't have chairs. Yet a lanky kid with dirty-blond hair waved more people over. I turned to see which attractive/athletic person was being beckoned. The only thing behind me was a wall.

I looked back to what was literally the center of attention, and the kid changed his gesture. He pointed at me, mouthed the words "Yeah, you."

I moved toward them, reluctantly. In a different lunch period, Zach Lynch would be the alpha in this popularity pack, and going to his lair would lead to something stupid or violent. Probably both. The influence of the school's football star might extend beyond a single lunch period, meaning I could still be walking into a bad situation. The worst thing: that realization came when I was already among them.

The kid that waved me over sat on a table, his legs swinging. His skinny jeans were so tight they looked like scar tissue. He wore an equally tight black T-shirt under a denim jacket. All in all a lightweight. One punch would knock him into his next class. I sized up other, more formidable guys in the group as most of the conversations tapered off. Everyone became aware of my presence, and my skin went clammy, making my underclothes stick to me.

Skinny Jeans said, "You're new. Nick, right?"

"Yeah. Who are you?"

"Carrey." He tapped a large black guy in a letterman jacket on the shoulder. Seeing other brown faces relaxed me. "This is Lorenz."

"'Sup." Lorenz offered his palm and I slapped it.

Carrey introduced me to a few more people, who were friendly enough, but I still didn't get where this sudden burst of goodwill was coming from. I'd eaten here all last week and no one cared. Why the change now?

My cold pizza got colder and I noticed a couple of hot girls at the end of the table with a dark-haired guy wedged between them. He was twisted away from me—to better manage the girl in his lap. With his free hand, he stroked the thigh of the second girl, who sat on the table, kind of like Carrey, but with her legs spread so that the guy and girl #1 were positioned between them.

They all wore jeans, so it wasn't like the girl on the table was full-on panty vision, but still . . . it was raunchy. I guess I'd brought a little bit of Idaho with me. There, *couples* couldn't get that close at a school dance, forget about a broad-daylight *three-way* in the middle of the cafeteria. I expected some teacher to break it up, but all of them seemed interested in something other than the erotic powwow I was witnessing.

Carrey said, "Hey, D, he's here."

The dark-haired middle of the people sandwich craned his neck and spotlighted me with bright, traffic-light green eyes. "My man!"

He nodded and the girl in his lap climbed off, pouting. The girl on the table swung one leg up and away, but slowly, for the boy's benefit. The move might score her bonus points at a future strip club audition, but today it just allowed "D" an escape from her thigh lock.

"D" stood, his long cargo shorts exposing half of his muscular calves, and a loose, natty sweater hung over his torso. He was my height, but lighter, fitter. He bounced when he walked. All swagger.

Hey, D, he's here. . . .

What did "D" want with me? When he introduced himself, I knew. Because of Eli. "What's up, Nick. I'm Dustin. Heard some good stuff about you."

"Then he's all like, 'People said Zach's boys jumped you but you gave them the business,' and everyone started laughing," I said to Eli in the J-Room after school.

He leaned back in his chair with a serious look on his face. "Go on."

I told him the rest, about how Dustin kept giving me props for standing up to "Roid Rage Zach" and then invited me to his party on Saturday.

"Anything else?" Eli said.

"No, the period bell rang and everyone jetted. But he told me to come to the"—I felt stupid calling it a Dust Off, a horrible play on Dustin's name—"party. Just like you said."

He stroked his chin like there was hair there. "It happened faster than I thought, but I think we're still okay."

"About that . . ."

"You want to know how I knew he'd invite you," he said.

I shook my head. "No. I got that part figured. You told me Russ had been running his mouth, and that got my schedule changed. Thing is, I don't think Russ would've told people I put up a good fight. Makes Zach look bad. But Dustin couldn't shut up about all this respect I had because of the way I handled myself. Funny how neither version mentions you showing up with your trusty camera."

He went silent.

"Eli?"

"Okay, I leaked the story. With some edits."

My fingers curled around an imaginary roll of quarters. "What do you think you're doing, man?"

"I knew if you had enough buzz, people would notice, and you'd get an invite to the Dust Off. It's a good thing."

I don't like people telling me what's good for me. We hardly ever agree. "Let me guess, *you* didn't get an invite."

He wouldn't look me in the eye. "I'm not into cliquey stuff like that."

"What, I'm supposed to go spy on the kids at this party, bring you some dirt to print in your paper? Then they can treat both of us like outcasts?"

He jerked like I'd jabbed him with something hot. "It's not like that, Nick."

"Right now it seems like you're using me for . . . hell, I have no idea what this is about. Here's what I do know: the story you 'leaked,' that's going to get back to Zach, if it hasn't already. You think he's going to pat me on the back and invite me to his house? I don't need you making more trouble for me, Eli."

I grabbed my stuff, for once heeding all the warnings I'd heard from the U.S. Marshals over the years. Whatever Eli was trying to pull me into smelled bad. I didn't need details; I just wanted to steer clear. Plus, I had to get to the conference call with Bertram. "I'm gone."

"Nick, wait. You have to go to that party."

"I'm going, but as a normal freaking guest. Not your spy."

Eli stood, searching for something to say. I wasn't going to give him the chance. He seemed like a decent dude, and I appreciated him helping me with my Zach Lynch problem last week, but I didn't need his covert schemes. I had enough of that going on at home.

If there was one thing I was good at—one skill I'd honed through all my identities—it was getting people to back off. For good. I puffed up to say some truly foul things to Eli. Not that he deserved it, but it was kind of like *Modern Battlefield*, sometimes it took a big bomb to end the game. Things would be easier if I left with him hating me.

Before I could launch my offensive, we were interrupted.

"I'm not your answering machine, Eli." Reya Cruz stepped into the J-Room. "Turn on your phone, you *pendejo*. . . ."

She and I stood there staring at each other, and I couldn't think of one harsh thing to say.

The last time I saw her up close she'd been in gym gear, and incredible. In street clothes—stretchy low-rise jeans and a tight tee—she shamed a few fashion models.

She swept dark hair behind one ear. "Nick, hey, you haven't been in gym."

"Schedule change."

"Right." She looked at her shoes.

"I solved the mystery. I know what the *R* stands for."

That pulled a smile from her, one that faded fast. She blurted, "I heard about what happened between you and Zach. I'm so sorry. He—I, I mean, I shouldn't have been talking to you right in front of him. We've *been* over, for two months now, but he still likes to pull the stupid macho crap as if it's cute. It isn't. I'm sorry." She met my eyes again. "I heard Zach bit off more than he can chew with you."

Eli chimed in, "Really? That's what you heard?"

I looked to him, knew what he was getting at. His "leaked story" had scored me some cool points with his sister. That didn't change anything between me and him.

Reya told Eli, "What's it to you? By the way, you're about to lose your phone privileges. Mami's been calling you. 'There's no reason to have it . . .'"

"'. . . if I don't pick up,'" Eli finished, grabbing the phone from his bag. "I know. I know."

Reya turned her attention back to me, asking me about my classes and how I liked Stepton. Good and good, I told her. With her, everything was good. I wanted to stay longer, but Bertram's call was in fifteen minutes.

"I gotta run. This thing with my parents . . . ," I said, letting it hang on purpose.

"Sure," Reya said. "It's nice talking to you again."

Eli interrupted, "Reya, you going to the Dust Off this weekend?"

She said, "You know it. What about you, Nick?"

"Yeah." Eli stared me down. "What about you?"

"I'm thinking about it," I said as coolly as I could manage. Eli, still manipulating.

She said, "I hope you do. I'll look for you there."

I nodded and backed into the hall. I was still pissed at Eli, but seeing Reya again sapped some of my irritation. I checked the clock on my phone as I walked. Now I had ten minutes to get home. I could make it, but I was thinking beyond the conference call. To the Dust Off.

Where she'd be looking for me.

CHAPTER 7

THE CONFERENCE CALL WAS SOME STRAIGHT bull. Bertram asked us the exact same questions he asked last week, with an added bonus.

"I need each of you to rate your experience in Stepton on a scale of one to ten," he said. "One being completely unsatisfactory and ten being completely satisfactory. You first, Nicholas."

"Negative four." No, I didn't really say that. I rated it five, my parents gave their ratings (Dad said seven, Mom said three), and we hung up. I retreated upstairs while they went into their usual fight mode. Except it wasn't usual this time. No snippiness for the sake of being snippy. This fight had purpose.

I paused on the second-floor landing while Dad tugged on his jacket.

"Where are you going now?" Mom said. "More 'fantasy football'?"

She said "fantasy football" the way a teacher might say "your dog ate it." I thought of Dad's late Friday.

"I've got to take care of some things at the office."

"You don't have an office, Robert. You fill out tax forms in a storefront.

I heard it used to be a Froyo."

"Jesus, Donna, back off. I've got work to do. I'll be home later."

Their voices were lower, and they weren't in each other's faces, but this felt more serious than their louder arguments. They used their real names.

Dad grabbed the doorknob. Mom placed her hand on top of his. From where I sat it looked like a loving gesture. Then he winced and I knew she'd dug her nails in. What she said next was just above a whisper, but I still caught it. Being the sole kid in an unstable house over the last few years had led to some finely developed hearing.

"With you it's always secrets on top of secrets," she said. "Haven't you learned anything? I won't stick around for WitSec to toss us from the Program. If you're up to something, again, I'll take Tony and leave. Try me."

My real name. I couldn't remember the last time I heard it. This *was* serious. She'd never threatened to leave before. She couldn't mean it.

I expected Dad to say something sarcastic, or mean, or bark some wall-rattling profanity. He pried her hand off his, gently almost. "I gotta go, Donna."

He left Mom in the foyer alone. Her head tilted forward, hand clamped over her mouth. I went to my room, didn't need to see this part.

I got why she was so fed up. Dad, unsatisfied with the jobs WitSec arranged for him or the tiny monthly stipend they provided in addition, always returned to his old ways to earn extra cash. We lived lavishly back in the day. He wanted some of that again. But he got busted every time, resulting in our constant relocations.

Bertram made it clear there would be no more relocating. Even if the threat was empty—and I didn't think it was since Dad had been a useless witness, with his old boss Kreso still being on the run—the pattern suggested we'd go to a place worse than Stepton next time. Would Dad risk it?

Likely.

In my room, my cell phone buzzed on my desk from missed texts and a voice mail, from Eli.

The texts were all some variation of "hit me up." I must not have been fast enough for him, though. I played the message. *"You're really going to make me use my voice here, huh? Okay. Nick, um, I'm sorry about what happened today. For reals. I line crossed. From now on, I'll keep you out of my more . . . troublesome obligations. As a peace offering, I wanted to let you know that my guild is going to quest for Urilium Gauntlet tonight, and I wanted to invite you to join our brotherhood."*

His guild? What?!

In one final squawk—spoken so fast that I could barely understand it—he said, *"You can lead the war party if you want."*

I stared at the phone for a good thirty seconds trying to wrap my mind around what I just heard. My head felt foggy, overcrowded with thoughts about Bertram, Mom and Dad, and quests for the something-something.

I texted Eli back.

Me: What's da Urethra Gauntlet?

Eli: Urilium Gauntlet. U got my message.

Me: I got it. What wuz it?

Eli: I'm talkin Finite Universe. An MMORPG

Me: wuz dat a typo?

Eli: Massively multiplayer online role-playing game

Me: Like Warcraft??

Eli: Hellz no. Better. More scifi than fantasy. No weirdo stuff like dwarfs & fairies

> **Me:** What do u play as?
> **Eli:** A techElf

I fought a laugh.

> **Me:** will stick 2 modern battlefield
> **Eli:** We cool?

I hesitated. Not for long, though.

> **Me:** we cool
> **Eli:** J-Room 2morrow?

I considered it, thought about what my life already was, and how I didn't want it more complicated. Yet—I don't know—Eli was growing on me.

> **Me:** 1 condition. No secret schemes. Normal school paper stuff
> ONLY

There was a long delay before his next text. I booted my computer, wondering if he'd make me regret my concession. I went to pee, and his response was waiting when I returned.

> **Eli:** Thinkn of startn a game review column. May b u can handle
> that?

Now that I could do.

Me: Maybe

Eli: Sweet. Gotta go. Cant b fashionably late 2 the war party

Um, okay.

Me: Ltr, E

That was easily the strangest exchange of my life.

Thing was, I'd felt cruddy before, thinking about what Dad might or might not be doing. Now I didn't.

I opened the browser and googled *Finite Universe*. Just for kicks.

CHAPTER 8

THE NEXT FEW AFTERNOONS IN THE J-Room presented me with an education that was more interesting than 90 percent of the stuff my teachers covered during normal school hours. Eli gave me this whole "History of the American Press" bit while walking me through the production schedule of the *Rebel Yell*. I probably wouldn't remember half of it, but his enthusiasm for the material was enough to trump the disinterested Stepton High faculty.

He started with a breakdown of colonial papers from the 1700s and how . . .

Okay, I forgot it already. There was something about tyranny. What did stick with me—for the wrong reasons at first—was the jargon.

"You've seen a newspaper before," Eli said, handing me some old copies of the *Yell* to review. "They're broken into columns. Because we have to print on regular copy paper, we only use three columns per page instead of the standard six you'd see on a paper in the supermarket."

I said, "Narrow paper, less columns. Seems simple enough."

"It is. And because we use columns, we measure content in column inches. Instead of my telling you to write a page, I'd say 'give me eight inches.'"

My head nearly *exploded* with dirty jokes. "You'd want me to give you a good, strong eight inches?"

He nodded enthusiastically. "Of course I'd want it to be strong, what else would I—" He caught on and hurled a pen like a circus knife thrower. I dodged it and we both cracked up.

He said, "I walked right into that one, didn't I?"

"You did."

"Hey, it's one of the most important things you're ever going to learn in this business."

"Doesn't *business* imply that we're making money?"

"*Business* implies we act professionally," he said, the laughs dying. "At least that's how I was taught."

"By who?"

"My dad, Carlos Cruz, editor in chief of *El Mejor Día*, 'The Better Day.' It was the Puerto Rican community paper he used to print from a shed in our backyard. He charged a quarter a copy, just enough to pay for ink. He always said we needed people to tell *our* stories."

Used to. Was.

I asked my next question cautiously. "How long's he been gone?"

"Four years. Cancer." Eli shrugged. "He used to say ink was in his blood. Me too."

"Inches," I said, no longer seeing the joke in it. "One of the most important things. Got it."

That week went much better than my first at Stepton High. I settled into my classes and actually learned some stuff without worry of embarrassment or bloodshed. Whoever handled my schedule change should be, like, a military strategist because I barely saw Zach Lynch. The couple of times we crossed paths, there were a dozen kids between us, limiting him to dirty looks. He might as well have been blowing kisses.

The extreme downside of my schedule change was I didn't run into Reya at all. Every day in the J-Room, Eli assured she was looking forward to seeing me at the Dust Off. I wondered if he was gassing me, hoping I'd reconsider being his party spy if he said her name enough. But he kept his promise, no more secret schemes. I kept mine and showed up. By Thursday, I wasn't even doing it out of obligation. I took a crack at writing a review of *Modern Battlefield* for next month's issue of the *Yell*. Eli marked it all to hell with a red pen that I could see myself growing to hate, but otherwise things went well in the J-Room.

The same could not be said for life at home.

Dad missed dinner every night that week. I fell asleep before he got in but was always awakened by the harsh tones from the late conversation with Mom. They'd found a volume that concealed most of the details from me, but one single syllable still managed to make it through the walls.

Why?

Why are you so late?

Why aren't you telling me what you're doing?

Why? Why? Why?

I got sick of the questions. By the time the weekend hit, I decided Dad needed to give up some answers. If not voluntarily, so be it.

All day Friday the school buzzed about the Dust Off. I didn't sit with Dustin Burke in lunch again, but he got my attention as we left the cafeteria. "See you there?"

Two girls—different from the pair I saw him with on Monday—ushered him away before I could answer, but yeah, I planned to go. How could I miss it? Or Reya?

After school in the J-Room that day, I expected Eli to "casually" bring up the party, then allude to whatever recon mission he'd wanted me to perform originally. He didn't. Which gave me crazy respect for the guy. We spent the afternoon formatting some story files, and agreed to hook up on Monday. Dad came home late again and avoided an argument with Mom by crashing on the couch.

That bothered me.

As bad as things have ever been, my parents always spent the night in the same room. At least I thought they did. I remember a couple of times in San Diego when I was up early on a Saturday and found Dad making waffles, strange because he always slept in. When I went to the living room for cartoons there were pillows and a blanket on the couch. I asked him about it, and he said he dozed off watching a movie.

There were other questionable times—like him staying a night or two at a hotel when we were in Texas—but there was always an excuse. He had the flu and didn't want to infect us. Or it was business. Though what sort of business requires you to stay in a hotel a mile from your house was beyond my thirteen-year-old mind to contemplate. I wasn't stupid; I bought the excuses because I wanted to.

My point: there used to be excuses.

Not in Stepton. Dad came home, went for the spare linen, and made a pallet on the couch, whipping the sheets around like a magician's cape, like he'd pull a comfy mattress from thin air.

Is this how divorce starts? For normal people?

Divorce meant lawyers, and paperwork, and attention. Mom would have to leave the Program since it was Dad's testimony that the marshals wanted. And Kreso Maric wasn't the type to care about marital status. The ex-wife of a snitch was as bad as the snitch himself. Kreso would take whatever blood he could get. Staying alive meant staying together. Mom and Dad *had* to put up with each other. I *had* to tolerate their private little war.

Right?

On Saturday morning I raked leaves and washed Dad's SUV—the requirements for my allowance—and an idea started to form. I dismissed it almost immediately. It was dumb.

Dusk came. I showered, dressed in fresh, never-worn sneakers, baggy painter's jeans (I tried skinny jeans once; they hurt my junk), a vintage concert tee, and hooded jacket. Then I heard the fight tones ramp up through my wall and my dumb idea returned. Not so dumb now.

"Again?" Mom said. "Is it a Saturday-night tax emergency?"

"I'm not going to do this with you," Dad said, then sank into their routine anyway.

He was going back to "work." I made a decision.

Dad's keys were still on my dresser from the afternoon car wash. I grabbed them and my cell, jogged downstairs to the driveway. I popped the locks on his ride and contemplated the best hiding place.

Not the glove box. Dad always went in there. It's where he hid his lottery play slips and the hand-rolled cigarettes he thought we didn't know about. The backseat and cargo area were a no go, too. He'd developed a habit of checking those thoroughly ever since I was eleven years old.

Dad wouldn't argue with Mom for long. He never did, having mastered the art of storming out. I settled on the passenger seat, or under it. I wedged my phone beneath one of the slide tracks, locked the doors, and worked the spare key off his key chain before entering the house.

He met me on the stairs. "Still got my keys?"

I handed them over. "Have a good night, Dad."

In my room, I called up the TrackApp website. A phone number and PIN later, a real-time GPS map appeared on-screen, giving a bird's-eye view of a blue dot sailing through the streets of Stepton. My phone . . . and Dad. I couldn't answer *why* Dad was spending so many late nights on the town. Not yet.

But I could do *where*.

After seven minutes the blue dot stopped moving. I waited another five minutes to rule out a pit stop. Satisfied, I zoomed in on the map, magnifying a grayed-out area simply marked *Downtown*. Stepton didn't warrant a more detailed description.

I switched to a satellite map for a street view. Fail. All I got was a *Coming Soon* message. *Really?*

Well, I had to get the phone back anyway. . . .

The temperature dropped as I sailed through Stepton's dark streets, my breath streaming behind me. My bike gears clicked as loud as gunshots in the eerie quiet. The October-ish scent of burning leaves hovered, and boxy suburban houses gave way to commercial buildings. Lawyer and doctor offices.

I hopped the bike onto the sidewalk before stopping to check the map I'd printed. I was a block away from my destination, "*Downtown*." I resumed my course, unsure of what I'd find. A bar? Maybe a bowling alley?

I spotted the SUV around the next bend, parked ahead of a dark BMW. I dipped into an alley diagonal from the vehicle and settled into shadows. There were very few cars on the street. And the landscaping was immaculate. Much nicer than Dad's usual dives.

Squinting, I read the marble sign a few yards from Dad's car.

No way.

The sign read: CITY HALL.

CHAPTER 9

DAD WAS ROBBING CITY HALL.

That was my first thought and I wasn't ashamed of it. Considering Dad's track record, he might've considered it a compliment.

But it didn't add up. If he was into something shady, he wouldn't have driven his own vehicle or parked directly in front of the target building. I cursed my stupidity. If Dad was starting his "empire" again, he'd need contacts. Accomplices. This might just be a meet. He drove here, dropped the car off, got picked up by some enterprising local. Which, of course, meant my entire scheme was useless.

I walked my bike across the street and fished the SUV's spare key from my pocket. I retrieved my phone, relocked the vehicle.

Thumbing the Contacts button, I brought up Dad's cell and hit Talk. At least I could screw with him. Hit him with a Daddy Guilt Trip for fighting with Mom. The phone rang.

Twice.

Once through my phone's receiver, a second time from the city hall lobby. Dad's old Isley Brothers ring tone was clearly audible from where I stood. Worse, Dad was clearly visible.

Tracing the sound toward the plate-glass entrance, I spotted Dad exiting the elevator with a large box cradled in his arms. I jogged my bike to a nearby hedge, where I ducked and killed the call.

From the bushes, I watched Dad push through the exit door, then do this weird bobbling/balancing act, shifting the box under one arm while unclipping his phone from his belt. He looked at the display, frowned, then pressed a button.

A chill crawled through me when I couldn't remember if I'd silenced my cell.

I snatched it up and tried to work the menu. My fingers felt too fat and too slow as I accessed everything from the internet to the memo recorder. Before I could pull it together, my phone lit up like plutonium and my Lil Wayne ringtone betrayed me.

A thud, followed by the *whip-flap* sound of pages in the breeze. Dad whisper-yelled, "Nick! Are you here?"

I emerged from my shrub cover, righteous, indignant. "Can you blame me, Dad?"

I expected some snap remark. So much so, I thought I heard, *"Boy, I'll beat the black off you for taking that tone with me."*

Something in my mind clicked, rewound, then replayed what he really said.

"Nick, you have to go before he sees you."

Not angry.

Afraid.

He knelt, crab-clawing papers that had spilled from the box he dropped. I ran to him, concerned by the quake in his voice. Kneeling, too, I helped him retrieve the papers.

"No, son," he said, snatching loose sheets from my hands.

"Dad, wha—"

DING.

Another elevator reached the lobby, and the doors parted, spilling a column of light across the marble floor. Dad's neck craned, then whipped back to me. "Go!"

I returned to the hedge for my bike but was too slow to make a clean getaway. The mystery man stepped into the city hall courtyard. I couldn't see him from the bushes, but their conversation was clear.

"James," the man said, his voice loud and fake pleasant, like a department store Santa Claus, "I'm sorry to interrupt our meeting, but I had to take that call."

"No sweat."

"What happened here?"

"Tripped. Stupid, really."

The other guy grunted and I heard dual firecracker pops from stubborn old knees. I pictured him doing what I'd done, helping Dad clean up the mess. "Let's make sure we get it all. We don't want to lose any of this critical info because of something *stupid*, now, do we?"

"No," Dad said, quieter now. "Sorry, sir."

Sir? It was like hearing a priest curse. Who *was* this guy?

They finished gathering the box's spilled contents. Dad made his way to his vehicle with the guy beside him. I shifted, got a partial view of their backs.

Dad stuffed the box in the backseat. A few more words were exchanged, but I couldn't hear over the wind. Mystery Man shook Dad's hand, then strolled to the BMW. Dad hesitated, his eyes on my bush.

The other guy said something else. Dad forced a laugh and climbed into his vehicle. The other guy did the same, flicking on sun-bright headlights that made Dad wince behind the wheel. A moment passed. Neither car pulled off. Finally—reluctantly—Dad drove away, and only then did the Mystery Man leave city hall plaza.

Shifting to my feet, I registered the sound of rustling paper. A sheet was balled in my hand, damp from palm sweat. It was from Dad's box; when he told me to run, I took it—didn't mean to.

I smoothed the paper against my stomach. Just two columns of random numbers that meant nothing to me. I checked the header, expecting to see *Page 54* or something just as useless. The page number was there, but that's not what sucked all the air from my chest.

Next to the number were two words: *Designate Whispertown.*

Whispertown isn't boring at all. It's pretty big-time.

I remembered to breathe and visually traced the path Dad's truck had taken, as if I expected to see some explanation in his exhaust fumes. No answers. Just questions. Two big ones.

What was Dad into this time?

And what the hell did it have to do with Eli Cruz?

CHAPTER 10

I CALLED ELI, UNWILLING TO DEAL with the delay of texting on this. His voice was bland when he picked up. "How's the party?"

"We need to talk. In person. Now."

"Um, okay," he said, wary. "Your house?"

"No way. Is there a place where we can meet?" The cold wind gusted, and it felt like getting slapped with an ice pack. "Someplace warm?"

A few minutes later I rolled into the desolate business district I'd found after my first day of school. Of the occupied storefronts, most were dark, with Closed signs facing the street. The exceptions were a pharmacy and a shop I'd missed before. RAGE AGAINST THE CAFFEINE—the caps lock is theirs, not mine. Its sign was airbrushed in neon reds, yellows, and purples, like graffiti. It was barely lit inside, but I spotted Eli in a window seat. I dropped my bike on the sidewalk next to a parked lime-green Volkswagen Beetle, and went in.

The blast of furnace heat was amazing, and I realized my hands had gone numb only when I sat across from Eli and couldn't feel the table.

There were seven seats in the whole place, and five were still empty. An elderly barista in young clothing shouted from behind the counter, "Get something started for ya?"

"Large hot chocolate," I said, assuming it was on the menu.

She went to work and Eli said, "You forgot to ask for extra marshmallows."

"What's *Whispertown*?" I wasn't in the mood for jokes.

He stiffened. "Did something happen at the party?"

"I didn't go to the party. This doesn't have anything to do with the party." Another assumption. I had a bad habit with those. I said, "Tell me."

He sipped from his own drink. Slowly. Gazed through the window. "No."

"What?"

"I said no, Nick. I'm not going to tell you because you told me not to."

"When did I—?"

"'No secret schemes.' Your words. I can show you the text. You didn't want to be involved in my more . . . troublesome projects. Remember?"

My frustration spiked. Before it erupted in the form of foul language, the barista arrived with my drink. "Four fifty."

I paid with a five and waved off her halfhearted effort to fish change from her pocket. When she disappeared into the back of the shop, I said, "Forget before, Eli. What's so secretive about Whispertown?"

"Tell me why you want to know."

I resisted another urge to curse. I still had the paper I'd taken from Dad on the city hall steps. Showing it to Eli wasn't the right play. He'd want to know where it came from. How I got it. I couldn't go there with him. Ever.

He said, "Now who's keeping secrets?"

I tasted my drink. It was lukewarm and gross. I chugged it down anyway to avoid talking, reverting to a game me and my old babysitter played before she got fired.

It was called Keep Quiet. When two people were alone, the one who kept quiet the longest was the smartest in the room, she said. It was really her way of getting me to shut up when her favorite shows were on. That didn't mean there wasn't something to it.

Eli broke first. "Since you moved here, have you looked around? I mean *really* looked?"

I looked. At the tiny coffee shop, at the empty street. "I guess."

"There's something wrong with Stepton, Nick. No one's talking about it. I'm trying to figure out why."

"Wrong how?"

"There's a guy on my street, Mr. Languiso, his house got burglarized last month. A week ago, a teacher's car got stolen right out of her driveway, broad daylight. Two days ago, a couple of kids dealing meth on the west side of town got freaking shot, Nick. Shot!"

"That, um, sucks." What was he getting at?

"Not sucky. Invisible. Like it never happened." He leaned forward and lowered his voice. "Did you know that most cities' crime stats are public record? Like, if you wanted to buy a house you could go online and make sure the place you like isn't in gang territory."

I shrugged. I didn't know that, but whatever.

He said, "The Stepton Police Department releases their stats online every month. None of those *major felonies* show up in the reports."

"You just said two of the crimes happened in the last week. The month's not over. How could they be in the reports?"

He shook his head. "Not those crimes specifically. Others like them. If you look at the available information, Stepton's like the safest town in

America. The crimes making the list for the last six months have been mostly misdemeanors, and those numbers seem exaggerated."

"What does all this have to do with the high school paper?"

"Nothing, except I'm the only paper in town. The *Stepton Chronicle* stopped printing years ago. There's no one else left to look into this *but* me. This isn't about printing a few hundred copies for everyone's homeroom. I've got bigger plans for this story."

"Big plans? Yeah, right. Prove it," I said, hoping he'd feel challenged and try to impress me.

He didn't take the bait. Instead, he sat back like he was done talking. "Your turn to share. What's got you so interested?"

I said the only thing I could say without revealing information that protected the lives of me and my family. "I don't like to be half in. I want to learn everything. It's not right that you have to carry the whole load of running the paper by yourself."

He laughed. "I shouldn't have tried to play you over the Dust Off, now that I know how crappy it feels."

I played Keep Quiet again.

"Okay, here's the deal," Eli said. "I accept your offer."

"You'll tell me more about Whispertown?"

"No. Not until I see how serious you are about learning everything."

I chewed the inside of my cheek.

"Hit the J-Room before *and* after school starting Monday so I can get you up to speed on some other parts of the operation."

"How long is that going to take?"

"As long as it takes. Unless you want to tell me the truth about why Whispertown's on your mind this evening."

"I'll be there, Monday." I got up to leave.

"You want a ride home?" He pulled a set of keys from his pocket and pressed two buttons on a silver remote. Three seconds later the lime Volkswagen at the curb grumbled on, its headlights cutting the dark like blue lasers.

I said, "That's you? I didn't know you drove."

"Never got around to taking my driver's test. But laws seem to be more fluid around here these days. When in Rome . . ."

I didn't feel like talking on the way home, but Eli wasn't letting me off that easy.

"Your newfound dedication to the paper is admirable, Nick."

"Glad you think so." I wasn't. I could feel the setup coming. What kind of reporter would he be if he didn't keep pumping me for information on my interest in Whispertown? Well, he could ask all the questions he wanted, I wasn't cracking.

That's probably why he went with a different tactic.

"I'm sure Reya will forget about you blowing her off when she discovers your passion for reporting."

"I didn't blow her off," I said, with more concern in my voice than I intended. "Let me out, I'll go to Dustin's now."

Eli was a shark smelling blood. "Too late. Someone set a couch on fire. Party's over. There are photos on Facebook if you want to see. That's *almost* like being there."

I stared through the window, playing it cool while cursing myself.

"We could explain it to her," he went on. "Let her know it's my fault you didn't meet her at the party. She'd buy it. Thinking I'm somehow screwing up her life is like a hobby for Reya."

He wanted me to talk about her, to ask for his help, give him some leverage. Nope.

"I'll see her in school," I said, knowing how unlikely that was thanks to my banishment to alternate schedule land. If I'd messed things up with her, I'd have to deal. Keeping my secrets was more important.

Eli nodded. "I understand."

I detected grudging respect in his tone. Maybe he admired my play, too.

Outside my house, Eli popped the Beetle's hatchback so I could retrieve my bike. When it was on two wheels again, I rolled it to the driver's side window, gears clicking.

He lowered the glass with a mechanical hiss. "Yeah?"

"Those meth dealers you told me about, the ones who got shot, did they live?" I don't know why I asked the question. I'd spend a lot of time thinking about it later, but not nearly as much as the answer he gave.

"They did. It was a good thing, too. The way things are going, if they'd died, it probably would've been ruled a suicide." He laughed. "*Mierda*, bet you didn't know I was such a cynic."

Oh, I had a feeling. I slapped the car's roof. "Monday, man."

"Monday."

He pulled off and left me in the cold.

CHAPTER 11

SUNDAY. THE PEARSONS WENT TO CHURCH, a Southern Baptist fire-and-brimstone sermon. Not that we were particularly religious, but the legend—an exercise in contradictions—insisted we were good, God-fearing folks. Afterward, Dad flopped on the couch to watch football while Mom announced she was going for a walk. Talk of meth dealers being shot made me offer to walk with her.

"I'll be fine on my own," she said. I was set to protest when she shut me down with a look. "I'm okay. I need some time to think."

"About what?"

"When that's your business I'll let you know."

When she was gone I joined Dad in the living room, waited for a commercial break. While some rock band sang a love song to a pickup truck, I said, "About last night—"

"Nothing happened last night." He cranked the volume on the TV, and I didn't push. I'd only brought it up as a courtesy before I did something I knew him and Mom would flip over. If it ever came to their attention.

I biked to a convenience store to purchase a disposable phone. After that, I needed privacy.

The day we moved here, while Mom and Dad fought over which wall the couch should go against, I went exploring for the first time and found Monitor Park, a couple of miles from my house. Pavilions, grills bolted to short concrete posts, a playground, and a gravel path leading to a man-made lake. Quiet. Secluded.

I dropped my bike along the lakeshore and dialed a number.

It rang twice. "Hello."

"This Lucky Dragon Chinese?" I asked.

CLICK.

I tossed stones in the water, waiting. The first few I threw for distance, making it about twenty yards offshore. The flatter stones I threw underhand, skipping them across the surface. Fifteen minutes later my new phone rang. The man who taught me to skip rocks was on the other end.

I picked up. "Can you talk?"

"I'm free now," he said.

"What took you so long to call back?"

"Business, kid."

His name was Stefan "Bricks" Bianchi. *His* business meant that the world's seven-billion-person population just got decreased by one, at least. He was a hit man. And my godfather.

Not *the* Godfather. Just mine.

"You doing okay, Tony?"

Tony. He never knew any other name to call me by. Safer for both of us.

"I'm cool," I said, without much conviction.

"Don't sound like it."

We hadn't talked in months—our system worked because we didn't do this frequently—and I felt a need to spill everything. Whispertown. Dad. Eli and Reya. Even Zach Lynch. *Especially* Zach Lynch. Though Bricks didn't know what school I attended, or what state I lived in, I was still tempted to drop a dime on Reya's psycho ex-boyfriend to my loving professional killer.

I knew better, though. Anything specific was more info than Bricks wanted; ignorance was his protection. But there was something he might be able to clear up for me. "Are there any reasons, other than for the sake of reputation, that would make a city downplay their major crime stats?"

A pause. "You watchin' old episodes of *The Wire*?"

"Hypothetically."

"A bunch of reasons. Mostly political."

Politics. The only thing I knew about politics was how to spell it. Still, I'd caught Dad at city hall, so what Bricks said lined up. It was the only thing that lined up. "Would altering crime stats ever make a difference in *your* business? Like, could you benefit from making things seem better than they really are?"

"I pride myself on there being *no* stats on what I do." He chuckled. "Unless you count missing persons reports."

"Bricks, you're being creepy again."

"You asked."

I threw another stone. "Say there were felonies that weren't making it into the—"

"Tony, quit the hypothetical crap. If you got a real question, spit it. Or else let me know you're healthy, and happy, and you're looking after your mom so we can end this call. We're taking a risk every time we do this.

Everybody up here knows I ain't no fan of your old man, but they also know how I feel about you."

I nodded like he could see me. I was the son he never had. He'd said it a million times. I've often thought he was the dad I *should've* had, despite his career choice. He was right about our calls being risky, but it was good to hear his voice. I didn't want this time to be a total waste. "I met this girl."

"That's what I'm talking about." I heard his smile through the phone. "She good-looking?"

"Think young JLo."

"Nice, kid. So"—he hesitated, which was unusual for him—"do we need to have *that* talk?"

"Aww, gross. No. I've already had that talk."

"Glad your old man's good for something."

Actually, it was Mom who decided she should "be frank about how the body works." She walked me through it with a picture book back in Texas. One of the more horrible days of my life. I didn't see the point in giving Bricks more fuel, though.

He'd brought up Dad—an eternal sore point, since they used to be best friends before Dad snitched—and I knew where the conversation was leading. It always happened this way.

Bricks asked, "How's Donna?"

Here we go. He asks about Mom, I answer, then he rants about how Dad don't deserve us and *da blah, blah, blah.* I knew how to stop it.

"How's Kreso?"

He started grinding his teeth. "You and me don't talk about the boss. You know that."

"Just wonderin'."

Another phone rang on his end. "Hang on."

His side went mute and I contemplated my big ol' bag of WTF. A hard gust shoved its way across the water, hitting me with a light, cold spray.

Sound crackled through my receiver again. "Tony, I gotta go. You good?"

I wasn't, but there was nothing he could do about it. "I'm good."

"Don't call this phone again. I'll get you a new number through the usual channels. Love you, kid."

"Same."

I thumbed the End button, then tossed the phone in the lake. It had been as useful as the stones it was joining.

CHAPTER 12

ELI WAS A TOTAL DICK THAT week. And so was I.

According to him, the monthly ritual of prepping the *Rebel Yell* for print was pure hell. I thought he was exaggerating. I thought wrong.

Eli was one of those annoying perfectionists who triple-check everything, then check it again. He wanted me to be the same way. He was cutthroat in his insistence that I prove my loyalty, and I was pissed about being at his mercy.

We said messed-up stuff to each other in the worst moments. There were times when I felt like a kickboxing match would've been more productive than what we were doing. But I wanted to know what Whispertown was about, so I hung in. Though, I made it a point to be as hard on him as he was on me.

Inefficiency was his Kryptonite. So I asked repetitive questions and made him walk me through processes we'd covered already. Take that, SuperJerk.

Monday was the toughest day, worsened by me leaving early to make that week's conference call with Bertram.

"Is that what 'all in' looks like?" Eli said from behind his desk while I gathered my things. "I always mistook that for leaving."

"I gotta be home. Relax, I'll be here in the morning."

"Maybe."

I stopped packing. "What's that mean?"

"I overheard Reya talking to one of her friends about how you didn't show at Dustin's party. She seems to think you have reliability issues. I'm wondering if my sister might be right about something for once."

A small piece of me perked up to hear Reya was talking about me, but Eli was clearly trying to push a button. "Whatever."

He said, "It's good you didn't go to the Dust Off. I heard Zach crashed it."

I shrugged. "I'm not scared of Zach."

"Of course you aren't. I just meant I heard him and Reya were together most of the night. That probably would've been awkward for you. Had you been there."

I grabbed my bag, walked to his side of the desk, and mashed down all the keys on his keyboard. The piece he'd been working on was instantly overrun with random characters. "Good night, Eli," I said, then left. I could push buttons, too.

He was on edge nearly every morning and evening we spent in the J-Room after that. Had I not been so consumed with wanting his insider information and giving him a hard time about it in the process, I might've seen that his bad mood wasn't all about me. Maybe things would've gone differently.

I don't know if I'll forgive myself for that.

So it went. Me and Eli still managed to get the latest issue of the *Rebel*

Yell finalized and formatted by Friday, minus a front page.

"What's our lead story going to be?" I asked, proofing the drafts of the other finished pages, again. He'd succeeded in making me a triple-checker. If we planned to print on Tuesday we needed to fill the empty space.

"The Portside game." He slouched low in his chair, only the top of his head visible over his laptop screen.

I'd heard rumblings about the district rivals coming to town all week. "That's tonight. We just going to paste it in on Monday?"

"Provided your copy isn't terrible."

I stopped proofing. "*My* copy?"

"You're writing it. I want art, too, so take the camera."

"I hate football. And it's for the front page."

"You don't have to like it to write about it. That's your assignment. I want eight inches."

I didn't find that phrase nearly as funny as I used to. "Eli, *it's the front page.* I thought you cared about the quality there more than anywhere else."

He closed his laptop and looked me in the eye. "I do. I look forward to reading your story on Monday."

I checked the time on my phone. The game started in two hours. I could probably get there early and scope some good vantage points for the photos. Get some pregame spectator quotes, even from the away fans, and . . .

Whoa. Where'd *that* come from?

"If I do this," I said, "I want you to tell me what Whispertown is. On Monday."

He rubbed his bloodshot eyes—he really did let this paper get to him. "If you do it right, I'll *consider* telling you."

"You'll tell me." I got everything I thought I needed, took the camera bag off his desk.

Eli said, "One more thing, Nick."

"What?" I snapped, expecting another asinine task.

He slid a lanyard across his desk, held it out with a blue laminate dangling from it. The plastic badge read: Stepton High Press Pass. "This will get you into the game for free."

I took it. "I'll bring this back next week."

"That's yours to keep, Nick." One side of his mouth turned up in a half grin. It was the first time he hadn't been a stone-faced troll in days. "We're almost done. You did good."

I rolled my eyes. "Don't go asking me to the prom or anything. I want that info Monday morning."

I left. Didn't bother to see if I'd hurt his feelings, or made him angry, or had no effect on him at all. I wish I'd looked back and taken note.

I wish that more than anything.

CHAPTER 13

THE PORTSIDE PIRATES BATTLED THE REBELS on the gridiron and I snapped pictures of everything, barely taking the time to focus. The camera had a massive memory card so I figured I'd get at least one good piece of art for Eli. In the third quarter, our star wide receiver caught a thirty-yard pass one-handed for a touchdown that tied the game. I got a great action shot of the catch. Best picture I'd taken all night.

He hung frozen in midair, wedged between two jumping defenders, stretched to his full six-foot-three height to snag the ball. Great lighting, incredible composition, probably good enough to sell to a real newspaper. One problem: the receiver was Zach Lynch.

I deleted the photo.

That douchelord wasn't getting any shine from me.

Walking the field's fenced-in perimeter, I scanned the crowd with the camera's zoom, then panned over to the Stepton cheerleaders on the sidelines, spotted Reya. Her face filled the frame, sparkling with gold glitter. She smiled as if she knew the camera was on her.

Startled, I lowered it. Realized the crowd's cheers and Zach's sad, sad end zone dancing were what triggered her smile. I raised the camera and looked at her one more time, almost snapped the picture, but decided against. If I'd had a chance with her, I blew it being distracted with all this Whispertown drama. Time to move on. Better for everyone.

Swinging the lens toward the far end of the field, I spotted an ambulance sitting prepped and ready in case someone got folded backward or something. The EMTs leaned against the vehicle, drinking Cokes. Twenty yards from them, in the bleacher shadows, a small group gathered. I zoomed tighter.

And saw my dad.

Him, a plump Asian man, and a wispy-haired white guy huddled together. I took a couple of shots.

Their conversation seemed . . . active. A lot of hand gestures, everyone participating, everyone a little on edge. Then chunky guy pressed a cell to his ear, said a few words, and ended the call. He motioned to the others, and they made for the exit.

I moved toward them. The game ended at the same time—winner: Rebels—and people crowded the walkways, slowing my progress. The surge of football fans kept me from tracking Dad and his buddies.

That was fine. Monday would be here soon enough.

Sunday I worked on giving Eli his eight inches (hehe . . . it was funny again).

All jokes aside, it was hard (hehe). Seriously, it was difficult. I'd never concentrated on writing before. Of course, I'd done the term-paper thing, and made a sucky attempt at that video-game review—which Eli cut from the *Yell*—but I never really *cared* about the quality of my writing before. My motivation had more to do with not giving Eli an excuse to withhold info than any other real journalism aspirations. When I finished writing what I thought to be front-page-worthy copy, I had three pages. Or thirty-odd inches.

Cutting everything I could only got it down to a page and a half. I was about to make another go when I noticed the clock. Four hours had passed.

In terms of *my* attention span it was the equivalent of an eight-hundred-pound man running a half marathon. I spent another hour revising, got my story to the exact length Eli requested. The amazing thing was, even though I cut stuff, it seemed *better* than before. My story kicked ass.

Shortly after eleven I said, "That's all you're getting from me tonight, Eli."

I went to bed proud of what I'd done. Sleep came easy.

I haven't had a peaceful night since.

Not only did I stay up late typing my article, I got up early, anticipating the shock on Eli's face when my copy crushed whatever low expectations he probably had.

I printed it and backed it up on a flash drive. Walking into the J-Room, I reread the printout, mentally flagging areas I thought Eli might ding me on. The normal mushroom scent of old books and neglect had been eclipsed by something else. Something worse.

"Eli, I think you created a monster, man—" I cracked the J-Room door.

My stomach seized and I took in too much red for anything to make sense. Though the smell pushed at me, I kept walking until my foot stuck in something gummy, like old syrup, but rancid. The tacky pool covered most of the floor, and my friend lay in it like an island, his head resting between two books that were so saturated, the pages were bloated.

"Eli?"

My stupid article drifted to the floor. I knelt next to him, in the congealing stickiness. Ugly slashes ran up his arm, and a triangular X-Acto blade rested next to his limp fingers.

I ran then, tracking red residue through the school, past the first string of early bird students. At the main office I screamed for help. The vice principal and security guard tried to calm me. Too late for that.

"My friend . . . in the journalism room. He's hurt. He needs help."

They reacted like they were supposed to, even though I was lying.

Eli was as far beyond help as anyone could get.

CHAPTER 14

THE VICE PRINCIPAL, MR. HARDWICK, AND the sheriff, Hill, argued over what should be done with me while I stared at the blood on my shoes.

I shook my head, had a hard time focusing. I came to school early to surprise Eli with my stellar writing. I half remembered this thing my godfather once said. It was about the best way to lay plans. And mice. Or something.

Me, surprise Eli.

That didn't go too well for either of us.

Sheriff Hill, his cheeks rosy and his chest puffed, said, "I just want to get a statement."

"After what he's seen you're really going to press this? He's a minor, and his parents are on the way. You can talk to him when they get here, if they allow it." Hardwick was Hill's opposite in many ways. His skin was brown, slightly darker than mine, while the sheriff's was a blotchy beige and pink. Hardwick was stylish in slacks, a dress shirt, and a tie while the sheriff wore a blue-on-tan uniform and shiny gold badge. He fought for my well-being, while the sheriff wanted to pump me for info before I had time to "formulate a story." That's how it seemed. Mr. Hardwick looked at me, sighed, forced a smile. "It's going to be fine, son."

I remembered something else my godfather said, fully this time.

When it hits the fan, don't trust anyone in a suit or uniform unless you're payin' them. If they're grinnin', trust them even less. They're all the same.

Them. They.

Us.

"Nick," Mr. Hardwick said.

I didn't answer because I forgot what my name was this time, in this town.

It occurred to me that sudden amnesia—a life-threatening condition in my family—was a sign I wasn't handling this in the best possible way. Was there a best way? Eli's blood was on my shoes.

"Nick?"

I looked up. Not because I remembered my fake name but because I recognized a new speaker's voice. My mother. When did she get here?

I left my chair. She hugged me, and I let her. Where her head rested on my chest, I wondered if my heartbeat was loud in her ears, like the bass from good speakers. As we stood there, her squeezing me in a way that wasn't comforting, I noticed she'd come alone.

"Where's Dad?" I was glad I had to say only two words, because my voice cracked on the second.

Mom pulled away, looked at my forehead—her trick for when she wanted me to think she was looking in my eyes. "Work, sweetie."

"Mrs. Pearson," said the sheriff, "I was wondering if I could speak to Nick about—"

"Is my son under arrest?" Mom said, facing him.

The color drained from his cheeks; his blotchiness became a smooth gray. "Ma'am, it's not that kind of situation."

"When you figure out what kind of situation it is, you can contact me, and I'll determine if there's anything for you and Nick to speak about." To me, she said, "Let's go. And don't say a word."

The room felt too bright. I noticed everything at once but failed to put any of it together. The sheriff reacting coolly to, but not surprised by, my mother's refusal to cooperate. Hardwick eyeing us with a mix of shock and pride. Teachers on the other side of the office windows, ushering kids toward the auditorium, away from the J-Room, where Eli was. Everyone present and accounted for in this totally f'ed-up moment. Everyone except my father. Because of "work."

Eli liked science fiction and fantasy stuff. Talked about it all the time. *Finite Universe*. Superheroes and laser beams. There, in between thumping heartbeats, the brightness of the room became a single laser that burned a question into my brain, one I couldn't ask or answer.

Which job was Dad working?

Was it the crappy, strip-mall-accountant job our handlers set up for him, or was it the *other* job? The job that had him acting shady, sneaking around with the Mystery Man in the BMW? The job that Eli was investigating?

"Mrs. Pearson," said the sheriff, barely opening his mouth to speak the words, "I'm just trying to find out if your son has any clue why the young man did what he did?"

The laser kept going, burning one last word in my mind. *Whispertown*.

Mom said, "If Nick can think of anything useful, we'll be in touch." She grabbed me by the arm, pulled me toward the exit.

Eli was going to tell me about Whispertown today. Then I'd know what it had to do with my dad's new secrets. But Eli didn't really know me, or my family, or how we came to this place. If he did, he would've known better than to deal with us—*me*—at all. He knew about Star Wars and journalism and video games.

Now Eli didn't know anything. Because he was dead, lying in a pool of his own stinking blood.

Outside the office, Mom looped a trembling arm around me. "It's all going to be fine. We're all right."

A shriek froze startled students and teachers. Hardwick and the sheriff sprinted from the office toward the J-Room. To Reya.

Two teachers and a custodian held her at the intersection of the main hall and the J-Room corridor. Three on one, and the three were struggling.

"That's not my brother," she screamed, lunging forward. "That's not my brother in there!"

Two EMTs—the same two I'd seen drinking Cokes by the football field on Friday night—wheeled a covered gurney toward the exit. Reya stopped bucking, stared at the still lump under the sheet, then collapsed, boneless. The three who'd been fighting her had to react quickly to keep her from crashing to the floor, and they almost screwed that up.

Hardwick and the sheriff knelt beside her, calling for assistance from the EMTs. The men complied, chocking the wheels on Eli's gurney and leaving him in the middle of a near-deserted hall. They had to help the living. Eli was now a delayed errand.

Outside, it was a day that didn't deserve to be so sunny. Mom pushed me through the doors into its brightness, and I didn't know which of us was shaking more.

CHAPTER 15

AT HOME, MOM LEFT ME IN the foyer, instructing me not to move. She returned with a garbage bag. "Everything goes in."

"Only my shoes and jeans are stained, Mom."

She held the bag open like I hadn't said a word.

Barefoot, in my boxers, I went to my room, pulled on some b-ball shorts and an old 76ers T-shirt. Mom brought me water and an orange prescription bottle I'd never seen before. When she moved, the contents rattled like mints. She popped the top, shook out two white ovals, and passed them to me.

"What is it?" I asked.

"Something you won't be getting used to. Take them."

After I took the pills, the rest of the day stuttered by in a few eyeblinks. One blink and it was lunchtime—I ate only half the sandwich Mom gave me. Two blinks and the sky turned darker. On the third blink, I opened my eyes to pure night and new weight pressing my mattress farther into my bed frame. Dad sat by my feet, patting my thigh in a weird, too-fast rhythm, keeping time with a dance track only he could hear.

"Son, are you awake?"

I groaned. "I'm up."

"Sorry about what happened to your friend."

"Why?" Mom's pills still had me groggy.

"What's that supposed to mean?"

I swung my feet to the floor so we sat side by side. I was almost taller than him. He had big muscles in his arms though, and stubble, and hard eyes. He had to have been the most intimidating bookkeeper on Kreso Maric's payroll back in the day. A scary guy to meet if you were alone in a dark alley. Someone who didn't feel sorry about much. I couldn't remember the last time he'd come into my room for anything. Apologized for anything.

"I meant 'thanks,' Dad."

"I would've come earlier, but I couldn't break away from work. I wanted to, but I couldn't."

"Don't worry about it. I saw a dead body, nothing new there."

Our height difference became more pronounced as he stiffened. "I'm gonna let you get some rest, Tony."

"It's Nick," I said, rolling onto my back. I didn't feel sleepy, just foggy and forgetful. I couldn't remember what we'd just talked about. I blinked and he was gone.

Of all the time jumps that day, the one featuring my Dad's remorse seemed most like a drug-induced dream. Pure fantasy.

Until I saw Eli's ghost.

Just after nine o'clock, metal scraped concrete outside, a low vehicle turning into our steep driveway too fast, catching the incline with its fender. I rose, cracked the blinds, and looked down on Eli's green Beetle parked behind Dad's SUV, exhaust rising like breath. The driver's door swung open. I saw his dark hair and tanned skin as he exited the vehicle. He turned, looked up at me. Smiled.

I blinked, cleared away tears. With them went the image of the dead boy, though the car remained. The door opened, for real this time. Not a ghost but the surviving Cruz sibling.

Reya.

The medicine Mom gave me was filtering out of my system quicker by the minute, but I still felt clumsy dropping my b-ball shorts and pulling on jeans from the closet floor. I wedged my feet into the first pair of sneakers I saw, then made it to the bathroom to brush my teeth as the doorbell rang. When I left the bathroom I heard Mom speaking to Reya in low tones, and I found Dad standing at the second-floor landing eavesdropping and gripping the banister.

He saw me, returned to his room, and closed the door.

I met Eli's sister downstairs. Her eyes were dark and puffy, like she recently got punched. In a way, she did. I stood there unsure of what to do or say, but she took away my first uncertainty by embracing me. I hugged her back.

"I'm going to get your friend some water," Mom said, and disappeared into the kitchen.

Reya backed away. "Is there somewhere we can talk?"

I led her into the dining room, still didn't ask the question on my mind since I saw her from my window. It seemed rude somehow.

She took a chair, set her bag on the floor, and scanned the room. Her neck craned from the tablecloth to the walls to the curtains. "You have a nice house."

"Uh, thanks." WitSec had good taste.

Mom came in with two glasses of water, then left again. Reya stared at her drink like she didn't know what it was.

Somebody needed to say something. I walked to the window and made a weak attempt. "That your car?"

"Mostly. I'm supposed to share it with—" She broke off, took a long gulp of water, and wiped dribble from her chin with her sleeve. "It's mine now."

"I'm sorry about what happened."

Her eyes hardened like stones plugged into her swollen face. "What did happen, Nick?"

I felt defensive all of a sudden. "How should I know?"

"You found him. What did you see?"

Red. That wasn't what she wanted to hear, though. I didn't know what she wanted to hear.

She said, "They're telling Mami that he slit his wrists. That sound right to you?"

It didn't sound right at all. Kids did it every day, though. See, I *still* wasn't getting her meaning. Maybe it was the drugs, or maybe I was just. That. Slow. "Was there a note?"

She laughed, a breathless cackle I never wanted to hear again. "No. He had two books with him. This *pendejo* cop said *those* were his note. Some kind of symbolism crap."

I remembered seeing books this morning. "What were they?"

"*Brave New World* and *Robinson Crusoe*."

They seemed *familiar* somehow, but I never read them, couldn't say if they were symbolic or not. Making that sort of statement seemed like the kind of I'm-smarter-than-you move Eli might pull. I didn't tell her that. No point.

She said, "When you saw him last—before today, I mean—was he acting strange?"

"Strange is a relative thing. In the time I knew him, he seemed . . . consistent. I was with him on Friday afternoon. He wanted me to cover the football game."

"Was anyone messing with him?" she asked. "Did he seem scared?"

I shook my head and made the stupid choice to play amateur counselor, spouting off stuff I'd heard on TV a thousand times. "Look, Reya, when things like this happen, you can't always rationalize it. I don't know why Eli did what he did. Maybe we'll never know."

She snapped, "My brother didn't do anything."

Eli did plenty. I had a pair of shoes covered in what Eli did. "What are we talking about?" I asked the question I was scared to ask before. "Why are you here?"

I regretted it almost immediately.

"I'm here because my brother was murdered."

CHAPTER 16

MURDERED.

"Wow." I blanked, too shocked to form a sentence. Eli would've dinged me for that. "Wow."

She pulled a thick envelope from her bag and slid it across the table. It was addressed to Eli and had an embossed blue crown where the return address would be. I recognized the symbol from Eli's laptop, the one I'd mistaken for Lord of the Rings. I lifted the envelope, read the words beneath the emblem. "Columbia University?"

"Open it."

The seal had already been broken and the contents were stuffed in badly. I removed a new arrival catalog with a diverse cast of campus models smiling on the cover, several blank forms, and a short letter that I assumed she wanted me to read.

"'Dear Mr. Cruz, we are pleased to inform you that your application for our Scholastic Press Association Summer Journalism Workshop has been accepted . . .'" I looked up, wanting the CliffsNotes. "What is this?"

"A journalism program he's been trying to get into for the last two years," she said, like that explained everything. To her, maybe it did. "You two were working on the paper together, right? He didn't tell you about this?"

"No."

She blinked rapidly, looked away. I could tell what she was thinking: if Eli didn't tell me the great news about getting into his coveted program, he obviously didn't share whatever case-breaking clue she'd fooled herself into believing I had.

"Don't you see?" she said, begging. "That's *Columbia*." She snatched back her precious letter. "Columbia University has the best journalism school in the country. He'd been dreaming about going there since he was like eight. He just got that letter a week and a half ago. Why would someone who was so close to having his dream come true slit his wrists in a dirty closet?"

The answer to that one was between Eli and God. "I don't know what you want me to say. I wish I could tell you something, I do. But this caught me by surprise just like everyone else."

Reya shrank. She gathered up the rest of Eli's acceptance letter. "I'm sorry to bother you."

I chased her to the front door. "You shouldn't drive like this."

"I'm not drunk. My brother's just dead."

"That's worse than drunk."

When we stepped onto the porch the cold bit into my neck and arms. I fought a shiver while she fished keys from her bag and pressed buttons on her auto-start remote. The Beetle purred to life in the driveway. A little over a week ago Eli had done the same thing at the coffeehouse before he took me home. The memory hit me with such force I almost stumbled.

"Nick, are you all right?"

"Cold out here."

Her eyes narrowed. "Is that all?"

I said, "That's all."

"Please let me know if you think of anything strange from last week." She reached into Eli's envelope, tore a corner off one of the forms, and produced a pen. She scribbled her number on the slip and shoved it in my hand before rushing off my porch.

She climbed into the car she no longer had to share and became a pair of taillights in the distance. For the first time since I met her, I was glad to see her go. I needed time to think this through.

I played it out in my room. . . .

Say Eli killed himself, for whatever reason, then that meant Reya was in one of those grief phases. The denial one. That's supposed to be normal and she'd get over it eventually.

Unless she was right.

You found him. What did you see?

I saw the ugly purple slashes running up his arms and the blade lying next to him. Body. Blade. Blood.

And books?

I sat up.

Brave New World and *Robinson Crusoe* weren't some symbolic riddle left behind. They were the books he'd used to keep his desk from wobbling. That's why they seemed familiar. I'd seen those titles every day in the J-Room. But what did that *mean*?

It meant the desk was moved.

No, not just moved. Pushed. Hard enough to knock it clean off its paperback braces.

There's something wrong with Stepton, Nick. No one's talking about it.

He told me that when we met for coffee. And when I asked him if the drug dealers survived their gunshots . . .

The way things are going, if they'd died, it probably would've been ruled a suicide. . . .

Oh, hell.

———————

This isn't about Whispertown. No way.

Yes it is, I thought immediately, *it has to be.*

I went back and forth like that for hours, until exhaustion crept in. If what happened in the J-Room was more than a sad decision and a final flick of a razor—if it tied to that damned story Eli was working on—then . . .

. . . Dad was involved. Somehow.

The flip-flopper in me piped up, *That's crazy, no way Dad's involved in the murder of a—*

My denial voice knew better. Dad could very well have played a role in the murder of a kid.

He'd done it before.

REWIND

Four years ago . . .

Summer. Our real home. Off the Philadelphia Main Line.

People still called me Tony.

Dad spent a lot of time working on his "business." At school, when kids asked what he did, I said he was a consultant, like I'd been told to do. Even at ten, I knew I was playing a part, and so were the other kids. They asked because their doctor/lawyer/pro-athlete parents whispered about how the Bordeaux family *really* made money; they wanted in on the grown-up stuff. I answered—always with a cheesy grin and overly casual tone that didn't quiet the rumors—because it was cool to be *that* guy. The gangster's son.

Summers were different, though. A lot of the kids in the neighborhood went on vacation, to the Jersey Shore, or even Europe. Of those who stayed, only a few had anything to do with me. Their parents couldn't control whose money their kids' school accepted, but they could control the company their kids kept, leaving me with desperation friends. Kids whose parents were too busy to care.

In some Disney Channel movie, it would've made us closer. But the Main Line wasn't the Mouse House. Instead of Disney, we had discord.

A hot-weather ritual of ganging up on whoever's identity quirk irritated someone first. The NFL player's son stuttered. The venture capitalist's daughter had underarm hair that curled from her short sleeves like tentacles. The gangster's son . . . wasn't.

"My dad *does* work for the mob," I blurted one afternoon, incensed by name-calling, violating my oath of secrecy.

"You're a l-l-liar! Your d-dad's a big old p-p-pus—" said you-know-who.

"I'm not." A fat lip was in somebody's future. "My dad and my godfather tell stories all the time."

"*The* G-g-godfather?"

"No, just mine."

The VC's daughter jumped in. "How do you know *they're* not lying? You ever *see* them do mob stuff?"

I huffed, "Your pit hair is hungry."

That argument got uglier than usual. Of course I'd never *seen* Dad or Bricks do any mob stuff. Didn't mean they made it up. I might've let it go. Except when I got home, Rachelle, my go-to babysitter, was waiting. Mom had a charity dinner to attend. Dad had to work.

I knew because he was on the phone with Kreso Maric. The boss.

Dad would have to go run some kind of errand late tonight. Some Cool Mob Stuff.

I planned to be there.

CHAPTER 17

WHEN MY ALARM SOUNDED AT 6:00 a.m., Mom cut it off and informed me school was closed because of what happened. I was asleep before she stopped talking. Not good sleep, only what my body demanded.

It was almost noon when I dragged my butt from bed to shower and I still felt drained. A note on the fridge said Dad was at work and Mom had gone grocery shopping. It also said to be home by four. Conference call today (moved from yesterday because I hadn't been up for it).

Seriously, Bertram? Rescheduling just so I can answer your stupid one-to-ten questions? Ass.

Searching the net, I found the only Cruz residence listed in Stepton. I pasted the address into Google Maps. Reya lived on the west side, in the center of the crappy neighborhood I rode through a few weeks ago.

I grabbed my jacket. Time for a return trip.

Reya's block rushed at me fast, and the surrounding houses looked just as sketchy as last time. A couple of guys lounging against a telephone pole eyed me hard when I turned onto Granger Avenue, Reya's street. I nodded to show respect. They looked liked they'd eat me if I fell and broke a leg.

I kept pedaling, spotted Reya's place about fifty yards ahead, well before I could read the numbers on the mailbox. Her lime Beetle was like a flare in this gloomy neighborhood. Three cars blocked her in while another half dozen lined either side of the street. A couple of Latino guys and a very pretty—very pregnant—Latina crowded the porch. The guys wore dark slacks, dress shirts, and loosened ties. The girl sat in a flowing teal maternity skirt that stopped midcalf. I felt like an underdressed jerk in my jeans, sneakers, and bomber jacket, but I was here now. "Is this the Cruz residence?"

A long moment passed with no one acknowledging my presence. I willed myself not to look at my shoes. Only the girl seemed to notice me, offering a half smile. I pressed on. "I was a friend of Eli's."

Someone screamed.

Both men turned toward the house, where rapid-fire Spanish followed the shriek. The pregnant girl stared at the ground. Inside, the voice was high and shrill. A woman. I plucked a few familiar curse words from the air.

A deeper male voice sounded, attempting to cut across the woman, but she wasn't having it. The storm door swung open on squealing hinges, and a short, bulky man with brown skin emerged, shoving aside the two guys on the porch and sidestepping the pregnant girl, who was suddenly on her feet.

From my initial impression I thought the young guys might retaliate—violently—at such rude behavior. Didn't happen.

The old guy came at me like I was a ghost he couldn't see. I stepped aside to avoid being run over. He went for one of the cars at the curb, a freshly waxed Jaguar, and fishtailed onto the main drag, smoking skid marks the only evidence he'd been there at all.

This seemed like a bad time, and I would've left if one of the guys hadn't spoken in such an exhausted, defeated tone. "If you want to go in, go in."

Pregnant Girl stared after the car as it screeched around the corner, then flopped back down on the stoop like her legs had given out.

I moved past them all and entered the open front door. Stepping inside the house was like stepping through a portal. Outside was the definition of hood, decrepit and barren camouflage. Inside was like something on HGTV, one of those makeover shows. Marble foyer, fresh paint, thick carpet leading deeper into the house. All well kept.

Inside, a dozen people were packed in a tight circle with their heads lowered, creating an oven with their body heat.

". . . *sea tu nombre. Venga tu reino. Hágase tu voluntad en la tierra como en el cielo. Danos hoy nuestro pan de cada día . . .*"

I hovered at the back of the crowd, unsure and uncomfortable. I was witnessing a prayer, that much I got. Strange, after the screaming from like five seconds ago.

This was private. Sacred. I turned to leave, quietly and without incident.

A hand fell on my shoulder.

The owner of the hand sidled next to me. Three black teardrop tattoos dotted his face beneath his left eye, and a puckered slash ran from his temple to jawline, curling at the end like a candy cane. His hair was like peach fuzz, coating his scalp with no definitive hairline, as if the barber handled the clippers with prosthetic hooks. The suit he wore could not hide how ripped he was. I'd seen his type plenty when I was a kid. He couldn't have been home from jail for long.

The closed circle in the living room continued muttering, "*Dios te salve, María. Llena eres de gracia: El Señor está contigo. Bendita tú eres entre todas las mujeres . . .*"

I found myself facing the group again, my new buddy beside me now, his heavy hand still on my shoulder.

He whispered, "It's a *Rosary*, little homey." An answer to a question I did not ask.

"What is?"

"The prayer for Little Cuz. It's what they say when someone dies."

Eli never mentioned being related to felons. Come to think of it, neither did I. "Them? Not you?"

He flashed a row of precious metal teeth, pointed toward the ceiling. Beyond the ceiling. "The Big Guy might find it funny coming from me."

The Rosary continued for a while, long enough for me to contemplate a quick dash to the door, or a flying leap through a nearby window. I'd been in this sauna for five minutes, had yet to be introduced to anyone, and was being courted by a fresh parolee. I should've stayed in bed.

When the Rosary ended, the members of the circle broke apart as if awakening from a trance. An elderly woman with her silver hair in a bun sensed me at her back. She turned, her expression suspicious. "Who are you?"

Her question drew the attention of the others in the room, all Latinos and Latinas of varying ages, heights, and sizes. I spoke quickly, afraid of what might happen if I didn't. "I was a friend of Eli's. I'm sorry."

My new big homey steered me into the packed living room. The crowd parted for me, creating a path to a love seat where a tiny woman with smudged mascara waited. Eli's mom, I guessed.

"Are you Nick?" she asked.

I was surprised she knew my name. "Yes, that's me."

"He talked about you. He never talked about people from school."

Something in me shrank, thinking her next words would be a string of accusations. That she thought I had something to do with her son's death. Then I'd be torn apart. Scanning the room, reading the characters in it, I had no doubt about that.

"You're the one who found him, aren't you?"

My stomach cramped so hard I thought I'd double over. "Yes, ma'am."

"Did he—" Her voice cracked, and a plump lady rushed to grab her hand. Mrs. Cruz waved her off. "Did he look peaceful?"

Oh God. I thought back to the moment I walked into the J-Room. Nothing in there looked peaceful. I caught sight of the ex-con who'd ushered me in. He gave a slight nod.

"Yes, ma'am," I said, not meeting Mrs. Cruz's eyes. "He did."

Her face folded and fresh tears watered her cheeks. She motioned for me to come closer. I hesitated.

"Please, Nick."

I got so close I could smell the soap on her skin. She stood and planted a light kiss on my cheek. "*Gracias*. For being a friend to my boy. I know he didn't have many."

What do you say to that? Before I could force words, Mrs. Cruz said, "You must be hungry." She yelled, "Reya! *Preparale un plato de comida*."

She'd called Reya. But the rest could've been a scene from *Scarface* for all I knew. *Reya, bring the chainsaw.*

I heard her voice from deeper in the house, in English. "Well, Mami, tell whoever it is to come in the kitchen." Her voice grew in volume as she drew nearer. "I'm not letting anyone else spill food on the—" Reya saw me and went mute.

In her silky dress, hair in curls, makeup done—she was the polar opposite of how she had looked at my house the night before, and I lost my words as well.

"Do you know Nick?" Mrs. Cruz asked.

"We've met," Reya said quickly. "Come with me, Nick."

She disappeared around the corner and I followed, throwing out a few nice-to-meet-yous on the way.

Serving trays wrapped in foil covered every horizontal surface in the kitchen. Reya had her back to me, holding a sectioned paper plate and grabbing a chicken breast with some tongs.

"Reya—"

"Save it. You decided I'm not crazy. We'll talk more in my room." She faced me, annoyed. "Do you like rice?"

CHAPTER 18

I FOLLOWED REYA TO HER ROOM, balancing a cup of iced tea and a massive plate that could've fed three people. Our backgrounds were different, but the traditions of death surpassed culture. Everyone mourned with food.

Real random, Reya asked, "Was there a pregnant girl on the porch?"

"Yeah."

"*Mierda.* She's due, like, any minute. I wish her water would break so she'd go away."

"I take it you're going to be the kid's godmother."

Reya hit me with a wicked stare. "She's my cousin. Pilar. We hate each other."

"Kind of like you and Eli."

I didn't think before I said it, a trait I inherited from Dad. If Reya had smashed my fully loaded plate into my face, she'd have been justified. She only redirected her gaze, what little fuel the hatred of her cousin ignited gone. "Sit down. Eat."

She motioned to her bed and I accepted the offer, sinking into her spongy mattress.

Like with the rest of the house, my attention was drawn to the decor in Reya's room. Dark wood floors. An orange-gold shade coated three walls, while burgundy adorned the fourth accent wall. Crown molding trimmed the ceiling border. The furnishings and linen complemented each other. I was acutely aware of the effort all this took because I'd spent a lot of grounded Saturdays hovering around my mom while she was glued to various home improvement shows on TV.

"Who's the decorator?" I asked, hoping to ease some of the tension I'd caused.

"Me."

Wow, the girl had skills.

I set my plate on her dresser, craving info, not food, and noticed a picture of Eli wedged in the mirror frame. There were many other pictures obscuring the glass, too. *Beneath* Eli's. His picture was a new addition to her collage of friends, one long overdue.

"What was all the screaming when I pulled up in your yard?" I asked.

She shrugged. "That was my mother's brother, Miguel. He's rich so he thinks that gives him the right to say anything. My mother was discussing funeral arrangements with my aunt Amaya when Miguel says, 'It won't be a Catholic funeral, not since Eli, you know . . .'"

"Oh man, what an ass."

"Yeah, he's stupid anyway," she said. "They all are. Eli didn't kill himself and I'm going to prove it." She flopped onto her mattress, visibly fatigued. "So what changed your mind?"

Knowing the question was inevitable, I'd thought about this carefully. I couldn't tell her too much. Not yet. Because if Eli didn't kill himself—

and I was leaning that way—then someone with the capacity for murder, and the skill/connections to make it look like something else, was still out there. Possibly living in my house.

It was safer to keep her at a distance, while getting what I needed. More info.

I told her a piece of the truth. "I sat up last night thinking about what you said. You asked me if Eli had been working on anything strange. This one story popped into my head."

She leaned forward.

"Whispertown."

Reya slid off her bed, paced past me. "Okay. What's that?"

"I'm not sure. I was thinking he might have some notes in his room. Maybe on his laptop." That's what I came for, hoping to ransack my dead friend's stuff.

She nodded. "Maybe. But we can't go in there now."

I refrained from a snappy *Why not?* and tried for friendly persuasion. "If you're busy, I could look."

"I'm busy, but that's not the reason. Mami's treating it like a shrine. I'll have to do it when she sleeps. If she sleeps." She passed a hand over her face like a squeegee, as if she could wipe the tension away. "Do you know anything else about this story? Why do you think it's important?"

"Um." Reya's bedroom door opened, a relief since I wasn't prepared for her follow-up questions.

Relief faded when a familiar ape in a dingy dress shirt and too-short necktie barged in, having fixed his own plate *before* coming to console his grieving ex-girlfriend. "Hey, babe. I would've been here sooner but Coach called an early practice since school was—"

He froze when he saw me on the bed.

Hello, Zach Lynch.

Reya said, "What the *hell* are you doing here, Zachary?"

He looked as shocked as I felt, though my brand came with a little smile. Had Eli exaggerated about these two reconciling at the Dust Off? Seemed that way.

Zach's cheeks flared; he flicked eye daggers at me, then puffed his chest. "I'm here to be a shoulder for you to cry on. I know you're going through some stuff, so I'll let your little outburst slide."

"Let *me* slide?" Reya crossed her arms, popped a hip one way, and cocked her head the other way. If he thought she had an attitude before . . .

The rapid string of Spanish that followed sounded like machine gun fire. I caught like every fifth word. All foul. Funny how I could translate obscenities in multiple languages.

Zach interrupted her, though his eyes were on me. "Hey! I came over here to be supportive. Stop acting bitchy and show some courtesy."

My fists clenched. I wanted to drop this guy. The last thing I needed was a brawl in the house of the only person who could help me get to the bottom of Whispertown. But I was *so* tempted.

Reya said, "You should go now, Nick."

"*I* should go?"

She seemed calm. Determined. "Yes. Zachary and I need some privacy."

"Disappear, dude. The grown-ups need the room." That dumbass took a seat on the bed, smiling, completely misinterpreting the nature of her request. I was sorry I was going to miss this.

Reya said, "I'll get some foil to wrap your food." She led me back to the kitchen, packed up my plate, and dropped it in a leftover grocery bag with a can of Sprite and some plastic utensils.

"Are you sure you want me to leave you with him?"

She said, "You're not the only one who can handle Zachary. I'll text you."

"Don't you need my number?"

"I've got it."

"Since when?"

She produced something close to a smile. The true gesture may have been beyond her reach today, understandably. "Since I stole it from Eli's phone a couple of weeks ago."

"Why didn't you let me know?" I said.

A sigh. "Sometimes I can be a little old-fashioned. Let's talk later. I've got something I need to do."

She returned to her room, was yelling at Zach before she closed the door. I left her to it, sneaking past the adults consoling Mrs. Cruz. My big homey was nowhere in sight, so I thought I'd make a clean getaway. Not so much.

On the porch, the two guys from before were gone, but Reya's cousin sat in her same spot. She leaned forward, her face cupped in her hands, like she was trying to catch her hitching sobs. Today's visit could be easily summarized as Nick's Invasion of the Personal Moments. The awkwardness never ended at the Cruz house.

There was no way to get around her unseen. I let the door swing shut on its own, the resulting slam notifying her to my presence. She stared over her shoulder, sniffed loudly, an unsuccessful attempt to compose herself.

"Figures," she said. "First cute guy I've seen in forever, and I'm smearing my makeup."

She smiled at me, but she looked haggard. Not just from crying but from . . . whatever.

I said, "Pilar, right?"

"Someone actually uttered my name to you? Did they cross themselves after they did it?"

"Reya told me."

"Oh, well, I know *she* didn't cross herself. She would've burst into flames." She touched her bulging belly, laughed. "Guess I'm one to talk."

I hadn't planned on this conversation, but it felt weird to just leave her there all alone, upset like she was. "I'm sorry about what happened to your cousin. He was cool."

"No, he wasn't. But he was sweet. A sweet, sweet kid." Then, "Do you want to sit down?"

She made room on her step like I'd said yes.

I checked my phone, only one thirty. I sat.

"What's your name?"

"Nick." I shook her manicured hand.

"How'd you know Cuz?"

"He was trying to get me to join the school paper."

She nodded. "He loved to write. Not just articles; he wrote short stories and stuff. Used to make me read them. Back in the day, I did it just because he asked, but they weren't very good. In the last couple of years, though, it's like he upped his game. I don't really like to read, but I started to look forward to Eli's stories. I—" A wrinkle creased her forehead. "There aren't going to be any more Eli stories."

The moisture in her eyes glistened in the afternoon sun, and she wiped away what she could with her palm, turning her eye makeup into dark raccoon circles. In spite of the smudged mascara, I noticed how pretty she was.

Her face was full, an obvious symptom of her pregnancy, but it didn't short her looks. She had olive skin, black hair that fell on her shoulders like dark waterfalls, and incredible brown eyes. It wasn't hard to imagine that, prior to Pilar's delicate condition, some of the animosity between her and Reya probably stemmed from how much they rivaled each other in hotness.

"You and Eli were close?" I asked.

Nodding. "He was such a nerd, but I loved him. When we were kids and Reya wouldn't let me play with her dolls, he'd invite me to his room and we'd have like this big action-figure war. This one time I put bleach in a water gun and sprayed Reya's Easter dress with it, he stood tall and said he was in on it. Eli always had my back."

I thought of the thwarted locker room beat down. "Yeah, he was that kind of guy."

Pilar popped up, startling me. "He's also the kind of guy who gives up like a *puta*, and slices his—" She didn't finish, more sobs cutting the statement short. She ran inside, the storm door slamming behind her, and left me on the porch alone. The very situation I thought I'd saved her from.

Somehow, that was my most awkward moment so far.

CHAPTER 19

BALANCING MY PLATE ON THE HANDLEBARS, I biked across town. With school closed for the day I crossed paths with a lot of classmates I knew by face but not by name. Guys playing touch football, and girls looking for the guys. I was more than aware of their stares as I passed.

That's him, he found the dead kid.

I put my weight on the pedals and pushed on until my legs burned.

At Monitor Park I'd planned to eat on a bench overlooking the lake. It was quiet except for the crickets, and some good-sized throwing stones made up the gravel path leading to the water. Before I could claim a spot and settle in, the vibrations of heavy bass and grumbling rapper-speak upset the calm.

A bright yellow Xterra came my way, spitting rocks from oversized tires. It passed me and I made for my bike, intending to find a new spot on the other side of the lake, when its brake lights flared. It slowed, stopped, then white reverse lights flashed as it backed toward me.

At first I thought it was Zach Lynch's goon squad, and my mood was just bad enough *not* to run. But when the music ceased and the vehicle stopped beside me, I saw a set of familiar, somewhat friendly faces.

Dustin, shirtless in the driver's seat, said, "Nick, what up? I thought that was you."

"Nice ride," I said, the SUV's paint job blinding me. Heavyset Lorenz reclined in the passenger seat, barely visible from where I stood, and Carrey occupied the seat behind Dustin.

"Getting the day off is sweet, right?" Carrey said.

I shrugged. "People should die on school grounds more often."

Carrey laughed, missing the sarcasm.

"That stuff with Eli's messed up," Dustin said. I wouldn't have expected him to know Eli's name on any other day, but the circumstances would have created a certain amount of notoriety. Eli, Patron Saint of Canceled School.

Lorenz worked his seat lever and swung into view like a vampire rising from his coffin "We 'bout to throw some burgers and dogs on the grill. Got some beer, too. You in?"

I didn't feel much like socializing. I showed them my bag of grief food. "I'm good."

"You're going to need a table to eat that," Dustin said. "Come to our pavilion."

He jerked the Xterra into gear and motored down the path before I could decline.

I climbed back on my bike, reaching the pavilion as they popped the tailgate to unload their goods. There were bags of charcoal, boxes of frozen beef patties, four dozen hot dogs, a stack of Styrofoam plates that was half my height, cases of soda, and a cooler I assumed hid the beer. The sheer amount of food confused me until new cars arrived, more classmates.

Dustin cranked his sound system, assaulting everyone with a thumping mix that startled a flock of birds to flight. My schoolmates cheered, throwing hands in the air and shaking booties even as more people came. I moved away from the festivities to a weather-beaten bench and table beneath the pavilion, while Lorenz and Carrey fired up the grill.

I worked through the food Reya gave me without much appetite. Dustin sat next to me. He'd located a shirt somewhere.

"We should talk," he said.

"About?"

"Eli. Everyone's saying you're the one who found him."

I bristled. What kind of morbid freak was this guy? "I'm not trying to be rude—you've been cool about inviting me to your parties—but I don't think Eli's any of your business."

I expected him to spaz and get some of his party groupies to toss me from the pavilion. Instead, "You weren't his only friend. Meet me by the lake in five minutes."

He left me, and his party, and disappeared through a path in the trees. I sat a moment thinking I'd misheard him. I hadn't.

Five minutes? Why wait?

I tossed my plate and followed.

Dustin stared across the lake with his hands stuffed deep in the pockets of his cargo pants. He didn't look at me when he said, "Bet you wish you never came here."

Did he mean his park party, or Stepton? Either way, "I wasn't given much say in it."

He wouldn't look at me and that pissed me off. I wasn't some airhead girl who sat on his lap and followed him around. *Let's get to it.* "Why'd you say I wasn't Eli's only friend?"

"Because you weren't." He faced me, his green eyes as murky as the lake. "He was my friend, too."

I said, "Bullshit."

"What?"

"Bull. Shit. I spent almost every day of the last two weeks with Eli. You know what I never heard? 'This one time, me and Dustin' stories."

His head jerked. "He never said anything about me?"

"Just that you don't invite him to your parties, which is strange with you two being best buddies and all." I skipped the part about Eli wanting me to spy on Dustin, though I was starting to rethink the motivation behind that strange, strange request.

I stepped closer, forcing him back so the lake lapped his heels. "What kind of a game are you running, Dustin? Trust me, I'm in no mood to play it."

"No games, I just—I need to tell someone else about Friday night."

That hit me like a slap. Friday night?

"What about it?"

"I need to tell someone what happened with me and him in that room where he puts the newspaper together. Where you found him."

Dustin was there *after* I left to cover the game. I knew I was among the last to see Eli alive, but that club was getting bigger. Me, Dustin, and a killer.

CHAPTER 20

"YOU WENT TO THE J-ROOM ON Friday *night*? Why?" I verbalized two of the billion questions I had. All while stepping deep into Dustin's personal space.

He sidestepped to keep from being forced into the lake. "You need to understand," he said, "how me and him got to that point."

"What point?"

"We had precalc together last year, and he was acing it. Me, I struggled, and my dad can be a hard ass about stuff like that. I asked Eli if he could help me and he did. I passed that class because of him. That's how we became friends."

That didn't sound like friendship. It sounded like tutoring. Maybe that's what friendship was to this party guy, surrounding himself with people who could meet needs at convenient times.

It occurred to me that my definition of friendship might be the same.

Didn't Eli have info I wanted? Wasn't that what kept me coming back to the J-Room every day? My irritation toward Dustin tapered off.

Dustin continued, "Sometimes it was cool having him around. He always knew the answer to stuff. Like, if you wanted to know just what the hell a hot dog was made of, he'd tell you. You might not ever eat one again, but you learned something new."

I agreed. "He was a *Jeopardy!* champion in the making."

"I know, right? We hung at my crib a lot this past summer. Whenever it was just us, anyway."

"What do you mean?"

"You know how it is, home all day, Pops was working. Sometimes the guys would come over. Girls, too. We've got a pool, so people like to chill at my place."

"Eli had a problem with that."

"Right. Like, like"—his eyebrows rose and I just about saw a lightbulb flash over his head—"someone who played starting QB all of a sudden had to ride the bench."

"Like someone took his spot," I said, condensing his clunky metaphor. I wondered if Eli ever tutored him in English.

Dustin nodded bobblehead-style.

I remembered how cold Eli got when I didn't immediately jump at the chance to be on the newspaper staff. He seemed sensitive to rejection. Needy. But I still didn't get what any of this had to do with how him and Dustin parted ways. Or Friday night. "What happened?"

"Nothing. Not then. He still came around from time to time, but only when he was sure it would be just me and him. Truthfully, it got creepy."

"Why?"

"Because he started to say weird stuff. Stuff about how everyone who dissed him was going to be sorry when he was some famous newscaster. He was always comparing himself to guys on CNN and PBS. I guess that's where they were from. The only news I care about is on ESPN. He had serious delusions of grand hair."

Delusions of—*wow*. "You mean *grandeur*. Delusions of grandeur."

"Yeah. Whatever."

Despite Dustin being an idiot, he wasn't far off base. Eli was sort of stuck on himself when it came to his journalism talents. He did get into that Columbia program, though. Maybe he was justified.

"I started ignoring him," Dustin said with little pride. "He'd hit my cell and I wouldn't pick up. If I did, I'd tell him I was busy. I never bothered to invite him to my parties because . . . he was a buzzkill. Okay? The problem was he didn't take the hint.

"There would be nights when I'd come home and he'd be at the dinner table talking up my dad or watching a ballgame in our theater room. He was like the crazy guys in those Lifetime stalker movies."

Again, I couldn't deny the truth in his statements. Eli never came close to creep status with me, but I remember all too well the day he showed up at my house uninvited and got cozy. It didn't bother me, but if he made a habit of it? I said, "Your dad was cool with him just popping up?"

"Yeah, because Eli was a computer whiz and he fixed my dad's machine one night when it was like crapping code. Dad needed to access files for an important call. He thought Eli was his digital savior. He didn't know what Eli really did to his computer."

That sounded weird. "What *did* Eli do?"

"He installed some sort of spyware on it. Like, whatever my dad did, Eli had a way of tracking it."

Whoa. Eli was spying on Dustin's *dad*? "When did he do that?"

"A few months back. He told me, at the school Friday. That's how we started fighting."

I tilted my head toward him, made sure I heard him right. "You two fought?"

"It was crazy, I—"

My phone rang, interrupting.

I checked the display. It was Mom's cell. Anyone else I might've ignored, but it was the first time she'd called me since we moved here. This couldn't be about the conference call; that was over an hour away. What *was* this about?

"Dustin, hang on a sec."

"What?"

"Hang on." I pressed Talk. "Hey, Mom."

The alarm in her voice hit me. "Tony, get home now."

I took a step away from Dustin, afraid he might've heard my true name. "What's wrong?"

In the background Dad yelled something I didn't catch.

Mom yelled back, "I told you not to test me. Me and my son will not sit by and let your selfish schemes destroy us."

Dad was closer, clearer. "Donna, put that suitcase down."

Uh-oh. "I'm on my way."

I ended the call, turned away from Dustin. "I needed to be home five minutes ago. My parents . . ."

"You're leaving now?!" He grabbed my arm, roughly. Almost earned a right hook for it. I shook loose and faced him, aware of a sort of mild panic in his eyes. Was this about to be a thing? Seconds passed as we sized each other up.

He exhaled. Backed off. "Sorry," he said, "I didn't mean to do that. Let me put my number in your phone. You're going to want to hear the rest of this."

I handed my phone over. Dustin stabbed it with his thumbs, his aggravation at being put off for later apparent. He was right; I wanted to hear the rest. But he was going to have to wait. Mom came first.

He gave my phone back and faced the lake, in his own world. I swear to God he looked like he wanted to walk into the water until he disappeared beneath it.

What in the world happened the night Eli died?

"I'll call you tonight," I said, more as a comforting gesture than a promise. If things had really hit the fan—and that's what it sounded like—come nightfall, Nick Pearson might be a fading memory.

CHAPTER 21

I RUSHED HOME BUT TOOK THE porch steps slowly. The front door only opened partway, impeded by two pieces of heavy luggage in its path. I muscled the bags aside, closed the door behind me. There was no yelling like I'd heard on the phone. In the quiet, my mind went to dark, dark places.

"Mom?!"

"In here." She sat in the living room. An umbrella and hat rested across her lap, even though it wasn't raining. "Pack a bag. Fast."

Dad rushed in from the kitchen. "Tony, your mother is overreacting. Go upstairs and let us talk."

"I don't talk to liars," Mom said. "Not anymore."

He said, "I should've told you what I was really doing on those late nights. I'm sorry, you know that."

"You mean you're sorry your boss let it slip that there are no late nights at your office. 'We lock the doors at six every day, Mrs. Pearson.' His words."

"I shouldn't have lied to you. I'm really into my league and I got carried away."

Mom huffed, "Again with the fantasy football? Tony, go get your things like I told you."

Fantasy football? You're going to ride that one out, Dad?

"Donna," he said, using his calm voice, indistinguishable from his condescending voice. "Where are you going to go?"

"It would defeat the purpose if I shared that information."

"That's not what I mean. You won't last on your own."

She popped up, defiant. "I have friends. You'd be surprised how many!"

Dad waved her off. "Sure you do. Are they good enough to keep you safe once you're out there alone? Remember what Bertram said about witnesses on their own? You willing to stake our son's life on your great friends?"

"You make me feel like a fool every day I'm with you. You're not going to make me feel like one for leaving you."

"I'm not playing you for a fool." Dad's voice had a high rasp I'd never heard before. It was as close to pleading as a man like him was capable of. Instead of actual begging—something that may have worked here—he resorted to that stupid excuse: "You can't do this to me after all we've been through, not over me hiding a silly little sports thing."

"After all we've been through? No, Robert. After all *you've* put us through. It's always been about *your* plans, and *your* dreams. Even when they went sour. We've lost everything, and every year, you feel the need to put us through it all over again. But I don't know if I blame you or myself more for letting it continue to happen."

"Baby, it's just football."

"STOP LYING TO ME!" Her calm was gone.

"I'm not. I can prove it. Ask Tony. He followed me to my league meeting the other night." Dad turned to me. "Tell her, son."

"What?"

"Tell her about the other night, when you saw me."

I couldn't believe the man's nerve. Bastard. What could I say other than I saw him downtown with a guy I didn't know? I couldn't get into the juked crime stats, or Eli. He'd spin that into whatever he wanted.

Also—as much as I hated to admit it—Dad was kinda right.

Mom hadn't thought this through. She wouldn't last without funds and a plan. I knew because I'd run the same scenario in my head plenty of times. Saving her from a short, hard life on the road—from her pride—was part of my reasoning for doing what I did next.

The other part, the *bigger* part, was *my* pride. If we left Dad to whatever twisted game he was really playing, I'd never know the truth about all this Whispertown stuff, or what it had to do with Eli's death. Dad won by forfeit.

I needed to know.

"I don't think he's lying, Mom. I tailed him Friday, after the Portside game. Him and two dudes went into this sketchy coffee shop. I snuck in with a crowd from the game and overheard them talking about stats and lineups before he saw me."

She glared. I counted my heartbeats. *Keep Quiet.*

"And you didn't feel the need to mention this?" Mom asked.

Dad said, "I told him not to say anything. A man's got to have some privacy."

"Fantasy football's big with some of the guys at school," I said, holding his gaze. "I'd love to talk some strategy with you later, Dad. It can be like, I don't know, bonding time."

Mom's eyes bounced from me to Dad, her face unreadable. "Glad to know you two have so much in common these days. Guess I'll have to find myself a hobby, too."

She stepped past me, kicked her luggage aside, and left the front door gaping as she disappeared into the day.

───────

I said, "What were you doing at city hall?"

"We're late for Bertram. Come on." He retreated to the kitchen like he cared about that stupid call. Anything to avoid the question.

"Dad, I lied for you. The least you can do is—"

He'd already dialed the number and passcode, put the phone on speaker. Bertram's voice came through. "My father had this saying, 'early is on time, and on time is late.' Since we're ten minutes past our scheduled meeting time, I wonder what he'd call that?"

"I'm sorry, Bertram," Dad said. "I just had an argument with my wife and she left. It's my fault, and I didn't mean to waste your time because of it."

Only static on the line. Bertram was likely having the same reaction as me. My dad—usually hostile—had apologized. And it sounded sincere.

Bertram cleared his throat. "So I understand, she's not present for the call?"

"She's not, but please don't hold it against her. Like I said, my fault."

Now Dad was accepting blame for something. I peeked through the window, making sure I hadn't missed nuclear Armageddon. The world didn't appear to be ending, so I was tapped for explanations.

"Are you two all right?" Bertram asked.

They said things about marriage I couldn't relate to, those conversations where people tell half the story and cap it with "you know how it is." I zoned while they cultivated their bromance. Then Bertram said something I missed, forcing me to snap back. "What?"

"I said I'm done with your dad, Nicholas. I'd like to spend a few moments talking with you. In private. Would you mind taking the phone off speaker?"

I grabbed the handset off the base. "Yeah?"

"I'm sorry about your friend." Papers rustled. "Eli Cruz?"

My jaw tightened. "Yes, that's his name. I can spell it if you want to make sure you've got it right in your files."

"I think I've got the spelling. Thanks."

Dick.

He said, "I want you to know that the Program offers counseling services. I recommend you take advantage of them. I already spoke to your mother about this when she informed me of the unfortunate situation."

"I'm not crazy."

"Counseling doesn't mean you are. It's talking with someone objective, and it helps."

For the first time since we started this conference call business, Bertram wasn't a robot rattling off his preprogrammed questions. He sounded decent. It didn't last.

"How's the rest of your acclimation going? Do you have any other friends?"

Welcome back, RoboBert. "You mean to replace the dead one?"

"I need to gauge how you socialize. You can answer the following questions using the one-to-ten scale. One being . . ."

We went through the routine, a half-dozen questions, like every week. When we were done, I planned to ask Bertram the point of it all. But I realized that, aside from the sound of me droning numbers, the house was quiet.

Dad was gone.

He's got to come home sometime, I thought, amused in spite of myself. This is what adults must feel like when a kid sneaks out. But the amusement diminished the longer I waited for one of my parents to return. I stomped around my room like I wanted to kick holes in the floor. Dad wasn't the only source for information in town.

I dialed Dustin on my cell. The phone rang four times before going to voice mail. Faint music and girlie laughter tinkled in the background. "Hi, this is Dustin, as you can tell"—a girl screamed joyfully—"I'm a little busy. Leave your name and number and I'll get back to you. If I'm still standing."

I threw the phone at my pillow like a pitcher aiming for the batter's head. I tried to walk off the frustration, noticing all the breakable things. The lamp. The TV. The camera.

The camera.

I'd forgotten about it. I picked it up, clicked through all my pics from Friday's football game in reverse order, rewinding time. Abruptly, the images switched to random stuff around the school, Eli's art for the last, unpublished *Yell*. A dozen more clicks and I came across another of my shots, the earliest one.

A picture of Eli at his desk in the J-Room. I took it on my first day, mostly to distract him while I erased the pictures he'd taken of me. Him recruiting, me scamming.

Of all the places I'd been, all the kids I met, he was the first to ever ask me to be a part of anything. Mostly, people were scared that I'd come to their school to take something from them. Their girl, or their spot on the team, or whatever attention they craved. So they pushed back, with attitudes or fists. Not Eli.

I spoke to the camera. "I'm going to find out what happened to you, man."

Grabbing my phone, I called Reya. She picked up before I heard a full ring. "*Sí.*"

"Hey, it's Nick. I know you said you'd call me, but I was really curious if you got a chance to check Eli's room for his laptop?"

Pots clattered against plates in the background, only to be eclipsed by loud Spanish voices. "I'm sorry, Nick, say that again."

"The laptop. Did you find it?"

"Uh-huh." Distracted, she said, "*Un minuto.* I looked, didn't see it any—" More noise, something breaking. "*Really?!* Nick, I've got to go. I'll call you tomorrow."

The call ended quicker than it began.

No Dad. No Dustin. No laptop.

I looked at the camera display, where Eli sat frozen in a moment. "I'm still going to find out what happened. But probably not today."

CHAPTER 22

I TRIED DUSTIN A FEW MORE times. Sent texts and left voice mails. No luck. My eyelids got sumo heavy as I pondered what else he could give me on Eli. I didn't know I'd fallen asleep until morning sun turned the insides of my eyelids blood orange, waking me. Bacon sizzled, maple permeating the air. I went down after I showered and dressed, found a cooling plate waiting. A cooler Mom didn't greet me; she stayed overly focused on *Good Morning America*.

When did she get in? Where had she gone? I said, "You missed your curfew, young lady."

She gave me an evil, narrow-eyed stare but didn't respond.

I don't talk to liars. Not anymore.

There was no second plate for Dad and I didn't see him on the couch. I was sure he didn't stay gone all night, not after yesterday's fight, but it wasn't beyond him to make a predawn escape, especially since he owed me a conversation. My breakfast remained untouched as I left for school.

Classmates poured into the front entrance, clowning around as usual.

Many ignored the folding plastic tables set up in the foyer, a construction paper banner along the edge that read: Grief Counseling Available for the Rest of the Week.

Three counselors manned those tables, a couple of clipboards between them. A short line formed as students waited their turn to sign up for appointments. I doubted they knew Eli at all. Any excuse to skip class, though.

At the head of the line was Zach Lynch himself, his crew in tow. He clutched a tissue in his fist, pretending to be choked up. I wanted to clutch his neck.

He leaned forward to sign up for a slot and I found myself on autopilot, veering toward him. My hand whipped forward, hammering his elbow and causing him to scrawl a crooked line across the sign-up sheet before the pen went flying.

"What the—" He bucked, but Russ grabbed his elbow. Zach's grief had been replaced by much less subtle rage.

I told the counselors, "I just saved you guys a half hour. He's cured."

Zach's chest heaved. The morning buzz ceased, all eyes on us. Zach didn't seem to like the idea of so many witnesses. He did an about-face into the crowd, shoving aside smaller kids in his way. His crew followed like the lemmings they were.

I was retrieving the pen Zach had dropped when I felt a counselor staring me down. I laid the pen directly in front of him and went on my way. At the same time, Vice Principal Hardwick appeared from the main office and approached the table. They chatted, watching me until I turned the corner.

Three periods later I knew why.

The office runner appeared in the middle of a lecture on World War II and the Axis powers, handed my history teacher a slip of paper.

"Nick Pearson."

I ignored the barely whispered comment from the back of the room about "the dead kid's friend," and left with the hall pass in my fist.

My path to the office took me past the journalism hall, where the lights still flickered, making shadows jump and disappear. I noticed a sheen on the freshly waxed floor tiles. Did that mean some crew came in and mopped away all of Eli's blood? Was everything sterilized? Lysol clean?

I reread the pass in my hand: *Report to main office for grief counseling.*

A dingy yellow trash canister stood nearby, its flap smeared with years-old gum and grime. I tossed my pass in and made for the exit.

The bike rack stood at the end of the school bus driveway, in plain view of the cafeteria. We were still a period away from lunch. I wasn't worried about being seen. A mistake.

I worked my bike lock combination with shaky hands and blood on my mind. I thought of the way it coated the floor that day, that way it smelled like bad meat and made a wet kiss sound when I stepped in it.

A car approached, what I assumed was normal midday traffic. Only, it never passed. A man-sized shadow fell over me. I turned; two of me stared back from the reflective lenses of aviator glasses, the eyewear of choice for Southern law enforcers.

Sheriff Hill, the man who'd had a hard-on about getting my statement the day I found Eli, motioned to his idling cruiser. "Get in the car."

Scrambling, I pretended I was just arriving, not leaving, "I'm sorry, Sheriff. I'm running late and was on my way to—"

"Get. In. The. Car."

"Sir, I'm going to miss science."

He plucked his glasses off, leaned in, exhaled a hot cloud of cigarette and coffee breath, a smell like fresh asphalt. "Don't make me cuff you. At this point, I'm not above it."

At *what* point? Hill's cruiser door hung open like the jaws of a flytrap.

I heard Mom's voice in my head—pre-Program—talking about stranger danger and how I should never, ever get into a car with someone I didn't know. I knew Hill, sort of, but couldn't shake the urge to run screaming like I was eight and he was offering candy. I didn't though, because of an alternate picture: me running, only to get Tasered, then flung on the hot hood of his cruiser just in time for lunch crowd witnesses.

I slipped into the car. Hill slammed the door hard enough to break my leg if I hadn't snatched it into the vehicle in time.

This is okay, I told myself.

I wondered if flies told themselves the same thing?

———

The police radio squawked and we bumped over an occasional pothole. Two blocks from the school Sheriff Hill lifted the radio mic and thumbed the transmitter. "This is car eleven, I'm ten-nineteen to the station house. I have a truant in custody."

"Truant!? I wasn't truant." Not technically. I never actually got away.

He went on like he didn't hear me. "Pearson, Nick. Papa-Echo-Alpha-Romeo-Sierra-Oscar-November."

The female dispatcher snapped back, "This ain't the army, Rodney. You don't have to use all that Foxtrot-Delta stuff."

"Do you copy?" Sheriff Hill said, his words clipped.

A crackling sigh. "Ten-four."

"No one wants to do things right around here," he said, slowing for a stop sign. He twisted in his seat and spoke to me directly through the metal mesh between us. "I bet that's how you like it, huh?"

"Dude, I don't know what you're talking about."

"First of all, I ain't your 'dude.' And of course you don't see my meaning. Nobody ever does. I'm the crazy old-timer."

I'd just go with crazy.

He stomped the gas and we lurched into motion. I felt some mild comfort from him calling in my so-called truancy. At least I knew he was taking me to the station and not some dark alley.

I hoped.

***

"What's up on my phone call?"

Three times I'd asked that question. Three times that dick Hill picked up his Styrofoam cup, sipped the bitter-smelling coffee, and leaned back in the chair across from me as if he were on the verge of a nap.

Truth: growing up around the people I'd been around, being part of a family like mine, I used to think being dragged to a police station was cool—a rite of passage. I heard my dad's friends tell jail stories like they were vacation memories.

I knew better now. Jail was not someplace I ever planned on getting familiar with. Which made me being in this place, when I hadn't done anything wrong, that much harder to handle.

Sheriff Hill brought me to the station house unscathed and without any more crazy talk. Or any talk at all, besides issuing a command to empty my pockets at the processing desk. No fingerprints. No mug shots. Instead, he ushered me directly to an isolated room that locked from the outside. A table, two chairs, and an ancient chipped ashtray occupied the tiny booth. Of course there was a two-way (or is it one-way?) mirror along the wall. People said TV didn't teach you stuff, but I'd seen all this many times on many channels.

I smacked the table, because I'd seen that on TV, too. "Hey, are you listening? Give me my call. I know my rights."

Hill finally said, "That's where you're wrong, Mr. Pearson. Those rights you think you know so much about, they're for people who are under arrest. I have not read you your Miranda rights. I'm not charging you with a crime."

"Then you're holding me against my will. My mom already told you I didn't have to talk about anything." I left my chair and pounded on the heavy steel door. "Let me out of here!"

"You're not here against your will. You got into my car willingly, after I caught you skipping school."

"Willingly?"

He shrugged. "I didn't put a gun to your head."

"Dude, my mom's going to *own* the police department by the time this is done. There's gotta be like thirty lawsuits for holding someone without arresting them."

"Wrong again. You're truant. I don't have to arrest you. According to Stepton City statutes, and I quote, 'A minor found in violation of the established truancy policy can be detained by a city official until such time as custody is remanded to a school official or the minor's legal guardian.'"

My TV Land legal knowledge wasn't helping, but I recalled a bit of my third-period Axis powers lesson. "What kind of secret-police stuff is that?"

"Only one person in this room is trying to keep a secret. Ain't me, though." He sneered. "You people make me sick."

You people.

My parents, when they weren't at each other's throats, sometimes spoke about the racial stuff they'd gone through growing up. Mom was from the South and said she'd been called the N-word more times than she cared to count. Dad, who'd always lived in the city, said it wasn't as bad for him, but certain neighborhoods were off-limits if you weren't the right color.

I'd never had much experience with prejudice, maybe because they'd shielded me from it. Until now. "This is because I'm *black*?"

He jerked, his hard expression cracking. "Don't try to twist this into something it's not. That race card stuff's not going to work in here."

"You're the one who—"

"Just know you don't get a pass with me. I won't let this town fall apart because you and yours think you have some sort of diplomatic immunity. Witness Protection my ass. Who's protecting *us*?"

You people . . . as in me and my family. Witnesses. Criminals. Hill wasn't racist, just civic-minded. For me and mine, it came out to about the same thing.

CHAPTER 23

I SAT DOWN, SHAKEN. IT DIDN'T matter that he was an officer of the law. No one—*no one*—but our handler and some higher-ups should have known our identities. That was one of the things we'd been told. Now I questioned *everything* we'd been told.

In four years, we'd never been exposed. We kept the secret through Dad's indiscretions. We never swayed from the legend(s), stayed normal, and boring, and low-key. And Hill blows it up like it's not our lives at risk, like it's nothing. The interrogation room got smaller. Hotter. The ticking clock was a slow jackhammer pounding at the wall.

"Why am I here?" I asked.

He said, "Believe it or not, I wasn't at the school this morning for you. I might not have ever thought about you again—that's the way this thing's supposed to work, right? You don't bother us, we don't bother you."

He talked like I was a lion at the zoo. I waited for him to answer my question. And thought about mauling him.

"Stepton High is my daughter's school. *Was* my daughter's school. She graduated back in ninety-seven. When things were still good here. Nick, or whatever your name really is, I care about this town more than I can say. I raised a family here. I'm willing to fight for it."

He was losing me. "Is this a campaign speech? I'm not old enough to vote."

"I want to know what you did to the Cruz boy."

I leaned forward so fast I almost came off my seat. "What *I* did? I didn't do anything."

Hill's head bobbed while he looked at me. If this were science class and I was something he viewed through a microscope, he'd be twisting all the little focus knobs. He said, "Sure you didn't. I'm supposed to turn a blind eye, though. Let my town go to pot because you're some G-man's pet monkey?"

Okay, maybe *he* didn't think he was being racist, but—

"I get it, to an extent, but I never signed on to ignore a murder." He took another sip of his coffee while I replayed his last statement.

He didn't sign on to ignore murder. Which meant he's ignored other things. Like falsified crime stats, maybe. *Eli, man, what were you digging into?*

Hill threw me off by bringing up the Program, then implying I had something to do with Eli's death. I settled down quickly. Voices flitted into my mind, ghosts from my old life. Not so much advice but overheard tactics on the formalities of the legal system, how to use them in your favor.

Interrogation Room Tip #1: Assume they're always watching.

I checked out the mirror. Someone could be taking notes on the other side. Or there could be recording equipment. He'd just admitted he played a hand in sweeping crimes less severe than murder under the rug, though.

Not something he'd want on tape. Still . . .

Interrogation Room Tip #2: If you're talking, say stuff that makes you sound innocent.

"Eli committed suicide," I said. "I saw the razor he used."

Hill said, "About that, did you know we treat suicide like a crime? Obviously, if it's truly what it appears to be, there's no one to prosecute, but we don't skimp on our procedures. We take pictures, catalog evidence, all of it. Except in the case of your pal Eli. EMTs were bagging him up before I could get a crime kit going. Fouled the whole thing."

He talked about Eli like someone's freaking lunch sandwich. *Bag him up. Next order, please!* "Maybe you should be talking to those EMTs."

"Maybe you should tell me what happened between you two. That journalism room looked tossed a bit. You guys have a fight? He say something about your mama?"

"No," I said. "He did mention yours."

His chair legs screeched as his weight shifted. He reached across the table, grabbed me by the jacket while his fist hovered by his ear. I braced myself for the punch.

Interrogation Room Tip #3: Piss them off enough to hit you, and it's a Get Out of Jail Free card.

He vibrated with tension, an internal struggle that could go either way.

A hollow thud sounded on the interrogation room door. He leaped backward like someone had walked in, realized we were still alone, and shouted, "What?"

"Need you in the hall, Sheriff," a muffled voice said.

Hill rose with his Styrofoam cup. He walked past, switched the cup to his right in order to rest his free left hand on his holstered Taser. Subtle. He maintained eye contact until the last possible moment, then pounded the door with three hard strikes. The lock disengaged and he stepped outside.

I allowed myself a deep breath, sat calmly with my hands on the table.

When Hill returned, he kept glancing at the mirror as if he saw something he didn't like in the reflection.

He jerked his head toward the door. "You're free to go."

This was a trick. It had to be. I hesitated.

Hill grabbed me under one arm and yanked me from the chair. "You may think you've gotten away with something, but that's not true. One day, someone might just find *you* in some secluded room. Come on."

The school must've called Mom; I looked forward to her ripping Hill a new one. In the reception area, the only adult present, other than the desk sergeant, was a white guy in a blazer and khakis. His hair was mostly dark with a little gray. He was bald up top and the exposed flesh was tanned, brown speckled with pink and red. He smiled wide, joking with the desk sergeant until he saw me.

His smile got wider. "You must be Nicky Pearson."

"Nick," I said. What I didn't say was, "Who the hell are you?"

Smiley guy flashed his hundred-watt teeth at Hill. "I'll take it from here, Rodney."

The sheriff gave me one last vicious look, then stomped away. The desk sergeant handed me a Baggie with my cell, money, house keys, and a pack of gum. I checked my things while watching the stranger from the corner of my eye. When I was done I faced him, unsure of what would happen next.

He extended a hand. "I'm Rich Burke, the mayor of Stepton."

Didn't see that coming.

"The mayor?" I looked to the desk sergeant, who read the question in my eyes, nodded a confirmation, then went back to his paperwork.

"I know you're wondering why the mayor is picking you up from jail."

"Yeah."

"I'm up for reelection and I'm looking for a running mate."

An awkward pause. The desk sergeant snorted an obligation laugh, so I guessed that was a joke.

The mayor said, "Let's talk in the car, Nick."

Another ride from a stranger. Great. I followed him through the station doors, on edge. When I spotted the car, I longed for Hill and the interrogation room.

It was a dark blue BMW. The same one I'd seen outside of city hall. Mayor Burke was the guy Dad had been working for. The one he was afraid of.

Me and Dad had something in common after all.

CHAPTER 24

THE CAR CHIRPED WHEN MAYOR BURKE deactivated the alarm. "It's unlocked," he said. "Go ahead and get in."

I could've run. Almost did. Sheriff Hill watched me from the station window the way a hyena watches a gazelle on Animal Planet. I wouldn't have made it far on foot.

The longer I hesitated on accepting his ride, the more Mayor Burke's grin shifted to something less pleasant. "Get in." Not to be mistaken for a request this time.

I moved toward the Beamer. I palmed my cell and brought Mom's number up on the contact menu, my thumb resting on Talk. Worst-case scenario, at least she'd hear my screams and know I didn't just disappear from the face of the earth like people tended to do back in our old lives.

Burke entered from the driver's side, pressed the ignition button. The engine hummed while the automatic locks engaged with a volume that could've drowned a rock concert. At least that's how it sounded to me.

"I bet you want to know why I'm here." He pulled into midday traffic.

"Kinda." Ghostly building reflections sailed across my smudge-free window.

"Whenever an incident occurs at the schools, my office is notified. It's a policy that was instituted shortly after the Virginia Tech massacre. Do you remember Tech? You would've been awful young."

I nodded.

"When the call came in, it got routed through my secretary. I happened to see it pop up on the shared server. When I noticed your name, I came right along."

That sounded plausible enough, but also rehearsed. A lot of detail without an answer mixed in. "That's how, not why."

His fingers flexed around the steering wheel until his knuckles turned white. "Pardon me?"

"That's *how* you knew I was at the station. It doesn't explain *why* you came."

A moment passed. He nodded like I'd asked him a yes-or-no question. "Your father works for me."

The way he admitted it with, like, no BS'ing, threw me. I played dumb, hoping my shock didn't show. "My dad's a discount accountant."

"Yes, which is what got my attention. The man's good with numbers and I needed him on a special project."

"What project?"

He turned off the main road, south. Away from school, and his offices at city hall, *and* my house. We were leaving town.

I massaged the lock release button. This new stretch of road was wide, long, and clear. We accelerated to seventy and any thought of me making a dive for it was left in his dust.

He said, "It's complicated. Nothing for a child to worry about. But I have to tell you, your father is gifted."

"With numbers? So's that vampire on *Sesame Street*."

"You underestimate him. Boys never understand just how difficult, and sometimes unpleasant, their fathers' work can be. I know I didn't. Mine was a carpenter, and I never appreciated the lengths he went to—how much blood and sweat he spilled—to provide for our family. Not until I was a provider myself. You'll see one day." He laughed at a joke I couldn't hear. "If you're lucky."

He slowed down as we approached a side street. Thick trees bordered it; between them I caught glimpses of exposed cinder blocks and partially finished walls. Construction equipment became visible through gaps in the tree line, faded yellow-and-green backhoes, bulldozers, and cement mixers. We passed a big caution sign attached to a wooden post on the shoulder: HARD HATS REQUIRED BEYOND THIS POINT.

"What is this?" I asked. The asphalt snaked closer to the work area.

"Progress, Nick. Progress."

He turned onto an unpaved track. The BMW bumped and bounced for about a tenth of a mile before the road opened up into a level patch of mud. Buildings in various stages of completion surrounded us. Most looked as close to being torn down as put up.

"This is Stepton's new municipal campus." He brought the car to a stop and pointed to specific half structures. "Courthouse, police station, DMV, physical plant. Son, this is the new core of our town."

"Is this the project my dad's helping you with?"

"In part." He silenced the engine and popped the locks. "Come on."

I got out of the vehicle while he disengaged another lock. The trunk. He went to the back of the car and the sounds of him rummaging around in there reminded me of plastic sheeting, shovels, and lye for disguising the signs of human decomposition. I shook off old memories of a ride gone wrong.

The mayor lowered the trunk, held two royal-blue hard hats. "Here." He passed one to me. "Rules are rules."

I put it on; he did the same. Mayor Burke walked me toward the skeletal frame of a building in midconstruction. "Welcome to the new city hall."

There was no activity on the site. I observed the machines—the ones with closed cabins for people to drive when they needed to dig and lift and push. A thin layer of grime was on the windshields and digger buckets and wheel treads. They hadn't been moved in days. Or weeks.

"Where are the workers?" I suddenly wanted there to be workers around.

He sighed. "Unfortunately, this project has created cash flow problems for our city. My constituents look for me to be a steady hand on the till, something I can handle most of the time, but, on occasion, I need the assistance of a strong crew. That's why I brought your dad in on this, to help us right the course."

I couldn't tell if he was talking about money or sailing, but I was sure he didn't answer my question. "No offense, but this doesn't mean a whole lot to me. I'm just a kid. Like you said."

"Not *just* a kid. You're James Pearson's son. That's why I brought you here. To show you how important your dad's work is. So you can tell him how much Richard Burke appreciates him and wants him to continue on the path we started down together."

Burke faced me, gave me a smile that probably showed up on a lot of flyers and posters at election time. He stared thoughtfully into the distance. "I hope you'll let him know that I'm looking out for him. I always look out for my friends."

This didn't feel like he was doing me a favor. Or Dad. This felt like a threat. A subtle one.

Screw subtlety. "Does this have anything to do with Whispertown?"

The mayor's fake-friendly tone blew away on the wind. "Did your father tell you *that*?"

"No," I said, improvising, "I was in his office and saw it on a piece of paper. When I asked him about it, he told me to mind my business. With what you told me, I figured it was related." The best lies were the ones closest to the truth.

Burke gathered himself. "You were right. That's what we're calling our little project and it's best you keep it to yourself."

Whispertown struck a nerve. I didn't know much more than I did before, but the connection was huge. Eli was researching it. He died. My dad was involved in it. He was scared. The sheriff was covering things up. He was pissed. The town's freaking mayor was involved in Whispertown and he was . . .

. . . trying hard to convince me he's a good guy.

Half-constructed buildings surrounded us. A lot of deep holes. A cement mixer ready to go. A locked shed with a big, red sign: DANGER FLAMMABLE CHEMICALS.

Someone who believed the mayor wasn't being straight up could have an accident real easy.

"Are you all right?" he asked.

"Fine."

"You don't look fine."

"It's been a long day."

"I bet. Why don't I take you home?"

"That'd be cool." I handed over the hard hat, still thinking of construction site accidents.

As the mayor drove us away, he said, "Your father ought to know about your run-in with the police today. Be honest with him so he doesn't have to hear it from someone else. Word travels fast in small burgs like ours."

We took the rutted road to the main stretch leading back to town and I noticed a stone-and-mortar marquee that I had missed earlier because it had been on his side of the car. An iron plate was mounted in the stone, ID'ing the new town center as BURKE MUNICIPAL CAMPUS.

No wonder this was such a big deal to the mayor. His name was all over it. Literally.

"Is there something you want me to tell my dad? Specifically?" I asked, cutting through the crap.

"Tell him Mayor Burke had his back when he needed it. Tell him Mayor Burke hopes he can count on the same." He flicked on the satellite radio and some guy yelling about "civil liberties" and "big government" filled the cabin.

The mayor bobbed his head like he was listening to good music.

CHAPTER 25

"MAYOR BURKE."

He downed the radio volume with a button on the steering wheel. "This is the way to your house, right?"

"It is. But my bike's at the school."

All business now, none of that who's-yer-buddy stuff from before. "I suppose there's time."

The mayor corrected his course and swung me by the high school. Classes were finished for the day, giving the building a desolate feel. A few stragglers remained for after-school activities like football, cheerleading, and band practice, along with the lost souls of detention and extra credit. The mayor pulled into the arching driveway by the bike rack.

"Thanks, sir." I exited the car, relieved to put some distance between me and him.

The politician's grin returned. "Remember what we talked about."

"Sure, I—"

Yellow flashed from the corner of my eye and a familiar SUV double-parked next to the BMW. A horn blared and the mayor's head wrenched to the left with enough force to suggest an invisible backseat assassin had snapped his neck. His window descended, as did the SUV's.

Dustin, organizer and promoter of the Dust Off, yelled, "Dad, what are you doing here?"

Dad!?

"I'm running an errand, Dustin," said the mayor, "but I should be asking you the same question. You've been grounded. I would have expected you to be halfway to the house by now. Not loitering around the school with your friends."

Snickers from inside the SUV. Lorenz and Carrey.

Dustin sputtered, all the ladies' man, host-with-the-most confidence gone. "I—I just have to take the fellas home."

"That's what school buses are for."

All snickering ceased. I was an awkward eavesdropper in this exchange, but I couldn't walk away. Too many questions—too many connections— now. I wanted to hear everything.

"Take them," said the mayor. "Tomorrow, they arrange their own transportation. Losing your cell phone wasn't enough, I see. Now I want your car keys. We'll talk more this evening."

The BMW rocketed from the curb much faster than what was allowed on school grounds. Dustin leered at me, bright red circles flaring along his cheeks. More noticeable than his signs of embarrassment was the brighter—almost angry—bruising around his left eye.

That was new.

Something flickered in Dustin's face, like he was fighting for control of his expressions. A sarcastic grin won the war. "I see you met the old man."

I nodded.

"Need a ride? I'm already in for it bad." His laugh, it sounded as natural as the cloned goat we learned about in science. "One more stop won't hurt."

"I'm good, man. I've got my bike."

He was in motion before I finished.

I stood there, blown by the day's events. Dustin was grounded (for what?) and had lost his phone. That's why I couldn't reach him last night. Maybe he was still a good source of information, if I could ever get him alone.

But the real head-scratcher . . .

Dustin's father—the guy who Eli went all cyberstalker on—was the town's freaking mayor? Why didn't I know that? How could I *not* have known?

Easy answer: after almost a month, I was still the New Kid. Stepton's history and family relations and clique dynamics were common knowledge to everyone else. Old news. No one talked about it. Not when there are hookups and new music and parties taking up the valuable conversation minutes between classes. I needed an insider to walk me through this.

But first, Dad.

The strip mall where my dad worked was called Picket Square. I cruised past the brick marquee entrance, pausing by three flagpoles side by side. The Virginia State flag, the American flag, and tallest, a pole featuring the flag of the Confederacy. Was that even legal? I looked around like I might see ghosts in gray uniforms saluting it. I felt like shouting to no one in particular, *You lost! Get over it!*

Biking onto the empty sidewalk, I came upon the cleverly named Tax and Accounting Services storefront. Through the windows I saw two rows of bland half cubicles arranged along a center aisle that stopped at a manager's office. Of the eight available desks, only three were occupied, one of them by Dad. There were no customers.

Dad sat at his desk, chin propped in his palm and his eyelids fluttering. He looked like Homer Simpson dozing at the power plant. I dropped my bike and entered, triggering door chimes, and was struck by the strength of the garlic shrimp smell from the No. 1 Chinese Restaurant next door.

Dad jerked awake, saw me, got all stony faced. I stepped back outside and waited.

Door chimes sounded as he joined me on the sidewalk. He said nothing. Did he know about Keep Quiet, too?

"Fine," I said. "I already know you're not going to tell me anything you don't want to tell. So listen. I got picked up by the sheriff today"—his mouth ticked—"and he told me he knows we're in the Program. Your buddy the mayor sprung me from jail as a personal favor to you. I thought you should know."

I hopped on my bike and pedaled away slowly. I made it ten yards before he yelled, "Nick, get back here. Right now!"

I made sure to stop smiling before I turned around.

We sat in the restaurant next door with a plate of untouched House Lo Mein resting between us. When I finished, he looked stunned.

"'Tell him Mayor Burke's got his back,' he said that?"

"Yep." I twirled some noodles with my chopsticks.

"And this was at the municipal campus site?"

I nodded again, preparing to shovel food into my mouth.

"Did he threaten you, or your mother?"

I let my eating hand rest a moment. "Did you hear my story? He didn't threaten us in a, like, superobvious way. His way was worse. It was—"

"Slick." He lowered his head, his hand clenching and unclenching as if he were trying to work his knuckles through the skin.

"Dad, as much as I want to know what you've done to get on the mayor's bad side, I'm a little more concerned about the sheriff knowing"—my voice lowered reflexively though no one was around—"*about the Program*. Isn't that the one thing Bertram, and you, and Mom said can *never* happen?"

His breathing quickened. "Have you told your mother any of this?"

"No, I haven't seen her yet. I—"

"Listen to me. You can*not* mention a word of this to her. Not. One. Word."

"Because you're going to tell me why I'm keeping secrets for you?"

He leaned in. Food steam misted his forehead. "Because I'm your father and you do as I say."

I jammed noodles into my mouth, then talked as I chewed because he hated that. "Don't tell me everything. Tell me the rest. What's the purpose of Whispertown? Why are you and the mayor manipulating the town's crime stats?"

He jerked. "What? Where did you hear that word?"

"Whispertown? My friend Eli told me." I dropped the bomb on him *Modern Battlefield* style. "Before he was killed."

I waited for the reaction. Guilt. Or Rage.

His face remained blank, revealing nothing. "I thought that kid committed suicide. Did Hill tell you something different?"

"*Hill?* You know him?"

"Did he tell you that?"

"Yes, I mean, no. But he agrees, kind of." I struggled for words.

Whatever my expectations had been, we were in the alternate version.

"Cops will play with your head. They tell you stories to trip you up. I don't know what that low-pay deputy—"

"Sheriff."

"Whatever. I don't know what game he's running, but if something happened to that boy, which I doubt, it's not because of anything between me and Burke."

"Why do you doubt it? You didn't know Eli. He was going to be this big-time journalist."

Dad's eyes went glassy, like a doll's eyes. I knew the look from when he and Mom fought. This was the point where he would completely abandon the conversation. "Uh-huh" and random-head-nod mode followed.

"Uh-huh," he said, nodding his head. He balled his napkin, tossed it on his empty plate. "Go home. I'll take care of the mayor."

"What about the sheriff?"

He stood. "We're done."

"Take care how?"

"That's not your concern. He should've never brought you into it. If that's how he wants to play it . . ."

"Play what, Dad? Eli—"

His fist hit the table like something falling from space, rattling the plastic plates and utensils. And me. A lady in a soiled apron emerged from the kitchen and started ranting in Chinese. Though we'd already paid, Dad tossed a twenty on the table, which quieted her.

To me, he spoke in a whisper more seething than a shout. "Whatever you think you're doing, shut it down. You're a kid. At your age, everything that pops in your head seems clever and important. It's not. I'm sorry that your buddy took the emergency exit on life, but that's not my concern."

I hated myself because, like the kid he said I was, I couldn't look him in the eye. I was six again, being reamed for drawing on the wall. At least I didn't cry. The way he played Eli, like he knew everything about everyone, even people he never met . . . I did the only thing I could do, hit him below the belt. "Because we both know you're above that sort of thing."

He sat up straight and stiff. "Don't you have to study or something? Go home. And—"

"Keep my mouth shut? Yeah, I got it."

"Now, Nick." He stood, held the restaurant door open.

I stomped by him, mad as hell. A car on the far side of the nearly empty lot backfired, its moaning transmission wailing its departure. I thought nothing of the raggedy beater as I snatched up my bike to ride home.

That little oversight would come back to haunt me later.

CHAPTER 26

SAILING DOWN SIDE STREETS, I STEERED with one hand while holding my cell to my ear. The ringing stopped abruptly, replaced by creepy organ music and opera voices.

"Reya?"

"Hey, Nick," she said, sniffing like she had a bad cold. If only.

"Is this a bad time?"

"It's a horrible time. I don't think there's going to be a better one for a while so we might as well talk." That weird tune kept playing in the background.

"Where are you?"

"The mortuary. Mr. Massey needed Mami to bring a suit," Reya said. "The funeral's Saturday morning. If you can make it."

"I will," I said, and that felt like too little. "Thanks for letting me know. Listen, I called because I have a question."

"Okay."

"That guy"—I played dumb masterfully—"the one who throws those big parties . . ."

"Dustin."

"Right. Is his dad someone important?" The way I figured it, if I let her bring up the mayor, I never needed to get into my pseudoarrest and field trip to the municipal campus.

"He's Stepton's mayor."

Score.

"Why?" she asked.

"Because Dustin told me that Eli hacked his dad's computer. He'd asked Dustin to meet him in the J-Room on Friday night because of something he found."

"What?!"

"That seem right to you? Him going all secret agent on the mayor's PC?" Her answer surprised me.

"Totally. Once Eli got these tiny microphones off the internet and put them in our uncle's car. I thought Miguel was going to . . ." She trailed off. "You just don't do that to Miguel."

I saw some of her uncle's temper at her house yesterday. I could only imagine how he'd react to having his car bugged by his nosy nephew.

Reya said, "What did Dustin say Eli found?"

"I don't know. We got interrupted before he could tell me."

"Nick?" In all the ways I could imagine my name crossing her lips, this disappointed/frustrated gasp was not one of them. "Can you talk to him tonight?"

I said, "He's grounded. No phone, no car."

"What about Facebook? Or email?"

"Maybe, but I got the impression it's a face-to-face deal."

"Then let's go to his house."

This was what I was afraid of. One sliver of daylight and she was ready to claw her way to Eli's killer. I got it, but I couldn't let her get out of hand. My family was tied up in this, too, and I needed to understand why first. "Reya, wait. I want to know what Dustin has to say as bad as you, but we have to play this right. Let me work that angle."

"Alone? I need to help. Don't call me with stuff like this, then push me away."

"I'm not pushing. I want you—" I startled myself, pulled my bike to the curb so I could concentrate and not say anything dumber than what I almost said. "I want you to help. I just think your mom might need you."

I want you here. That's what I almost said. I didn't mean to help me look for clues. When I heard her voice, tears and all, my dad anger faded. I wanted to see her, would've biked to her right then if she'd asked.

Instead, I sensed her frustration, a clock tick from exploding. "I don't know how much more of this I can handle."

I'd called for information—or to make her think she gave me information—not to upset her. I didn't want the call to end with her thinking badly of me. That's where my head was. She was standing in a building housing her brother's corpse, and I was all about the Nick impression. Nice.

"I'm going to take care of this," I said.

"Sure you will, Nick."

I thought her disappointment was bad. Her disbelief was worse.

"Mom!" I called, stepping through the door, feeling the empty house sensation immediately. A spicy—and familiar—scent hung in the air. I followed it to the kitchen and flicked the lights on, obliterating the dusk shadows.

The meal waited on the table. White cardboard cubes with a note taped to them.

The food was from the No. 1 Chinese Restaurant.

My stomach clinched as I unfolded the paper, noting my mother's handwriting.

Nick—I hope you and your dad enjoy the takeout. It's your favorite . . .

I knew what was in the containers without opening them. House Lo Mein. What else but the meal me and Dad ordered at our (not so) secret meeting? I read the rest of the note.

Don't bother waiting up.
MOM

CHAPTER 27

I DIDN'T WAIT UP, AND THE next day I awoke before anyone. Mom's bedroom door was cracked, her soft breaths slipping through. Dad snored downstairs on the couch. There was no sign of Mom's note in the kitchen, but I didn't imagine it. She saw me and Dad yesterday, but how?

The whole way to school I contemplated the possibilities and watched for police cruisers. I made sure to get in the building before the bell rang, fearing Hill might ride up on a white horse, cowboy-style, and lasso me like a sprinting calf (hey, I did live in Texas for a year).

I thought someone might call me out about yesterday's missed classes. But no, business as usual. Another favor from Mayor Burke? If so, he wasn't the only Burke pulling strings. By midday I heard buzz of yet another Dust Off. Saturday night.

In honor of Eli Cruz.

On the surface, it seemed like a cool thing to do in memory of an old friend. It could also be a big old "screw you, Dad" for whatever got him grounded. Having met his father, I understood. Whatever Dustin's inspiration was, I still needed those deets on his last meeting with Eli. And I intended to get them before he got too busy party planning.

My goal was to gain some clarity at lunch—even if I had to drag Dustin away from his concubines. Only, I never made it to lunch.

Vice Principal Hardwick met me in the hall after fourth period. "Pearson."

"Sir."

"Let's walk."

We moved against the flow of students heading into the cafeteria, en route to the office. Had I written off those skipped classes too soon?

"Am I in trouble, Mr. Hardwick?"

"Trouble? No. Not given the circumstances."

I didn't like the sound of that. "What circumstances?"

"Your horrible grief, son." He led me beyond the main office, to a small conference room where a counselor waited.

"Sir, I don't need—"

"Either you're a student who's overcome with grief, or you're a misfit who cuts class. We sit misfits in a different room. After school."

Sighing, "Do I at least get to lie on a couch?"

Grieving kids get catered sandwiches, I discovered. Little consolation since I missed any cafeteria time with Dustin because of those worthless sessions. Yeah, *sessions*, plural. Thursday and Friday. Mr. Hardwick insisted, said it would do me good. I don't know how. The lady wasn't even a real counselor. She was a student at a community college. I looked older than her, and she kept referring to a textbook with Post-it notes protruding like hot pink tongues. She was all "you're in a safe haven" and "it's okay to cry."

At times detention seemed like a better option, but I decided against it. Everyone in my house was giving each other cold—like Arctic—shoulders, but a call from Hardwick might thaw my parents enough to accomplish one unified act . . . keeping me at home this weekend. That I could not abide. I needed to be at the Dust Off Saturday night.

But I had to get through that day first.

Eli's funeral.

Mom had barely spoken to me in three days. Dad was the same. I wouldn't give either of them the satisfaction of being the first to utter an actual sentence. Our house settled into an eerie quiet, upset only by an occasional slammed cabinet, rattled dish, or flushing toilet.

I donned my dress shirt and slacks Saturday morning, dreading the idea of biking to Our Lady of Mercy Cathedral in such attire. It took monk-like muscle control to hide my relief when Mom met me at the bottom of the stairs in a black dress, clutching a string of pearls.

"Help me with these," she said. It was all she said.

We took the SUV without asking Dad, which sort of rocked. I reached for the radio, needing to hear something other than engine noise. Mom shoved my arm away.

"What?" I said.

"I don't want things to be like this between us, Tony."

"Like how you're making them? *You* haven't been talking to me."

She tapped the steering wheel. "We've all been a little childish lately."

"I *am* a child. I'm supposed to act like that."

"You're right, of course. You are."

"What's the deal with that note the other night?"

"That was impulsive. I came to my senses before your dad saw it, and threw it away. Did you mention it to him?"

"No! But you've been watching him? Us?"

She shook her head. "Just that afternoon. I was angry after we fought, and you *helped* him cover his tracks."

The accusation wasn't lost on me, but I didn't confirm her suspicion—right as it was. Fantasy football. Yep.

"I wanted to see where he'd go after work," she said. "When I got there, you two were coming from the restaurant. I got nervous, so I left."

When I got there . . . I got nervous, so I left.

It hit me. That backfiring beater in the parking lot when me and Dad were coming out of the restaurant . . .

"It was you in that old car?"

A nod.

"Where did you get it?"

We came to a stoplight. She said, "Tony, are you happy here?"

The abrupt change bothered me more than if she'd openly refused to answer. An odd question to ask today. "We're going to a funeral."

"I know. That's a hard thing. Eli seemed like a nice boy. He's the first friend I've seen you with since we started the Program. Do you have others?"

"Yeah, Mom. I'm Mr. Popularity, future homecoming king."

"I could do without the smart mouthing."

"Are we going to run, Mom?"

The light changed, and we were moving again. "You're too much like your father."

I tensed, taking it as an insult. She rephrased. "I mean you're clever.

Too clever for your own good."

She turned the radio on. Never did answer the question.

We arrived at the church, slipping back into our roles as the Pearsons. The sanctuary had maybe fifteen pews on each side, only a few of them full. We stood in a line of ten people, waiting our turn to view Eli's body. I shifted to the right and saw the foot of the mahogany casket, then left, saw the tip of Eli's nose rising over the coffin's lip. I scanned the other guests, needing to look elsewhere.

There wasn't a large crowd to see Eli off. Hardly anyone from school. I recognized a few faces from the Cruz house, like Reya's distant cousin with the prison tats. He sat on the right side of the sanctuary in the center of a pew, his arms stretched along the seat's back edge, his suit worn around the collar and thin at the elbows. He caught me looking and gave a respectful nod.

A couple of rows ahead of him sat Pilar, crying harder than that day on the porch and rubbing her bulging belly. Uncle Miguel sat beside her, awkward, fiddling with a sparkling pinkie ring that could've paid for the casket. Seeing him next to Pilar, I noticed something I missed before. The similarities between their noses, and chins, and the way their eyes were set.

Pilar was his daughter.

Not a huge revelation—her being Reya's cousin, and him her uncle—but I was stuck on the way he'd exploded from the house and went NASCAR with his Jag, never sparing her a second look. A reminder that my family didn't have a lock on dysfunction.

The church murmuring dialed down as Reya entered with her mother, both in dark glasses, their arms intertwined. Like everyone else, I couldn't help but stare. I didn't realize the viewing line had moved.

"He looks like he's sleeping," the woman between me and Eli said before stepping aside. I faced the coffin.

Eli's glasses were gone and his hair was neatly trimmed. I was used to his sweatshirts and shorts, the only things I'd seen him wear. The suit wasn't him. He wouldn't play *Modern Battlefield* or *Finite Universe* in a three-piece. He didn't look like the guy I got to know, the guy who saved me, then told the school I was a badass ultimate fighter. Or the dude who taught me about newspapers and drank half a case of orange soda at my house. If he was just sleeping, he'd still look like my friend. Not this . . .

I stumbled to the nearest empty pew. Mom's heels clacked loudly behind me. I didn't think this would hurt so much. Only knew him a few weeks.

Sobs ripped the solemn atmosphere. Mrs. Cruz gripped her son's coffin, rocked it like he really was asleep and a good shaking would wake him. Reya pressed her face into her mother's neck.

I thought I'd be embarrassed about this, but I cried, too, like me and him had been hanging forever. You don't have to know someone your whole life to know them. Not really.

Lonely is the same everywhere.

———

At the gravesite, a small mob gathered around Reya and her mom. Me and my mother watched from a distance.

"How's she been doing?" Mom said.

"Who?" I knew.

She gave me a weird look. Squinty.

I said, "She's as good as you can expect, I guess. I haven't talked to her in a couple of days."

"You like her, though?"

Oh my God . . . it was so awkward I felt like asking the grave diggers to bury me, too. Mom rubbed my shoulder. "Give her a little time."

"For what?"

Mom just smirked. "You got a lot of good stuff from your dad, too. I hope you know."

"What's that mean?" The woman had suddenly become the Riddler.

She cleared her throat. "I think someone wants to talk to you, Nick."

Her gaze drifted over my shoulder. I turned and found a puffy-eyed Reya approaching.

"Hello, Mrs. Pearson," she said, her voice rough. "I hope I'm not interrupting."

"Not at all, sweetie. I'm so very sorry about your brother." She turned to me. "I'm going to go offer my condolences to Mrs. Cruz." Mom left us.

"I don't know what to say to you right now." I felt the need to be honest. A rarity.

"Admitting that is the best thing I've heard all day. I hate all these people who just talk and say nothing. 'He's in a better place,' 'grief is for the living.' I'm sick of it." Reya gave me a hug. "Thanks, Nick."

"What now? You going home?"

Her mouth turned down. "Yes, to get ready for the party. I'll pick you up at eight."

"You're going?"

"Aren't you?"

"Well, yeah—I just thought you might want to be with your family."

"I've been with them for the last five days. If we're together much longer, there might be a series of Cruz funerals next week."

I couldn't tell if she was joking. "Maybe a little fun would do you some good."

"Fun? I'm going so we can get the truth out of Dustin. You haven't been able to make that happen or I would've heard from you before now, right?"

No use denying it. I hadn't called or texted because I knew she'd press for info I didn't have. I didn't want to hear her disappointed voice again.

She said, "You want some alone time with Dustin? What better distraction than Grief Girl? Everyone will be all over me. You shouldn't have a problem."

It sounded so . . . strategic. Like Eli. "You sure you're up for it?"

She looked toward her brother's coffin, sinking slowly into the earth. "You shouldn't have to ask."

CHAPTER 28

REYA ARRIVED FIVE MINUTES EARLY. I was ready on my porch—had been for a half hour, despite swapping shirts four times and the tense moment where I temporarily blinded myself with the malfunctioning nozzle on the cologne I swiped from Dad.

Confession: I've never been to a high school party.

What? Is it that hard to believe? I've been in the Program since I was eleven. There were no middle-school parties those first two years, at least none that I got invited to. And I've attended only one other high school. The last time I went to a social gathering of my peers there was a Batman cake and a bouncy house. Now I was attending what seemed like some epic teen-movie bash, with the bonus objective of fishing for clues about my buddy's possible murder, to which I hadn't completely ruled out my father as an accessory. Most kids just worry about bad breath. I was stressed. Sue me.

I walked to the Beetle, not too fast, a conscious I-go-to-these-things-all-the-time strut, though I was already sweating from nerves and the unseasonably warm night. The car's interior lamps switched on like stage lights when I opened the door, and I lost my forced composure.

My eyes darted to the exposed flesh first. Calf, thigh, arm, back, and sternum. All twinkling moist from glitter lotion, like fairy dust in a cartoon. Her hair hung straight, stopping midspine, a change from her spongy curls at the funeral. And her makeup was pro level, erasing all signs of tearful mourning.

The clothing that kept this from turning into my most guarded fantasy consisted of tan shorts that she might've borrowed from a Barbie and a top that swooped around her neck and shoulders like a silk wave.

I stood with one leg in the car, one on the ground, comparing my typical sneakers-jeans-tee-hoodie combo to her glam-girl look. "Should I change?"

She appraised me. "You're fine. All the guys dress like you."

"Do all the girls dress like you?" I pictured the Dust Off in music video format.

She smiled in a way I hadn't seen since that day in the gym, about a hundred years ago. "I told you I'd provide your distraction."

It wasn't supposed to distract *me*. I climbed in and caught a whiff of her body spray, something with melon. It mingled with the citrus scent of my cologne. We smelled like we'd vandalized a Bath & Body Works.

Being in the Beetle again was a strange déjà vu, spooky even. I considered bringing it up. Some conversation about Eli might help us—*me*—refocus.

She shot that plan to hell when she said, "We're on a date."

"Hunh-what?"

"We're on a date. If anyone asks, that's our cover."

"Right," I said, "pretending."

She glanced sideways, then back to the road. "People are going to talk when we come in together. We better give them what they ask for. It will make the night go more smoothly."

"Hope I don't mess up your rep." I imagined our gossiping schoolmates, with hushed voices and scowls, linking her to the loner who found her dead brother, then consoling each other as if Reya had died, too.

She laughed. "Mess up my rep? Do you own a mirror?"

"What do you mean?"

"*De pinga!* I can't tell if you're being modest or you're one of those guys who got cute over the summer without realizing it."

Focus, focus, grin, focus . . .

She drove us into the only part of town I hadn't explored, North End, not just a direction but the neighborhood's actual name, where Stepton's rich residents lived. Home to requisite McMansions and driveways displaying their luxury vehicles, even though every house had a three-car garage.

"That one is my uncle Miguel's." Reya motioned toward a stucco-sided two-story. The way she said it, I knew she thought the house was spectacular. Envy and awe.

I wasn't impressed. Crime syndicate money could buy estates, and I'd seen a few. Still, I said, "Wow, that's nice."

"He actually acted like a decent person today. I barely recognized him."

"That's good, right?

She shrugged. "If it lasts. Which I doubt."

"Him and Pilar get along?" I said, testing my theory about their relation.

"When he claims her, which is like never since she got pregnant. *Was* pregnant?"

Was?

"Wait," I said, twisting in my seat to face her. "Shut up."

Reya gave me a sharp nod. "She popped like an hour after the funeral."

"Is she okay?"

"She's fine. Might still be in labor. Mami went to the hospital to be with her since her own mom's dead. I should thank Pilar and that kid. There's no way I could've left the house in this outfit otherwise."

Mention of the outfit popped it to the forefront of my mind. I should thank Pilar, too. Every guy at this party should thank Pilar.

We turned in to a cul-de-sac and joined a line of cars inching through an open wrought-iron gate. High hedges blocked my view of the house, but I heard a Kanye West track thumping.

"It's like we're going to the Playboy Mansion," I said, impressed now.

"Dustin always does it big."

"The neighbors can't be happy about this."

"There are perks to being the mayor's son. The police won't bust up your party, no matter how pissed the neighbors get. I've seen people catch major beat downs at these things, as long as no one dies it's—"

She trailed off. Someone already had.

Reya parked the Beetle behind a Honda where two kids were hooking up on the trunk.

I left the car, waited. Reya pried off the Nikes she'd worn while driving, replaced them with a pair of four-inch wedge heels that matched her shorts. Her lethal ensemble complete, she joined me, almost my height now, and grabbed my hand. "Date, remember."

Closer to the house, randomly scattered groups were involved in whatever activity was preferential to their clique. Smokers smoked.

Musical kids engaged in freestyle rap battles. Most had a beer can or plastic cup in hand.

A girl smoker flicked mini-meteorites into the bushes before touching Reya's shoulder as we passed. "Sorry about Eli, Rey."

Similar sentiments came from others but felt less genuine, like Reya showing up was an unwelcome reminder that the night was supposed to be a celebration for her dead brother, and not *just* a party. She squeezed my hand tighter through the halfhearted condolences. By the time we entered the house I was happy she hadn't broken my fingers.

She leaned into me and whispered, "Get ready to split up."

"What if I can't find Dustin? This place is huge."

"If all else fails, stand by the blender." Then louder, so others could hear, "Go get me a drink, baby."

She let go of my hand, kept moving until I lost sight of her.

I spent a moment totally paralyzed.

Some guy holding a bunch of neon lights bumped by, unfreezing me. I stepped into the path of the next person moving with purpose, a stocky girl who tensed as if expecting a fight. I held my hands up, peaceful. "I need some help."

"What?"

"You know where the blender is?"

<hr />

After twenty minutes of leaning on the Burkes' granite countertops while some shaggy-haired kid played Mixed-Drink Mad Scientist—I swear I saw him throw a cucumber into a swirling batch of strawberry daiquiris—I began doubting Reya's strategy. At least twenty people had come through the kitchen to either grab another beer from a sweating floor cooler or risk their lives on questionable cocktails. But no Dustin.

I ventured back to the foyer, tired of waiting. Two lengths of rope were secured to the staircase banister, marking the second story off-limits. Past the stairs was a dark corridor with a few people hanging around the entrance, but little activity beyond. That's where I'd start.

I knew I wouldn't find Dustin there, but I needed a break from all this normal teen stuff. My untuned social meter was on overload. Also, I had a suspicion about the corridor that I needed to satisfy.

A piece of wisdom from Bricks came to me. *When you're in a place you're not supposed to be, the best thing you can do is fake as much confidence as possible. People always notice the guy acting like a thief. They never notice the guy acting like the owner.*

I strolled down the hall like I was Mayor Burke himself and no one gave me a second look. I thought.

The first door I came to was ajar, and I saw a toilet and mirror in the shadows. Moving on. The next door was closed. I tested the knob and found myself staring at a large garage occupied by Dustin's yellow Xterra, the blue BMW that had taken me to the municipal campus, and empty bays for two more cars. I moved on to the last room, sealed by lacquered double doors that didn't swing but slid into the wall. I parted them wide enough for a view and found what I was looking for.

The mayor's office.

Inside, I flipped on the lights, revealing several full but neat bookshelves, an uncomfortable-looking leather couch, and a TV mounted on the wall next to a gun cabinet.

Like the bookshelves, the cabinet was full and neat, a couple of rifles, a shotgun, and several handguns. The pistols weren't like guns I'd seen when I was younger, scratched and scarred with tape around the grips and threaded barrels for illegal, screw-in suppressors. These sat on red velvet, illuminated by special lights like props in the Smithsonian. Clint Eastwood's .44 from those old cop movies, an Uzi from *The Matrix*. Display guns. Not *gun* guns.

I lost interest in the cabinet, moved toward the PC sitting on top of the polished glass desk in the center of the room. This was where Eli planted his spy software and stole information on Whispertown.

I sat in the mayor's chair and ran my fingers across his keyboard. Something about violating his space appealed to me. Payback for his nice-guy threats.

Mostly everything else on the desk was office normal—a coffee cup full of pens, a mail holder, a red stapler—except for the trophy. A single bronze boxing glove that punched the sky. The engraved base read: *VA State Golden Gloves—Richie Burke—1989*.

Mayor Burke was a former boxing champ? Proud enough of the accomplishment to keep this trophy around while not having a single picture of his kid anywhere in sight? I remembered Dustin's bruised eye. Must be nice having a sturdy teen for a stand-in punching bag. Keep the skills up.

Someone said, "What are you doing?"

Brief images of being tossed from the party flickered through my head.

It wasn't the mayor, or Dustin, or anyone who might care about me trespassing in this private space. The voice belonged to a gorgeous brunette.

She said, "I thought this was the way to the pond."

A gorgeous *drunk* brunette. I caught the slur in her voice this time, and if I hadn't, her stumbling over an invisible piece of furniture would've clued me. She went down on all fours, laughing. The way she leaned gave me a perfect view of bouncing cleavage in her low-cut tank top. She met my eyes, and I got the impression she wasn't offended.

"You thought there was a pond down this hallway?" I tried to measure her level of intoxication.

"Well, it's gotta be somewhere." She stood on shaky legs, came closer. She limped now, hunched, massaging the knee she had banged, giving me another view of her incredible chest. "Hey, can I check my email in here?"

I stood. "No, you can't."

Time to go before someone else caught me, someone who'd remember it tomorrow.

"I don't feel real good," she said, rubbing her stomach.

I could've—*should've*—left her. But I thought about that Golden Glove trophy and the mayor's reaction if he found liquor vomit in his office. Dustin might be making trouble for himself by throwing this party, but I didn't feel right letting this girl add to it.

"Come on," I said, hands on her shoulders, "let's get back."

"The pond!"

"I don't know where the pond is, uh—?"

"Callie, nice to meet you. What's your name?"

"I'm Nick."

"No, you're hot." She let out an ain't-that-clever? giggle and pressed her boobs into my stomach. The alcohol on her breath smelled like medicine. "Take me at the pond. I mean, *to* the pond." More giggles.

Gently, I pushed her away. "I'm here with a date."

I thought she'd press the issue more, forcing me to get mean, but instead she whined, "I don't feel good and I'm supposed to meet my friends at the pond."

She lurched forward, gagged, but nothing came up. Thank God.

"Okay, okay. Let's get you some fresh air and I'll help you find the pond."

Only then did she allow me to lead her away from the mayor's office, into the garage, and through a side door to the exterior. In the open, she seemed steadier and took point through a wooded path where no other partygoers were visible.

Callie pushed aside low-hanging branches and warned me about jutting roots. For someone who'd been so drunk and clumsy and unsure moments ago, she got us to the pond without a single misstep. Why didn't I see it then?

Water lapped like wet hands clapping, and the path opened onto a black mirror. A cedar observation deck, with large boxes of fish food mounted to the railing, marked the end of the line. A couple of dozen koi swam toward the deck, drawn by our movements, expecting a feast. Pumpkin-colored heads broke the surface, Whac-A-Mole-style. The moon hovered over the far end of the pond, its silver-dollar reflection rippling.

Callie approached the railing but did not take in the view. Instead, she faced me without meeting my eyes.

A sick feeling crept over me, no alcohol needed. "Where are your friends, Callie?"

An unwelcome voice sounded. "Right here, bitch."

Zach Lynch.

I turned slowly. They were all there. Russ, the twins, and, of course, their leader. Callie skirted around me, careful to keep her distance. Smart girl.

She pressed herself to Russ, kissed him on the lips, then jogged up the path, leaving me to my fate.

Skank.

CHAPTER 29

ZACH DRANK JACK DANIEL'S STRAIGHT FROM the bottle. The long bicycle chain wrapped around his knuckles scraped the glass when he sipped. "Heard you was talking junk about us. And you're here with my girl."

He shattered the bottle on the deck, splashing my shoes with backwash.

It could've been for show, him being a big man in front of his lackeys. But I didn't think so. Not the way Dee and Dum kept trading furtive looks, or the way Russ kept glancing at the path like he wanted to chase Callie. They didn't want to be a part of this, because Zach planned to do something worse than bloody my nose in the locker room.

His chain jingled.

Maybe they'd all been drinking. If I moved fast, I could probably beat them back to the party, where they'd be less likely to jump me. That was a good plan. A smart plan.

Instead, I took two running steps, made as if I was breaking right, and when Zach Lynch moved to intercept me, I stopped short and punched him in the spot below where the ribs met the sternum. He went bug-eyed, doubled over. With him off balance, I grabbed both of his shoulders for leverage, then rammed my knee into his balls.

First move Bricks ever taught me.

It took Zach and his crew by surprise, but their shock wouldn't last.

I ran at Dum. He tried to juke to one side, but I grabbed his arm, used his momentum to spin him around, then kicked him in his Achilles tendon. His leg shot up like a punter's and he landed flat on his back.

With two down, I had my best shot at escaping. I ran, craning my neck to make sure no one followed. Bad move. Callie had led me to the pond, pushing aside low-hanging branches as she went.

When I faced forward I ran full speed into an oak branch slung across the path.

It caught me in the mouth, put me horizontal to the path before dropping me on my tailbone. Dee pounced and held me until his friends recovered.

Pinned to the ground, viewing things upside down, I saw Zach approach, massaging his crotch and swinging his chain. He didn't talk, or threaten.

The whine of a low-powered motor interrupted the sound of that chain cutting the air. Light flashed on us, halting Zach.

"Back off, Lynch," said Lorenz, his mousy voice always odd coming from his huge frame. He stepped from a clownish-looking golf cart. Carrey followed, as did the wheelman, Dustin.

Zach said, "What are you doing here, Burke?"

"This is where I live. And Callie can't shut up about how clever you guys are. Figured I'd better get down here."

"This don't have nothing to do with y'all," Zach said.

Dustin. "My house. My party. It's all about me."

Zach's chest heaved. "This pussy has been disrespecting me ever since he got here. All in my girl's face. I'm supposed to let that ride?"

"I think you're confused about a couple of things."

Lorenz and Carrey helped me off the ground while Zach contemplated his next move.

He took a step toward me, still swinging that chain. Dustin signaled to Lorenz.

The big guy leveled Zach with a punch.

"Go home," Dustin told the rest of Zach Lynch's crew, "and take him with you."

Carrey and Lorenz walked me to the cart, kept me upright since I was still shaken from the tree branch. I took the seat next to the mayor's son. They sat in the back.

Zach rolled around in some dead leaves, groaning. His neutered friends circled their fallen idol.

"They won't bother you anymore tonight," Dustin said.

No, not tonight, but this wasn't over. With guys like Zach Lynch it never was.

Dustin puttered us back to the party, where the crowd was thinning. He noticed me noticing.

"Beer's gone," he said.

Dustin parked the cart. We entered a rec room, where stragglers abused all the things that didn't belong to them. I scanned faces for Reya but didn't see her.

I said, "I thought you were grounded. Where's your dad?"

"Business trip to D.C. He goes up a lot, and he can't rule with an iron fist when he's MIA." He held up a loaded key chain. "I've got the keys to the kingdom. Liquor cabinet, Beamer."

"You're not worried about getting in more trouble?"

"Life's short." He led us toward the foyer and the roped-off staircases. He ducked under the barrier, as did Lorenz and Carrey. I hesitated.

"It's cool," Dustin said. "Come on."

I followed them up to Dustin's room. Or apartment. It was massive, four of my bedrooms put together. I could see a jetted freaking tub through his open bathroom door. If this was what Dustin's space was like, I imagined the mayor's having a retractable dome roof like Cowboys Stadium.

Lorenz flopped on the unmade California king and rummaged through the drawer on Dustin's nightstand.

"Lorenz," Dustin said. "Stop going through my stuff."

Lorenz rolled his eyes and grabbed the new *Sports Illustrated*. When he lay back, he froze, sniffed. "Dawg, why's your bed smell like vanilla ice cream?"

"Alexis Carter works at the Cold Stone in Portside Mall," he said, matter-of-fact. "She brought samples."

Lorenz scrambled off the dirtier-than-he'd-anticipated sheets, and Carrey crowed, "Pimp!"

Dustin shrugged off the conquest. "I do what I can."

I fought the need to say something that might sound weird, like, *How was it?*, reminding me how little experience I had with my peers. I could trash talk the sheriff but couldn't get into a conversation on teen sex.

Thankfully, Dustin changed the subject. Sort of. "So, you and Reya?"

There was a moment of panic when I thought he was asking if me and Reya had done it. But he showed me his phone, the screen filled with a photo of me and her arriving at the party, taken and sent by someone with too much time on their hands. Reya looked red-carpet worthy in the picture. I looked lost.

"Yeah, we came together."

He examined the picture like a jeweler examines a diamond. "That ass is lookin' fine, dude."

"That ass" had a name, and I had a knee-jerk urge to break Dustin's nose. Again, I reminded myself that this was normal guy talk. And he just saved me from Zach. *Chill, Nick.*

Lorenz powered on Dustin's flat screen and popped in a Blu-ray. Carrey surfed the web on the opposite side of the room. While they were occupied, I said, "You want to talk in the hall or something? About Eli?"

"For what?" Lorenz said, fiddling with the media center controls. "His conspiracy theories are a rerun to us."

I had no idea what that meant. I wasn't in the dark for long.

Dustin said, "I told you I met him that Friday, right?"

I nodded.

"As soon as I got to his newspaper dungeon, Eli starts in on how my dad is a crooked politician and when he exposes him, it's going to be the story of the century. Eli was all like, I shouldn't have dissed him and I'll remember all the f'ed up stuff I did when I'm on the streets and he's living in a big house. It was crazy talk."

I wanted to say that didn't sound like Eli. But I couldn't get over his attempt to plant me in Dustin's last party as his inside man. Everything I had learned since Eli died suggested he had dirt on the mayor then and was looking for more. If Whispertown was all about Mayor Burke's shady crime stats, Eli planned to blow the whole thing up. He'd told me that himself.

Eli could be manipulative when he needed to be. Reya *and* Dustin confirmed he had no problem invading someone's privacy.

I said, "What'd you do?"

Dustin looked away, ashamed. "I pushed him. Man, I was going to beat him down."

I thought back to how I found Eli, the desk knocked off its book supports. Was that how it happened?

"You didn't though?"

"No. I felt it building up in me and I backed off. I—I don't like to use my hands like that." Absently, he touched the darkening bruise around his eye. "I left."

"Wait, so Eli was fine the last time you saw him?"

"The last time *I* saw him, sure."

What did *that* mean? "You're losing me. If Eli was alive the last time you saw him, what was the point of that story? Why the 'Nick, you need to know'?"

"Because when I came home, I told my dad about what happened." Dustin's phone buzzed, and he checked an incoming text. With his eyes on the screen, he said, "I told my dad."

No need to repeat. I got it the first time.

CHAPTER 30

WAS DUSTIN SAYING WHAT IT SOUNDED like he was saying? "You really think—?"

"He's crazy, Nick," said Lorenz. "Don't listen to him."

"Screw you," Dustin barked. "I'm not crazy."

"You do hate your dad," Carrey added.

"That's the thing about rich white boys," Lorenz went on, "they love hating their parents. It's true, I looked it up."

Dustin walked over and unplugged the TV.

"Hey!" Lorenz whined.

Dustin stood in the center of the room, pointed at his eye. "What did you think this was about? This wasn't me forgetting to dump the trash or turn on the dishwasher. He caught me going through his office. After Eli died I tried to see if any of the stuff he said was true. My dad lost it."

"You think he had something to do with Eli's *suicide*?" I used the *s* word on purpose, to get his reaction.

He glared. "You still calling it that?"

Lorenz rolled his eyes and plugged the TV back in. Carrey stayed glued to the screen. This made me question the dynamic here. Was Dustin prone to making up wild stories about his abusive father?

At your age, everything that pops in your head seems clever and important. It's not.

When Dad said that, I blew it off because he's Dad. Now that I wasn't the only one with the Mayor-Murder Theory, it felt silly somehow, like when you hear a little kid say they're afraid of something under their bed, and you're embarrassed that you used to be afraid of the same stupid thing. This was how it would sound to objective people. Far-fetched.

Lorenz lost interest in the movie and began rooting through Dustin's closet like some fashion archaeologist. "You still got that beast leather jacket, D?"

Dustin groaned. "Dude, stay out of my stuff."

My phone shook. I read the incoming text.

Reya: Where r u?
Me: Meet @ car n 5

"Reya?" Dustin said, not waiting for a confirmation. "Does she think her brother killed himself?"

"She's just grieving." I needed to be guarded about how much I said until I processed all I'd heard. "And she's ready to go."

Lorenz said, "You still here? I would've dived through the window to get to that girl tonight."

Chill, Nick. I focused on Dustin. "What now? Did you find any, like, evidence? To back you up?"

"No. He's got it all locked down with passwords."

I was at a loss. "Why tell me then?"

He shrugged. "Things have been getting tense around here. More than ever. I've got a bad feeling and I wanted someone other than the dumbass twins over there to know. Someone who was also Eli's friend."

This guy, who beamed confidence since the first time I met him, now looked unsure. Frightened. "Dustin—"

"Don't keep your girl waiting, Nick. Nothing left for me to do but clean up and get these jokers home. I'd rather be in your shoes."

I didn't take offense this time, had a feeling he wasn't talking about how fine Reya was.

We slapped palms, and he said, "Watch your back. Zach's gunning for you bad."

"I kind of got that impression."

He laughed a humorless laugh. "Trust me, there are worse people to have after you in this town."

Reya didn't ask me what Dustin said, or if I'd found him. Something was wrong. She drove us away from North End, but not toward either of our homes. She seemed . . . faded somehow, despite the lingering body glitter.

"Are you okay?" I said.

"Super."

No one knew sarcasm better than me. "What happened?"

"Nothing *happened*. Not other than being around friends again and seeing people getting on with their lives."

"Are your friends the Dementors from Harry Potter? Did they drain all your happiness with their Dementor's Kiss?"

A small smile. "I didn't take you for a Potterhead."

"I read a lot growing up." Another lesson learned during my time in WitSec: want to avoid kids who'd like to assault you . . . check out the library.

"Eli always used to bring up stuff in books and on TV like that. Only it would be things no one had ever heard of."

"I know. Sometimes I'd google stuff he said hours after I talked to him."

"Me too!" She brightened for a second. "If I'm *loco*, tell me now. Don't let me keep making a fool of myself."

"Reya, where's this coming from?"

She slouched in her seat, driving us in circles. "I cooked and cleaned and played hostess at my house this week because Mami couldn't do it. At the mortuary, I picked my brother's casket because Mami couldn't do it. I talked to this insurance guy about an old policy my papi had on Eli because Mami couldn't do it."

"That's a lot to ask of anyone. Not criticizing your mom, just sayin'."

"I know, and I was pissed. I kept thinking, 'Eli didn't kill himself. He wouldn't do *this* to us. This is somebody else's fault.' You know? But tonight, when the music was playing and I saw my old friends, I forgot all that. I wasn't obsessed about what 'really' happened to him. Just for a second. When I remembered, and the 'Eli wouldn't do this' thought snapped back in my head, this other voice was like, 'That's so stupid.'"

She swiped at her eyes, doubting herself. Possibly ready to let this go. I couldn't keep her in the dark any longer. "I need to tell you what Dustin said. Let's go somewhere, though. You probably shouldn't be in motion when you hear this. You know the lake at Monitor Park?"

She drove us there. And after I told her Dustin's suspicions about the mayor, she perked, regaining some of her previous drive.

"You think this Whispertown thing is what Eli pulled off the mayor's computer? And the mayor faked his suicide to cover it up?"

"Maybe? We can't tell unless we know exactly what Whispertown is. Did you ever find his laptop?"

She shook her head. "I called the school myself on Thursday, and they didn't have it."

"Damn it."

If—it was a big if—we were on to something, and the mayor, or most likely someone working for him, did this to Eli, they would've taken any evidence that was lying around. Nothing's easier to carry than a laptop.

"If it's gone," I said, "then that's a wrap. That data is lost."

Reya sat up and gripped the wheel like she'd been zapped with electricity. "Nick, Eli would never risk his data being completely lost. He was too type A for that."

I caught on immediately. "Backups. But where?"

"I didn't see any flash drives or anything in his room when I checked. He was hardly there anyway. Always holed up in—"

"—the J-Room."

Maybe we were doubling down on our delusions, but I couldn't lie about how right this part of our "investigation" felt.

"It's sealed off," I said, recalling the padlock I'd spotted. "We can beat that, though. It's too exposed to risk a pick set, even between classes. If I can get a look at the brand of lock, we can get in fast with a bump key. And—"

She tilted her head. "A what?"

"A bump key. It's a special key with the teeth filed down. You stick it in a lock, give it a little bump, and it shifts all the tumblers inside, unlocking it."

"You can get something like that?"

"Well, I can make one. I think."

"*For real?* You'd do that, break into school property?"

I mistook the tone of her voice for shock, discomfort at how easily I'd brought up breaking rules—*laws*—and I backpedaled. "It's just something dumb I saw on TV, we can—"

She leaned into me, pressed her mouth against mine, slid her tongue between my lips. It tasted like cinnamon gum, a flavor I was not a fan of before but could learn to love. Definitely *not* a Dementor's Kiss.

My hands found her hips, grazing the skin just above the waistline of her shorts, and I pulled her into my seat, on top of me. She reached down and jerked a lever; we fell back into a near-horizontal recline. I felt fingernails on my shirt, under it, lightly scraping my stomach and chest. I revenge fondled her back and thighs, our mouths sloppy on each other's faces and necks.

I didn't know how much further this would go—nowhere, everywhere—but some treasonous voice of reason suggested that to do more than kiss Reya, after all she'd been through, was taking advantage.

She licked my earlobe and my hormones dissolved that traitor like a baby tooth dropped in acid.

It was what it was. . . .

The initial heat cooled after a few minutes, saving me from any crisis of conscience I might've felt tomorrow. I convinced myself that guilt played third base, and I hadn't hit a triple. We stayed there for an hour, our rabid pawing becoming light kisses and conversation. She thanked me, verbally, for being there for her ("You know, after those kisses, saying the actual words seems kind of redundant"), I told about how her psycho ex got some girl to set me up ("Zachary's an ass and Callie's always been a tawdry whore"), and we agreed to scope the J-Room and work on a bump key ("I'll try to think of a better way, but that seems like our best shot").

Reya shifted back to the driver's seat, holding my hand instead of starting the engine. "You ever get homesick?"

"Huh?"

"You moved here from Detroit. Do you miss it?"

"Naw. Not really." I'd never even been to the place. Gotta love the legend. "Eli told you where I'm from?"

"No. Got it from the GAP."

Completely confused, "The place where you buy khakis?"

She giggled. "Girls' Associated Press, Stepton High's gossip wire service. That's what I call it anyway—you can't be in the Cruz house and not pick up some journalism talk. You had the female pop all chatty as soon as you touched ground."

Flattery and embarrassment rubbed together, started a fire in my cheeks. "No way."

"Your humility is really getting on my nerves."

"We can't all be movie star fabulous like you."

She grinned, more used to compliments than me. But was the truth really a compliment? She *was* fabulous. More so by the minute. I mean, anybody with eyes could see she was beautiful. What she'd done for her mother this week, though, and what she did for Eli tonight . . . I'd never met anyone like her.

I've also never tried to solve a possible murder, either. A lot of firsts this year.

"You don't believe me, do you?" she asked.

"About the GAP. I'd really, really like to. No one said anything."

She snatched her hand away, planted it on her hip. "Like you'd notice. You move in a bubble, Nick. I practically threw myself at you." She scratched her temple, rephrased. "Or into you."

"What do you mean?"

"The day we met—"

"When *I* bumped into *you*?"

She fidgeted. "I maybe could've sidestepped you, if I'd tried."

"But you acted so irritated."

"You've never heard of 'playing hard to get'?" Her expression changed into something less proud after she said that. "Then the thing with Zach happened. And I backed off. I thought you thought I wasn't worth the trouble."

I thought it. A few times. Being in the Program did have *some* benefits. "I'm used to trouble."

The kissing continued.

I could've stayed with her all night, but we both had creeping curfews.

She drove me home with one hand interlocked with mine. In front of my house, I leaned in for one last kiss, which might've been better than the first. It was a To Be Continued kiss, the one that left you thinking about the next.

She saw me zoning. "Something on your mind?"

"Got a sudden craving for vanilla ice cream."

Smirking, "Do I even want to know what that means?"

"Good night, Reya."

She motored down the block. The driveway was empty—Dad gone as usual—and I slid past Mom's open bedroom door, saw her buried under the covers. Soon, I was, too. I fell asleep thinking of vanilla and cinnamon, and missed Reya's 2:00 a.m. text about the car accident.

The one that claimed the life of another classmate.

The one that may not have been an accident at all.

CHAPTER 31

I FOLLOWED THE SCENT OF MAPLE bacon to the kitchen, where Mom had three skillets resting on blue flames. I said, "Smells good, Mom."

"Thank you. Set the table for the three of us."

Three? I knew me and her were better after our talk yesterday, but she'd called a truce with Dad, too? "Where is he?"

"Showering. I told him we're having a good family breakfast today. Even if it kills us."

A thirteen-inch TV sat on our counter. Mom kept it on the news while she cooked. I arranged the place settings in a foggy daydream state while Mom chatted and the anchor ran down the morning's top stories.

(Reya, Reya, Reya.)

"These have been tough years for us, Tony—"

"*Gas prices hit a record high . . .*"

(Reya, Reya, Reya.)

"—only given so much time on earth, and you end up regretting the things you don't—"

"... *tensions in Iran escalate, necessitating a trip by Secretary of State* ..."
(Reya, Reya, Reya.)

"—cherish the time we have, but it has to be ours, not the made-up people we pretend—"

"... *In local news, three Stepton High School students were involved in a fatal car crash late last night* ..."

The silverware I'd been holding rattled to the floor, my focus shifting to the reporter's voice. Mom went mute and increased the TV's volume.

"... *the teens were rushed to Stepton General, where one was pronounced dead on arrival.*" The broadcast cut from the anchorman at his desk to nighttime footage of emergency lights flashing over a familiar dark blue BMW hooked around a tree like a boomerang. "*The remaining passengers were treated for injuries, but we've received conflicting reports of their status at this time. No one witnessed the accident but one of the survivors alleges their vehicle was run off the road by an aggressive driver in a dark, late-model truck or SUV. Police are searching for the vehicle.*"

"Good Lord," Mom said. "Do you think you know them?"

Before I could answer, Dad entered with a damp towel around his neck. "Sure smells good. Let's eat." Something on our faces must've told him he was the only one who still had an appetite. "What? What'd I say?"

I ran upstairs and powered on my half-charged phone. The display blazed with like ten text messages. All from Reya. And I asked the question.

> **Me:** I saw the news. Do you know who died?
> **Reya:** Carrey. Everyone is saying it's him.

I was slow responding—what was I *supposed* to say? Another message came through.

> **Reya:** D was nervous when u talkd 2 him, right?
> **Me:** yeah
> **Reya:** They r sayin D was run off the road.

I looked through my window.

> **Reya:** I can't believe Carrey's dead. We just saw him.

Stared at my driveway.

> **Me:** Can we go 2 the hospital?
> **Reya:** We can, but we won't get past lobby. I've got texts from others, Family Only!

That was a problem. I needed to talk to whoever was conscious, Dustin or Lorenz. Today.

> **Me:** Only relatives? This the same hospital Pilar's in?
> **Reya:** OMG, Nick!! Ur a genius. Can u b ready in 30?
> **Me:** I'll b waiting.

I got dressed, returned to my window, the news report on my mind. It said the police were searching for a dark truck or SUV. I could've helped them; there was one downstairs.

The Beetle pulled up outside and I went to Reya, kissed her, expecting the touch/smell/sight of her to be a bright spot in my dark, dark thoughts. I was expecting too much.

Dad, where were you last night?

A lingering question. With an answer I was afraid I already knew.

REWIND

IT WAS ON. TONIGHT, I'D FIND out exactly where Dad goes when he does Cool Mob Stuff.

Once Mom left for her grown-up party, which sounded more like work than fun, giving my babysitter the slip was simple. I said, "I don't feel very good. I'm going to bed now."

Rachelle, being the attentive child-care professional that she was, disengaged from her iPhone for half a second. "If you throw up, you better be good with a mop. I saw you eat that corn earlier."

Phase two of my plan to see Cool Mob Stuff involved a little more finesse. I slipped on my jean shorts and sneakers, then tiptoed to the garage. I brought a blanket for camouflage; I planned to blend in with all the other junk Dad kept in his SUV. The extra jackets, dirty car-washing towels, and other assorted chaos that cluttered his seats and made Mom call his vehicle Oscar's Trash Can. That plan went by the wayside when I opened the door and found he'd removed the benches entirely.

I climbed in anyway, checking out the new stuff Dad had cleared space for. A shovel and a pickax clanked as I maneuvered a heavy bag of something called lye aside. A thick, blue tarp made a better cover than my blanket with the flowers on it. I slipped under the plastic sheet and waited. Not for long.

Dad took the driver's seat, raising the garage door—*Ka-chut-Ka-chut-Ka-chut.* The sound always reminded me of roller coasters climbing. Another noise, a heavy thud. I couldn't see, but I had this flash where I saw Dad's forehead bouncing on the steering wheel.

He said, "Jesus, get it together."

The engine rumbled and we were on our way. If this were a roller coaster, I'd put my hands in the air, waiting for the drop.

Some lady's warbling high note blared through Dad's speakers before being cut off by an equally high telephone ring, almost like it was part of the song. I was glad for the interruption. Not that the lady couldn't sing, but it was a religious song from the gospel station. Dad never listened to that stuff, and it felt, I don't know, creepy.

Dad took a long time to answer the call. He breathed deep before speaking. "Yeah."

"We're here." Kreso Maric's accented voice, in concert quality. *"Are you close?"*

"I'm about fifteen minutes from you."

"Be here in ten."

"Mr. Maric, I'll try, but maybe this is more of a job for—"

The singing lady picked up where she left off when Kreso hung up.

Dad stepped on the gas, urging the vehicle forward, faster.

Nine minutes later we slowed. I peeked from my hiding place and found the darkness startling. In our neighborhood, it was never *dark* dark. We had streetlights and porch lights and landscaping lights. Here there was no light other than a fingernail moon that I glimpsed through the treetops. Dad's brakes squealed and we were still; the engine went silent. His door seal broke, triggering the chime that meant he'd left his headlights on. He'd yelled at Mom for doing that once, because it drained the battery. He closed the door without noticing and I got scared thinking about having a dead battery in an unfamiliar forest.

I slithered from under my cover, careful not to rattle anything. On hands and knees I moved up, keeping my head low until I reached the console between the front seats. The headlights flared over an awesome Mercedes, two men leaning on it. I dropped down before they spotted me, then realized that wasn't possible. I'd played with enough flashlights to know that in the dark, you couldn't see the person *behind* a light. You might catch a shadow, but mostly you were blind.

I raised my head again, with confidence. Ready for Cool Mob Stuff.

One of the men was Kreso, his tanned face, neck, and hands in contrast with his pale gray suit. Beneath the jacket, his blue shirt hung open at the collar, revealing two golden chains. The other Mean-Face guy was less dapper—denim, sneakers, plain button-down shirt—and huger. He looked like he could bench-press the car.

Dad approached them. No words were exchanged.

Mr. Maric motioned toward the car with his chin and the back door opened. Two more guys left the vehicle. One was an undersized version of Mean-Face in a nearly identical outfit. The other was a skinny, bushy-haired blond in a Bart Simpson shirt. He looked like one of the kids that rode the high school bus.

Mean-Face #2 pushed the kid down on his knees. Kreso reached under his jacket and produced a square, black handgun. I'd seen pistols before, but never like this. Dark woods, four guys surrounding a crying, begging kid. This wasn't what I came to see. But I couldn't look away.

I shuddered, waiting for the bang, knowing what was coming.

Really, I didn't know anything.

Kreso handed the gun to Dad.

CHAPTER 32

GO HOME. I'LL TAKE CARE OF THE MAYOR.

Dad said that. Not even a week ago. Looking over the ER waiting room at Stepton General, packed with classmates like the halls at school between bells, I wondered if this was how Dad took care of things. The whole thing felt like a somber continuation of last night's Dust Off. Reya did the talking at the visitors' desk, and we were on our way to the maternity ward with a couple of visitor passes.

In a private room, Pilar lay propped up in her bed with MTV playing on a low volume, a *Teen Mom* rerun. Next to her bed an egg-shaped baby squirmed in a bassinet, imprisoned in a mummy-tight blue blanket.

Pilar turned to us slowly, fatigued. "What brings you here, cuz? Need some practice staring down your nose?"

"I came to make sure my favorite cousin was doing okay," Reya said, her voice flat. "Because I love you. So much."

Pilar said, "Really?"

Pilar wasn't being snarky about Reya's sarcastic shot. She sounded hopeful. My one and only hospital stay was a tonsils thing when I was five, and I remembered being terrified whenever Mom left the room.

Was it any less terrifying for Pilar now? Where was her dad? The *kid's* father?

Her new baby gurgled, then broke into a high-pitched cry.

She forced a smile, motioned to her son. "Reya, bring him to me please."

Reya went rigid. "Are you sure? He's so small."

"You won't break him. Babies are tougher than you think. That's what your mom told me."

Reya slid past me to scoop the kid up. When she did, his shrieking cut off like someone hit the pause button. He proceeded to shove his whole fist in his mouth. He was pale brown, and a knit cap covered most of his hair, though a few slick black strands slipped out. Big green eyes stretched wide like they might swallow his head.

I gave him a little wave as Reya handed him to his mother. "What's his name?" I asked.

"Absolut Citron Rios. Vodka played a big role in him being here, so it felt appropriate."

I winced. "Um, that's—it's—"

Pilar cracked up. A second later, Reya did, too, and pointed to a card taped to the bassinet. Ricardo Elijah Rios.

Elijah.

Reya blinked away fresh tears. "Best name I ever heard."

The kid got bored with his fist and resumed his shrieking.

"He's hungry," Pilar and Reya said together. A look passed between them, real understanding.

Pilar said, "Nick, would you mind stepping out? I have to—" She motioned to her chest.

"Say no more." To Reya, "I'm going for a walk."

She nodded, understanding that I wasn't strolling for the cardio. I closed Pilar's door and headed to the nurse's station.

"Excuse me, ma'am. I'm on the wrong floor. Is there any way for you to look up the room numbers for Lorenz Murphy and Dustin Burke?"

Lorenz wasn't an option. He was in the intensive care unit, immediate relatives only. Dustin, however, was on the second floor, room 214. I cracked the door into gray darkness.

"Who is it?" Dustin asked in a scratchy voice. "Who's there?"

I slid inside. "It's Nick."

My hand hovered over the light switch, and he said, "No! Leave it off. I want it dark."

My eyes adjusted. Dustin sat on his bed, in a shadow shell. The television glow flickered over him, bandages heavy on the left side of his head. His left arm was cast and in a sling, the fingers sticking from a plaster glove like fleshy plants poking through snow. More gauze covered his neck and lower jaw, where the skin looked mad infected. The pupil of his left eye, the one that was bruised before the accident, now seemed to float in cherry Kool-Aid. I fought a grimace.

I didn't hide my reaction as well as I thought. He said, "I know. Pretty hideous." He laughed the same humorless laugh from the last time I saw him.

"What happened? I mean, if you want to talk about it."

"I don't mind, if you answer a question for me. How are Lorenz and Carrey doing? No one's telling me anything. I would've gone to find their rooms myself, but I get dizzy when I stand up."

I know he said more, but I was stuck on the Lorenz and Carrey question. He didn't know? His red eye looked through me before tears spilled. The gush came so fast I thought he had splashed me. "Damn, dude. Your poker face sucks. Both of them?"

I'm ashamed to say I reacted to the "poker face sucks" comment first. After my time in WitSec, I took offense, as if I were in the NBA and someone told me I had a weak jump shot. I processed the rest—what he was asking me to confirm—next.

"Carrey died last night. Lorenz is in intensive care. I don't know how he's doing." I got angry. Someone should've told him before now. Why'd I have to do it? With everything else I was dealing with. "Tell me what happened to you all last night."

Dustin shook his head, flinging tears sideways, dampening his bandages. "You should forget this now. Forget everything we talked about. Jesus, *Carrey*?"

"I'm not forgetting anything. The news said you were run off the road by a dark SUV. Is that true?"

He nodded.

"You didn't get a look at the driver?"

"No. And I never want to. Leave it alone."

"Do you think this has something to do with what you told me, the stuff with your dad?"

He didn't answer.

"Dustin."

"No," he said, "I don't think this has to do with the stuff I told you because I didn't tell you everything."

That, I wasn't expecting. "Explain."

"I told you what I thought about Eli because, I don't know, it seemed—

relevant? Is that the right word?"

I couldn't tell if the question was about his head injury or poor vocabulary. "That depends on you."

"Right. Well, the day I got caught snooping in my dad's office, he wasn't alone. There was a guy with him; I'd seen him around the house a couple of times. Only, *he* was pissed, him and my dad were yelling at each other."

"About what?"

"I don't know. I didn't hear anything specific. All of sudden, they were in my face. When they came in, the guy started pointing at me and yelling at my dad. I think the beating I got later was more about Dad being embarrassed over the guy than me snooping."

The guy.

My dad knew the mayor, had some kind of shady dealings with him involving crime in Stepton. At some point they'd had a disagreement, evident by Mayor Burke's creepy interest in me and Dad's insistence that he'd "take care of" Burke.

While Dustin talked, I ran the timeline down in my head. Monday, I found Eli's body. Tuesday, I met Dustin in the park, his first attempt at clueing me in on his shady dad. Wednesday, the mayor took me for a ride and Dustin got a shiny new black eye. Most likely, this meeting between "the guy" and Mayor Burke happened sometime on Tuesday. Enough time for the mayor to work off some steam by abusing his son, then deciding to send a message to "the guy" by picking me up the next day.

"Who was the man yelling at your dad?"

I waited for it, waited to hear, "*I never got his name, but he's a tall, black guy. Maybe in his forties. Muscular, mean looking. Come to think of it, Nick, he looks a lot like you if you were older."*

After a labored sigh, "It's a guy people around here don't talk about much. He runs stuff in town, I mean, the bad stuff. Drugs and things. His name is Miguel Rios."

CHAPTER 33

WAIT. *WHAT?*

Was he talking about Pilar's dad? Reya's uncle?

He said the name again. "Miguel Rios. He's badass, Nick. Like a for-real gangsta."

I felt like the hospital was tilting. Nothing made sense anymore. "What kind of business would your dad have with a guy like that?"

"I don't know." He lifted his broken arm. "But I don't think it's going well."

I'd heard "dark SUV" on the news, connected it to Dad's beef with the mayor, and thought I was Sherlock Holmes. This was something else entirely. Reya's uncle was some kind of *boss*?

I remembered what Reya had told me the day I phoned her at the funeral home, how odd it sounded. *Once Eli got these tiny microphones off the internet and put them in our uncle's car. I thought Miguel was going to . . . You just don't do that to Miguel.*

What was going on here?

This was so far over my head. I needed some advice, like now. Of course, I ended up giving Dustin advice, because I'm so qualified. "Dustin, don't tell this to anyone else."

"I didn't even want to tell *you*. You're like a bulldog, dude."

One thing Deputy Marshal Bertram had stressed to my family during our years in the Program was the burden of information. Everyone thinks they can keep a secret, particularly a dangerous one. Most people are wrong. "I'm serious. Until I get back to you, keep this between us."

"Keep *what* between you?" The politician's boom of the mayor's voice made me want to jump.

Dustin sputtered, "D-Dad?"

I faced the mayor, which makes me sound braver than I felt. Given an option, I simply preferred not having him behind me.

"Keep *what* between you?" he said again, spittle flying.

I didn't say anything. Neither did Dustin. Fury flashed on the mayor's face like lightning inside a cloud. He pushed me aside—not hard, more like a nudge—but I felt the muscles in his forearm flex, latent power that could've sent me flying if he chose. I got a small fraction of what Dustin must see all too frequently.

"Get out of here, Nick! Don't come back. You're to have no contact with my son again."

I hesitated, fearing for Dustin.

"Now!" the mayor roared.

A passing nurse stuck her head in, concerned. "What's going on in here?"

"Nothing." I slipped by her and kept going down the hall. I hated the way I left, like a punk, but what could I do? Throw the boxing champ mayor out of his own son's room? Me and Dustin take him down together? Maybe in the movies.

I texted Reya from the elevator to let her know I'd be in the lobby, then took a seat in the waiting area, away from the other kids. I wasn't in the mood to hug or join in a prayer or do any of the stuff that was a thousand times more normal than what I'd just experienced.

They could keep their moral support. I wanted to talk to a killer.

<hr>

I lied to her. Again.

I told Reya that Dustin hit his head and was too weak to give me any good information. She bought it. Why wouldn't she? I was trustworthy Nick.

If what Dustin said about her uncle Miguel being Stepton's version of Kreso Maric was true, Reya already knew about it. But she didn't know about the thread-thin link between her uncle's activities and Eli's death. If there was one. I couldn't risk her going ballistic and confronting Miguel until I knew more. No telling what *that* could lead to. Better to keep her in the dark, for now.

"Back to original plan?" she said.

"Original plan?"

"The J-Room. Eli's backups. Whispertown, the key to everything."

"I guess." Whispertown might really be the mayor's construction project. All the dying could be something else entirely. Nothing made sense.

"You wanna come back to my house? Mami will probably go visit Pilar again. You can explain that whole 'vanilla ice cream' thing."

The words sounded good, but there was no enthusiasm behind them. Another teen was dead. She proposed a make-out session as a distraction.

Something to tarnish last night's perfect end. No thanks.

"My mom told me to be home." A lie. "I've got chores." Lie.

"Okay." She didn't sound disappointed.

She gave me a light, passionless kiss when she dropped me off. While our lips touched, I wondered if I'd saved enough allowance money to buy a disposable phone.

In my room, I logged on to my computer to start the process me and Bricks had rigged for when we needed to talk, a system he insisted on after we went into the Program, when I called him from a stolen cell in San Diego. I could still hear the rage in his voice. *Tony, you're in California! I can tell from the area code. You never let me know where you are. Never! You understand?*

I got it. He couldn't tell what he didn't know. Couldn't be *made* to tell.

Switching phones was key, but there was the little obstacle of sending each other the new numbers. Enter Facebook.

Step 1: With over a billion users, FB's the perfect way to hide in public. My page is a fake, obviously. To those floating around cyberspace, my name is Stan Humphrey, Cablon High class of '04. I enjoy sushi, massages, and Caribbean cruises. Every so often, Stan gets a wall post from a rival of his favorite sports team, the L.A. Lakers.

Kobe Bryant can eat %&^ and *#&@ die.

A casual observer would think it was just some flamer dick taking his sports too seriously . . . missing the code entirely.

The symbols correspond to numerals on a standard QWERTY keyboard. The way our system works, you add one to the number that corresponds with each symbol.

The symbols %&^ convert to 687, your area code.

Decode *#&@ and you get the last four digits of the phone number.

Step #2: Twitter. No decoding. Bricks simply posts his predictions for the pick-three lottery drawing: 555, for example.

I combine the pieces and—*boom!*—my godfather's latest number.

And if he hasn't gotten around to shooting the latest code into cyberspace, I just send a private message to his Twitter account. A simple *##*. Letting him know to start the process. That's what I planned to do.

Until I saw the private message in my Facebook in-box: *Call Me. Now. 856-555-8741.*

Bricks bypassed our codes, our slick system. A straight phone number.

That meant something urgent. Possibly life threatening.

Call me. Now.

Too bad the message was already two days old.

CHAPTER 34

PACING. I WAS AT THE EDGE of the lake, with my new disposable pressed to my ear, and a light drizzle falling. A hollow ring bleated through the receiver while I imagined the infinite horrors that might inspire such a sloppy move from Bricks. "Come on."

The ringing ceased abruptly.

"Is this Mama Luisa's Pizza?" I blurted, still playing our spy game.

"No need for that," Bricks said. "I'm alone."

"What happened?"

"You just got my message?"

"I don't check that account every day." Breathing on his end, that's all. Like some perv crank call. "Is this about Kreso? Does he know something about where we are?"

"This is about your mom."

I stopped walking, dumbstruck. "What? Mom?"

"She's been reaching out to old players up here, trying to call in markers and get her hands on some cash. Damn, I didn't think she'd be so stupid."

"Why would she—?"

I have friends. You'd be surprised how many!

Dad's lies hadn't fooled her, only delayed her. Got her to slow down before putting her plan in motion. What else had all her weirdness been about? The mysterious old car, the snooping on Dad, that weird conversation before Eli's funeral. It couldn't be a coincidence.

We *were* going to run.

"You still there?" Bricks asked.

"I'm here."

"What's she up to, Tony? Messing with the streets again is insane."

"Does Kreso know?" I said, evading.

"I don't think so. She's been hitting up some low-level sharks mostly. These guys aren't on the Big Man's radar. Yet. But if people keep talking . . ."

It would get to Kreso eventually. Mom had to know that. Which meant whatever she was planning would happen soon.

Bricks said, "If she needed something she should've come to me!"

I held the phone from my ear, stunned by the outburst. He had a thing for her when they were kids, I knew that. Those "remember when" stories used to be funny, with Bricks laughing as much as Mom and Dad over his childhood crush. There was no humor in him now. Just . . . *ick*.

"Thanks for letting me know about Mom."

"Tony, talk to her." He pressed on. "Give her this number if you have to. I'll help."

"What? You want me to let her know that we've been talking on the down low, for years, then ask if she wants to play, too?"

Dad might be involved in a political conspiracy and kid murder. Mom was planning to duck WitSec. Now Bricks wanted to reveal our secret calls. Was everyone going crazy?

"Do what I say, Tony. Call me back tonight and let me know—"

"Someone's coming, Bricks." No one was. "I gotta go."

I ended the call, tossed the phone in the water, and stared at my throwing hand like it was demon possessed. I couldn't talk to Bricks anymore today, not about Mom. But I never got to ask him any of the stuff I'd intended to. About the mayor and Miguel Rios and how Dad might be connected to them.

Would any of it matter if Mom told me to pack a bag today or tomorrow?

It felt like my life was falling apart. Since it wasn't really my life, I should've been cool with it. There's a difference between being cool and feeling cold fingers walking up my spine when I considered what might be coming.

I got in bed that night with my thoughts shifting back to two dead Stepton teens. Fatigue overlaid their faces with another kid's from long ago. A kid with a cartoon on his shirt who begged "Big Man" Kreso Maric for his life while my father held the boy's fate in his hand.

My buzzing phone interrupted the start of a nightmare.

Reya: Lorenz died 2nite

Three dead Stepton teens. My stomach clenched at the count.

Another text.

Reya: We r getting n that room 2morrow
Me: Count on it

CHAPTER 35

A HALF HOUR BEFORE FIRST BELL, I examined the J-Room padlock, a Schlage. I took a picture with my phone for reference. After school, Reya would drive us to a hardware store in Portside for materials to make and test the bump key.

I ran into a small group where the halls intersected. Three of them craning their necks the way people do in a building like the White House. *Wow, the president's lightbulbs work the same as my lightbulbs.*

New kids. Army brats, I guessed. Eli told me they get a lot of them here. They were escorted by a fourth kid decked in an orange vest that actually said Student Guide. The group moved on, down the main corridor and past the grief counselors, who'd extended their stay for another week.

Classes crept by. I'd memorized the bump key tutorial on YouTube, my hands mimicking small filing motions under my desk, ready to work. My bag shook. I snatched my phone before my teacher heard.

Reya: Meet @ science hall after bell, found a better way

Ring, ring.

—————————————

The bell stopped as I got close to the science hall, but the corridor remained packed and noisy. Voices. Shouting. Screaming.

Cheering?

People crowded, packed tight, which was weird this far from the caf. I wedged between classmates who stood on tiptoes or leaned sideways for a better view of . . . something.

I heard a voice I recognized and this crazy knocking sound again.

"Skanky bitch!" Reya shouted.

THONK.

"Messing with"—*THONK*—"my man."

Chants of *"Girl fight! Girl fight!"* An anthem. I broke through the crowd. What. A. View.

Callie, the girl who left me in the woods for Zach and company on Saturday night, slid on her knees across the slick tile floor. Reya stood over her, two handfuls of Callie's hair coiled in her fingers, dragging the girl from one side of the hall to the other. At the end of each trip—*THONK*—Reya rammed Callie's head into the closest locker before reversing her momentum and repeating the process on the opposite side. *THONK.*

I might be in love.

A linebacker in a starched white shirt and black slacks muscled me aside. Vice Principal Hardwick shouted, "Settle down!"

The crowd shushed. Except for Reya. She didn't miss a beat. *THONK.*

As Hardwick closed the gap between them, Reya released Callie and stumbled directly into Hardwick's embrace.

"Have you lost your mind, Ms. Cruz?"

"I'm sorry," Reya said, "but she—"

"Quiet! There's never an excuse for this." He clamped down on Reya's arm, then helped a wobbling Callie to her feet.

The VP walked them toward me, on his way to the office for the obligatory parental phone call. When the girls passed me, Reya bucked Mr. Hardwick's grip, hopped up and down like a lunatic. "Anybody else want to disrespect me?"

Reya ran past me and shoved some poor kid I didn't know. "You want some, too?"

Hardwick stepped up, snaked an arm around her waist, and lifted her off her feet. "Move," he shouted to anyone and everyone. The crowd parted. Reya kicked and screamed the whole way.

Kids dispersed quickly, anxious to get to the cafeteria and broadcast the events to those unfortunate enough to miss what was already being billed as the fight of the year. I stayed behind. Reaching into my jacket pocket, I removed the heavy key chain Reya slipped in after she shoved that last kid. A key chain she'd lifted off Hardwick's belt during the scuffle.

A better way indeed.

Seven keys on Hardwick's key chain were Schlage compatible and I hit the jackpot on the fourth try. I ducked under the yellow caution tape strung diagonally across the frame.

Red, tacky blood pooled ahead of me.

I blinked.

No blood, clean tiles.

"Breathe, Nick."

Mostly, the room remained unchanged from my last visit. Someone had taken the ancient Mac and printers, but reference books still lined the baseboard and teetered in stacks at each corner.

I had a half hour before next bell. I went straight for Eli's desk.

The drawers were unlocked. It saved me the time of breaking in but didn't bode well for me finding anything useful. As I suspected, they were all empty.

I sat in Eli's chair—nowhere near as creepy as I feared. If he'd hidden a flash drive in a locked drawer, as most rational people would, then the Eli Magical Mystery Tour was over. No clues, no evidence, no case.

The key word: *rational*.

Those books along the wall drew my attention each and every time I entered the room. He could've hidden a flash drive in one of them. I scanned the titles, everything from automotive manuals to the Chronicles of Narnia. I grabbed the closest one and leafed through it, found nothing. Moved on to the next. There was no time to get through all of them. I'd have to figure out a way to get back in here after school, before Hardwick realized—

The third book I chose came from a bulky stack in the corner closest to Eli's desk. When I removed it, a white plastic corner protruded from the area the book formerly concealed. I set the book aside and began to remove more volumes from that stack until I revealed the entire heavy-duty plastic beast.

A stepladder.

Above, I noticed a fiberglass ceiling panel slightly askew in the overhead grid.

Working quickly, I cleared the rest of the books and climbed the ladder.

I had Eli by a few inches, so it was easy to reach in and snag his stash. An insulated lunch box rested in the ceiling.

It contained a single flash drive and an ancient peanut butter and jelly sandwich. I pocketed the drive and put everything back the way I found it. The bell rang just as I emerged into the hall.

Mission accomplished.

———

By the time final bell rang I felt like a rocket about to blast off. I biked to Reya's in record time. She met me at the front door. "Did you find it?"

I glanced away and shook my head. She sighed. "It's okay. There was no guarantee that he—"

I held up the flash drive. She punched me in the shoulder for lying.

"Hey, I'm not Callie. Please, don't unleash your wrath."

"That crap got me kicked out of school for two weeks."

I'd heard. But what a genius move. I had a feeling Eli would've been proud. I know I was.

We plugged in the flash drive. Her machine booted and I dried my sweaty palms on my jeans.

A window appeared on the screen and my face went slack. Reya ran both hands through her hair. "No, no, no."

We had another mystery to solve.

Eli's password.

CHAPTER 36

A BUMP KEY WASN'T GOING TO get us past the flash drive's security. After a couple of hundred wrong passwords, I had to keep Reya from snapping the thing in two. Even though that's what I felt like doing.

It went like that for days.

I drifted through school, jotting down new password guesses when they came to me. Eli liked Star Wars, so I made a Star Wars list. My journalism list had things like "C0lumn$" and "1nch3s." All of them wrong. Reya, suspended for fighting and obsessed, spent *all* her time trying to crack the code, filling notebooks with her failed attempts. I went to her place after school each day to take a typing shift while she soaked her hands in ice like an athlete. Hackers we weren't.

I expected Mrs. Cruz to shut the whole thing down since Reya got in trouble over the Callie fight. All she said was, "It's nice to have one of Eli's friends over," like I was visiting him.

By day four, I found Reya wearing a pair of glasses with purple frames, kid's glasses. When I asked her about them, she said, "Contacts were irritating me."

I looked from her to the picture of Eli on her mirror, noting a much stronger resemblance between them. I would've said something, but she was into the work.

During one super-frustrating code-cracking session, my phone lit up.

> **Dustin:** I'm @ home now. Got my phone back (as u can tell)
> **Me:** U ok?
> **Dustin:** No. But I'm here. That's more than L + C can say ☹
> **Me:** Remember, keep quiet. Me & Reya r workn something thatll help
> **Dustin:** Lik what?!?! Dont make this worst, yo!
> **Me:** B cool. Stay low. Will b n touch

I snapped my phone shut and powered it down. I couldn't deal with him freaking right now.

Wait, *freaking*. Maybe with a *3* for the *e* and an @ for the . . .

The password window flashed red at another bad attempt while Reya dozed behind me. Hopeless.

Late was the new early at my house. There'd been no fights, and Mom kept insisting that we "eat breakfast as a family," but the evenings felt like I was an emancipated minor. Sandwiches and sodas in front of the TV, no parents to be found.

I took my dad's spot on the couch and surfed channels. One more day of school this week, then a long weekend of staring at the password screen. Hopefully.

If Mom was planning to run, how much longer did I have in Stepton? With Reya? I could've asked Mom directly, put everything on the table, but I was afraid. Afraid that if I mentioned it, I'd make it happen. Like now.

I powered on my phone intending to text Reya, but I accidentally touched the voice mail icon. One saved message. From Eli.

"You're really going to make me use my voice here, huh? Okay. Nick, um, I'm sorry about what happened today. For reals. I line crossed. From now on, I'll keep you out of my more . . . troublesome obligations. As a peace offering, I wanted to let you know that my guild is going to quest for Urilium Gauntlet tonight, and I wanted to invite you to join our brotherhood. You can lead the war party if you want."

Bingo. Video games.

I called Reya. When she picked up, I heard keys clacking in the background. "What?"

Ignoring the snap in her voice, I said, "I've got some new ones for you."

"Hang on." Rustling, crackling static, then, "You're on speaker."

"These are all video game based." I started with *Modern Battlefield* because Eli was so good at it. We worked through the names of maps, guns, co-op missions. Nothing. We switched to that *Finite Universe* game. "Try *Urilium*."

"Spell it."

I did. "If that doesn't work, try *gauntl*—"

"Nick! Nick! Oh my God," she screamed, forcing me to lower the phone. At a distance, I still heard her say, "I love you *soooo* much right now."

My stomach clenched. She was happy. That's all.

When her volume decreased, I said, "It worked. What do you see?"

"There's a folder called 'Whispertown,' but there's a ton of stuff in it. All sorts of files and subfolders. It's going to take awhile to sort through. Come by early tomorrow, I should have some answers."

"Hey, what you said a minute ago—" The line went dead.

CHAPTER 37

THE WORST DAY OF MY LIFE began with a kiss from my mother.

Her lips pressed my forehead, warm and comforting, waking me. I felt five again. "Come on, sweetie. I need you to get up."

The sky beyond my window was purple, gold streaks signaling the rising sun. Mom wore black, just like I imagined she would on our last day in Stepton.

No. Not now. Please not now.

I reached for the bedside lamp. The bulb flared, revealing her usual robe and slippers. "Get dressed and come downstairs for breakfast. I want us to have a bit more time together today. As a family."

What had we been doing all week?

"Downstairs in twenty," she said.

I stumbled into the shower and let the hot spray sting my face. Dad beat me downstairs, where a massive country breakfast waited. I sat next to him. Mom brought over biscuits from the oven.

Dad reached for the remote control on the counter. Mom slapped it from his hand so hard the cover popped off, sending two AA batteries rolling to opposite ends of the kitchen. Dad's jaw hung slack, in midchew.

"No TV during meals," she said.

It was scarier than if she'd spun her head 360 degrees and leaped to the ceiling like a human spider.

"We don't know how long we get with the people we love," she told Dad, like they were the only two people in the room. "You should know that better than anyone. Cherish the little time you're allowed. Things won't always be this way, Robert."

Dad brought his napkin to his mouth and spit the food he'd been chewing into it. He pushed away from the table, walked past Mom. "I'm going to grab a bagel."

In Mom's last words—*Things won't always be this way, Robert*—I decoded a warning that Dad did not heed. We wouldn't be around forever, maybe not even for long.

He slammed the door. Gone.

Today might not be the day, but me and Mom's time here was short. Especially if Eli's flash drive implicated Dad in the mayor's and Miguel's sleazy schemes.

Cherish the little time you're allowed.

I needed to see Reya. Now. I wanted every moment I was allowed. Unlike my dad. I left the table.

"You're leaving, too?" Mom said.

I kissed her on the cheek. "I love you. Whatever happens, I'm with you."

She looked past me, into the middle distance. "I know."

"I'll see you later, Mom." I grabbed my bag and left, preparing myself to tell Reya good-bye soon. Mom didn't respond.

I prepared for the wrong thing.

Reya, hunched and tired, led me through her house by the hand. We pushed past her mom, on her way to the kitchen.

"Good morning, Mrs. Cruz," I said on the move.

Reya pulled me into her room and shut the door. She bounced on the balls of her feet and chewed her nails.

"Was it what we needed?" I asked.

She nodded but kept chewing her nails.

"Well?"

She said, "Sit down."

I settled onto her bed, waiting. She took the swivel chair by her desk and brought up a text file, the font too small to read from where I sat. "Don't keep me in suspense, Reya. What is Whispertown?"

"It's us. Stepton." She finger combed her hair hard enough to tear some out. "*Our* town."

"I don't get it."

Her fingers curled as if she wanted to strangle me for not understanding. "It's a code name. For Stepton. A *government* code name. They're running an experiment in our town. A trial. Eli found out about it from the files he stole off the mayor's computer. It involves the Witness Protection Program, Nick."

My face felt like it had been soaked in lighter fluid and someone struck a match. She said "Witness Protection Program" and my name. *In the same sentence.* "What"—my voice cracked—"kind of experiment?"

"There are criminals in our town. Living with us, going to school with us. Anyone we know could be one of them, anyone at all."

CHAPTER 38

I STUFFED MY HANDS IN MY pockets, afraid she'd see them shaking. "What's so secret about that? Who doesn't know that the Witness Protection Program can set up a family with new identities?"

"I'm not talking about *a* family." She passed me a few sheets from a stack she'd printed. "Look."

The first was an email from Mayor Burke to a person identified only as Barkley.

> Barkley,
> I must say the numbers are even better than we anticipated.
> If you review the attached spreadsheet you'll see that the major crime stats remain steady in Stepton despite the integration of 50+ rogues.

I said, "Rogues? He's talking about WitSec families?"

"What's WitSec?"

I felt far away, like I was outside my body watching two people playing me and Reya. I heard me say, "It's another term for Witness Protection. I saw it in a movie."

Reya nodded. "Best I can tell from Eli's notes."

"Why does he call them *rogues*, though?"

"Keep reading."

> Certain individuals were concerned that placing such unstable people in a single locale would incite spikes in violence, larceny, and overall chaos. Being one of the few who lobbied for the Whispertown initiative, I don't feel a bit of shame in saying "told ya so" . . . LOL. The Program's so-called Worst of the Worst merely need a little TLC. That's southern hospitality for y'all . . . LOL. Take a look at what I've sent you and I'll have a formal report ready in a couple of days.

I put the email aside, feeling something between hurt, outrage, and fear.

Rogues.

Unstable people.

The Program's worst of the worst.

"This still doesn't make sense to me, Reya. How does the Witness Protection Program protect anyone if they dump fifty witnesses in the same place?"

She motioned to the next email in the stack she gave me. "There's more."

> Barkley,
> Attached is my official report and stats on the Whispertown initiative for the last six months. Additionally, I've included

*prime fiscal statements for our town. The funds are helping
us tremendously, and though I haven't been privy to the
numbers you're running, I'm willing to bet disciplinary
incidents are down for you. Your witnesses behave here.
Please stress that to your superiors. It can only help our cause
when this goes before Senator Rowell's subcommittee.*

"He's lying for the money," I said.

"It fits, right?" She pulled up several spreadsheets. "Eli discovered
something was off about the official crime stats from interviewing people
who'd been victimized."

I recalled some of what he'd told me in Rage Against the Caffeine.
"Like the teacher who had her car stolen from her driveway?"

"Exactly." Reya highlighted cells in a spreadsheet, several seven-figure
dollar amounts. "It was costing too much for—what did you call it?"

"WitSec." It was strange saying it aloud to someone other than family.

She spoke rapid-fire now, barely taking a breath. "The government
wanted a cheaper, more efficient process. They decided to try an
experiment. Stepton got two million dollars for allowing one percent of
the witness population to be placed here, unaware that they're guinea
pigs. The witnesses are monitored by two U.S. Marshals, utilizing a
'streamlined process' to observe and report on their"—she checked Eli's
notes—"'*acclimation.*'"

Acclimation. The very word that Bertram used on those annoying
weekly calls with the repetitive questions. *Nicholas, on a scale of one to
ten, how's it feel finding out that this whole Whispertown thing is about you?*

I said, "Why 'rogues' and the 'worst of the worst'? What's the deal with
that?"

"That's the most *loco* part. This program had been suggested years ago, but they had problems trying to test it. For one, WitSec didn't want to jeopardize any of their 'good' witnesses. People who could deliver the most damaging testimony over the most sought-after criminals got to stay put. Even witnesses who couldn't always deliver but managed to follow the rules got a pass. Mostly the bystanders."

Bystanders, people in the wrong place at the wrong time. They were the ones who happened to step out of the Starbucks at the exact moment a motorcycle hit man shoots a mob lieutenant at the red light. Or the honest worker who took the wrong job with a financial adviser/money launderer and saw files she wasn't supposed to see. The WitSec sob stories. Not career criminals who used Witness Protection as a pass on the penitentiary and retribution from former friends. Guys like my dad. I didn't need Reya to explain the rest. "Remove bystanders from the equation, and all you've got left are the snitches."

"And not just that," she said, "but the snitches who couldn't follow the rules. The most rebellious and dangerous protected witnesses."

I moved to the window, unwilling to look her in the eye as I secretly described my recent family history. I said, "The witnesses who screwed up the most—I'm talking three, four times—and were the least valuable, became candidates for this new program. What choice did they have? It was either that or be expelled, right? And WitSec didn't want anyone's blood on their hands, even if that blood belonged to criminal dicks. After all"—I swallowed hard—"criminal dicks can have families, too."

"The government couldn't do this without permission—" said Eli. Odd, him being dead and all.

I searched for the ghost, found a webcam video playing on Reya's monitor. It was recorded in the J-Room, the time stamp reading two months before I arrived at Stepton High. His sister said, "There were a few of these on the drive, too."

Eli continued, "—*wouldn't be nice to dump a bunch of malcontent criminals into an unsuspecting community without getting sign-off. It'd be like dropping a piranha in a stranger's fish tank, just 'cuz. When Uncle Sam proposed a million-dollar payday for the city's participation, good old Mayor Burke did the responsible thing and asked for two . . .*"

"Seriously?" I got closer to the screen as if I expected Eli to react. "The mayor *negotiated*?"

Reya tapped the space bar, pausing the video. "Not only that, if the program's a success, the town's supposed to get up to five million per year going forward."

"That in this video, too?"

"No. It's in another one. I've watched nearly all of them." She stared at the frozen screen—Eli's face—with longing, like she wanted to reach through and touch him.

"Nearly?"

"The last one he recorded is secure. We need another password."

I groaned. "Why'd he do that?"

She shook her head "Like I would know. That *Urilium* word didn't work and I don't have the energy to try and crack it right now. Besides, there's something on one of the other videos that bugs me."

Reya brought it up and dragged the time slider to a precise minute and second. Again, Eli was in the J-Room, the time stamp from last month, a week before my arrival. "*Things are much more complicated now. I may have enough to expose the mayor, but family concerns are stopping me. I don't know what to do.*"

She paused it. "Every other video is about the money, or the stats, or the rogues—"

"What about the rogues?"

"Common sense stuff. They're scum."

I chewed the inside of my cheek, drawing a dribble of salty blood. I shouldn't have taken offense. She wasn't talking about *me*, not directly. Still . . . *scum*?

"The 'family concerns' thing is totally random," she said. "I have no idea what it means."

"Maybe he's talking about your uncle Miguel." I said it harshly; the words felt jagged coming up.

She blinked slowly. Once. Twice. "What do you know about my uncle?"

Deflecting, I said, "He's family. Didn't Eli mic his car once? That could be about Whispertown, couldn't it?"

"That was like two years ago. Has someone been talking to you about Miguel?"

"Well, I don't have access to a Girls' Associated Press or anything, but I heard he's into some stuff. You might call it *roguish*." I stopped short of calling *him* scum.

Her defenses went up. "I don't know what you're implying, but if you think whatever my uncle does has something to do with . . ." She stopped short, maybe letting reason trump blood loyalty.

I might've told her about Miguel and the mayor's fight that Dustin witnessed, and how the car accident could've been an attack meant for the mayor. But the bedroom door swung inward, and Reya had just enough time to tap a key and minimize Eli's paused video before her mother saw. Mrs. Cruz eyed me like a stain, a far cry from what I was used to. "School's starting soon."

Reya said, "I'm suspended. Fighting. Remember."

Mrs. Cruz's eyes narrowed. "Someone who gets suspended for fighting probably shouldn't have company for a while. Wouldn't you agree?"

Looked like the grief trance was wearing off. Mrs. Cruz, reporting for parental duty.

"Fine. He's leaving. Just give me a minute."

"Make sure he does. I'm going to Portside to take care of some business." She turned to leave, stopped, faced Reya again. "I love you, *bebe*."

Alone again, Reya said, "You're not really going to school, are you? We need to figure what's next."

"I'm going." I needed to figure my "what's next" by myself. "Big test."

She tapped a pencil on the desk, tossed it aside. "Fine. I'm taking you."

"You're suspended. Fighting. Remember."

"Last I checked, there's no fence that keeps suspended kids from driving on school grounds."

"I've got my bike."

"Park it on the porch."

"But—"

"I'm going to pick you up from school, too. We can crack the password on that last video."

"Whatever."

"Why are you acting so pissy?"

They're scum. "I'm good."

She tossed her keys and I caught them one-handed.

"Start the car then," she said, bossy, focusing on the monitor. "Hold the two buttons on the key chain at the same time for three seconds."

I rolled my eyes and pressed the buttons.

One . . . two . . .

The overcast day went bright as summer. A sudden flare forced me to flinch and press my forearm over my eyes, a lucky reflex that probably saved my sight when the window blew inward. An invisible, oven-hot mitt smacked me and tossed me into the wall over Reya's bed. I rebounded off the drywall and landed on her mattress, dust raining on me. Only then did I hear echoing thunder that wasn't thunder at all.

I was stunned—sounds and sights took on a slow-motion quality. Reya rose, yelled in an unlikely deep voice, "Moooommmm!!!"

I coughed and smacked myself in the side of the head, knocking something right because the world screeched into real-time speeds. Fire crackled, metal groaned, and people I didn't know screamed.

Mustering what strength I could, I followed Reya's trail outside and felt the dry heat coming from the flaming remains of her Beetle. The neon paint crisped and bubbled from green to black.

Next to the Beetle, Mrs. Cruz's Camry had shifted diagonally. Its back tires had cut ruts in the lawn while the front tires melted in the all-consuming fire. The passenger door was closest to Reya's wreck, bowed inward as if sideswiped, all the windows shattered.

On the opposite side of the car, Reya. Unharmed by an explosion that would've killed her, had she been near the car. Lucky.

The same could not be said for Mrs. Cruz, who lay unmoving in her daughter's arms.

CHAPTER 39

SIRENS WHOOPED IN THE DISTANCE LIKE angry birds. Still, I ran inside the Cruz home and dialed 911 myself, needing to do something.

"Someone's been hurt in an explosion," I yelled into the phone.

"*Sir, stay calm and—*"

I cut her off. "Trace the call and come fast."

I dropped the handset, ready to return to the lawn, when I realized the opportunity presenting itself. Yes, as dire as the situation was, without knowledge of whether Reya's mother was alive or dead, I saw opportunity.

I made a side trip to Reya's room.

The gathering crowd had thickened by the time I made it back outside. The heat from the explosion formed an invisible wall, keeping people back, giving Reya and her mother a wide berth. I rushed to their side, mad that none of the onlookers had offered any help. My indignation faded as I felt the weight of my backpack bouncing on my shoulder; helping hadn't been my first priority either.

"Is she breathing?" I asked.

Reya simply rocked her mom, her voice a whimper. "Wake up, Mami. Wake up."

I reached toward Mrs. Cruz, intending to check her pulse. Reya slapped my hand away and rocked her mother harder. A fire engine blasted its air horn, parting the nosy onlookers.

An ambulance rounded the corner. The cops wouldn't be far behind; I couldn't be here when they arrived. They'd have questions and I needed to see my dad. Now.

I backed away slowly, grabbed my bike, and disappeared into the crowd with the items I stole from Reya's room feeling heavier than they should.

In charred clothing, I entered the Tax and Accounting Services office, the burned fuel vapors stronger than the garlic shrimp from the Chinese takeout next door. A single customer sat with his legs crossed and an elbow propped on Dad's desk, rattling on about minimizing his tax liability. Dad wasn't listening.

The customer noticed Dad's gaze drift over his shoulder. He turned around, gasped. "Son, you're bleeding from the neck."

I touched two fingers below my chin. They came back red with tacky, drying blood. "Just a scratch."

Dad came to me and dug his fingers in my arm. I bit back a groan. We exited to the tinkle of the door chimes and his coworkers' concerned muttering. No Chinese restaurant today, no secluded corner beside the building either. He dragged me to the center of the near-empty parking lot, where nothing or no one could get within thirty yards without us seeing them.

"Damn it, Tony. What did you do?"

"What did *you* do, Dad?" I yanked the zipper on my backpack and pulled a handful of emails out. "The Whispertown initiative? Fifty rogues in a single place? Two million dollars for the city—for the mayor?"

He backed away, stunned, a vampire facing a crucifix.

"How—?" He didn't finish his question, but closed the gap between us, snatching the emails from my hands, then taking my backpack and rifling through it. "You just don't listen."

"Keep the bag, Dad." I dug Eli's flash drive from my hip pocket. "I've still got this."

He tried to grab it, but I ducked him, sidestepped. "Everything's on here. Emails, financial statements, the whole history of Whispertown. Kids are *dying* over this."

His face sagged, a warm-dough blankness. "Please tell me you're not still on that kick about your friend's suicide."

"That kick? He's dead, Dad. Murdered. A couple of other good kids are, too. Because of this scam you and the mayor and Miguel Rios are running."

"Where are you getting this stuff from, Tony? Why do you smell like a gas station?"

"Ask your buddies."

"Enough!"

His chest bumped mine. It took all my willpower not to back down. "Tell me what's going on, Dad."

"If you have any more information on Whispertown you need to hand it over to me. Now. It's dangerous."

"But you just said you don't know anything about the killings—"

He exhaled slowly. "I don't. Whispertown's only dangerous to me, you, and your mother."

"What's that supposed to mean?"

"The information on that drive is, most likely, the only reason we're still walking this earth, son. Hand it over and I'll explain."

A large part of me screamed, *Don't do it, don't trust him.* I listened. "No. You explain, *then* I hand it over."

The way his eyes blazed and his chest heaved, I thought he might try to snatch the drive from me. I was ready to run if he made a move.

Maybe he sensed my intent, knew he was at my mercy, for once. "Have it your way."

Dad talked. Explained. Everything.

By the time he finished, I kind of wished he hadn't.

CHAPTER 40

"WHISPERTOWN WASN'T MEANT FOR US," DAD said. "Not me, you, or your mom."

It sounded custom-freaking-made for us. Rowdy witnesses, no useful testimony. "I don't understand."

"They can't find Kreso and I was on my third strike. We were done."

"We . . . *were*?" I repeated the words in my head, forcing my brain to absorb their true meaning. "They were going to kick us out?"

"They *did* kick us out." He spoke without looking at me. "When we left Idaho, we were supposed to be on our own. I needed to find a place for us to live, only there was nowhere to go. I couldn't go back to Philly, and I don't know any other place. We were a day or two away from being homeless."

Homeless? "What happened, Dad?"

"I begged Bertram for another chance. There wasn't much he could do, but he said he'd make some calls. Almost immediately he got back to me, told me there was a mayor in Virginia who wanted a word.

"When I got on the phone with Burke, I made my case. I told him all that stuff you're supposed to say. I'm sorry. I know better now. I want a good life for my family."

I want a good life for my family . . . that stuff you're supposed to say?

"The whole time I heard Burke typing and buzzing his secretary for more coffee. I thought it was a done deal until he asked, 'Got any special skills?' I mentioned bookkeeping, and he got damn near giddy. Two weeks later, we were here." He spread his arms high and wide, stared into the chemical cloud snaking overhead. "Basking in the glory." His arms flopped at his sides and he faced me.

"That's the big secret, Tony. Your old man is King Screw Up who managed to work one last con. I'm helping Burke cheat the federal government out of a lot of cash. Kreso Maric would *love* that. Are you happy now?"

Happy? No. I felt queasy, and not from the Stepton air. We were almost living on the street? Because he couldn't keep an honest nine-to-five like most people? "What went wrong?"

He stared. Either genuinely confused or trying to avoid my line of questioning. I clarified: "The mayor got mad at you for something. Why else would he drive me to that construction site so I could tell you about it?"

"Oh, that."

That? That *what*? "Dad!"

"You know about the kind of money we're talking about here, right? Millions. It's supposed to go to city projects, like that municipal center. Burke's been sticking his hand in the cookie jar."

I leaned into Dad, making sure I understood him. "He's *embezzling* the money?"

Dad nodded.

I said, darkly, "And you're good with numbers."

Another confirmation. "His money's as clean as your mother's floors when I'm done. I did such a good job making those funds look all shiny and legal, I felt I deserved a bonus. He didn't respond well."

I'll take care of the mayor. "You didn't respond well to him not responding well, either. What did you do, Dad?"

"I told him to stay the hell away from you and"—he dropped his head, shameful—"I let it go."

"You? Let it go?" My gaze shifted toward the parking spaces along the front of the Tax and Accounting Services office, where Dad's SUV sat, and thought about the mayor's mangled car, probably in some impound yard with blood on the seats.

"I *did*," he insisted. "I didn't want to risk the safety and security of my family again. I—I backed down, Tony."

This is the messed-up part: as convincing as he sounded, I still didn't know if I believed him. I was so used to his secrets, and lies, and general I-don't-have-to-explain-myself attitude that his confessions felt like game. Even when he was expressing concern for me.

"What happened to you?" he asked, plucking at my singed shirt.

I didn't need him pretending to care, I needed him to make sense of it all. "What's Miguel Rios got to do with this?"

"I don't know," he said, disgusted. "Rios is small-time. Some weed, some meth, a little bootlegging. He's no—"

"Kreso?" Was that some admiration for the old boss coming through in his voice?

Coolly, "No. He's no Kreso Maric. Him and Burke got something going on, but it's none of my concern. I focus on the money."

"Yeah, Dad. You do that." I went for my bike, and he followed.

"Where do you think you're going?"

To check on Reya and process all he'd told me. He didn't need to know that, or anything else about me. Not anymore. "Don't worry about it. Focus on the money."

He sped up, spun me by the shoulder. "You don't talk to me like that. I don't care what you're going through."

"Even if it's almost getting killed? Because that's what happened. Your pals, who are none of your concern, put a bomb in my girl's car. I could've been in it, Dad. And it would've been your fault because the whole reason we're in this crap town, with its crap air, and crap school, and crap"—I waved my arm, flustered—"crap *Chinese food* is you."

He repeated things I said like he was reciting a riddle. "A bomb? Your girl's car?"

"People are dying because of your final con. The mayor's dirty, Miguel Rios is dirty, and I'm going to stop it. For my friend."

Dad's jaw flexed. "If you stop him, you stop us, too. Do you understand that? Do you know what Kreso wants to do to—"

"To *you*? To you, Dad. All this is about you."

I didn't know what I had expected coming here. I guess the same thing I'd been expecting my whole life, for my dad to act like a dad. I walked away.

"Come back, Tony."

"Why, Dad? To hear more BS excuses about why we're in this mess?"

"No," he said. "You made a deal."

"What de—?" I remembered the plastic nub in my hand.

"Give me that flash drive."

I looked at it. Then at him. "Mom said we're a lot alike. Guess she's right, 'cause now I feel I deserve a bonus, too. I'm keeping it." I stuck the drive in my pocket.

"Tony!"

I mounted my bike before he could stop me, put some distance between us, then yelled the most hurtful thing I could. The truth. "I can't wait for me and Mom to leave your sorry lying ass. You deserve to be alone."

I pedaled in a wide circle, out of his reach. Stayed long enough to see my words hit him. Hard. Then I was flying, planning my next move.

With the wind in my face I ran down everything I knew. All the answers I'd gotten just created more questions. If Eli's death was about him blowing the whistle on Whispertown, what put his uncle and Dustin's dad at each other's throats *after* he was gone? Did Miguel find a link between the mayor and Eli, and decide to retaliate? Was it just about the money?

And Reya. How'd they know to try and hit her? With a car bomb?

I couldn't imagine that was in the mayor's white-collar criminal playbook. Miguel, then? He was the "gangsta," and a car bomb's classic mob movie fare. Still, hit his own niece? That's—

The black streak appeared in my periphery like a roaring demon, forcing me to veer hard to the right. My front tire hit the curb and I floated, floated, flo—

I hit the concrete on my side with a crunch, skidded, my limp arm shielding my ribs. I traded bone for skin as the friction rubbed away several layers, despite my long sleeves. When I stopped, I couldn't breathe, stunned.

The dark SUV rolled to a stop, its tires mere feet from my head. The engine revved, indecisive. Crush me or not?

Was this what it was like for Dustin, Carrey, and Lorenz in the moment before the BMW met the tree? *Ho-hum, this thing might kill me.*

The transmission clanked into park, and doors clacked open. Sneakers slapped the pavement in a rush to reach me. Dee and Dum dragged me upright and I saw the license plate. ZAC ATAK.

Zach Lynch joined his lackeys. "I'm going to end you."

Russ raised the back hatch. In that instant before Dee and Dum tossed me in, I recalled another time I'd ridden in the back of an SUV, on my way to a very bad place.

My feet left the ground and I collided with the backseat. Positioned awkwardly on my shoulder in the cargo bin, I twisted in an attempt to right myself. I wasn't fast enough.

Zach Lynch delivered a haymaker, no interference. I slumped but did not slip into blackness.

Instead, I time traveled. . . .

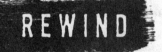

DAD DIDN'T TAKE THE GUN, NOT at first.

The boy's whimpering switched to screaming pleas that made me want to cover my ears and close my eyes, but I couldn't manage either. "Please, Mr. Maric. I'm sorry. Oh God, please."

Kreso slapped him silent. "Thieves do not speak to me." He waved the gun butt-first to Dad, impatient.

"Kreso." Dad backed up a step, changed his tone to something lighter, friendlier. "*Kreso*, that's not my thing. I run book."

"You think that I do not know what I pay you for?"

"You're the boss, of course you—"

Kreso stepped forward, jabbing the gun at Dad like a sword. "Say again."

Dad hesitated. "You're the boss."

"Take." He grabbed Dad's dangling hand and pressed the gun into it. "This imbecile steals from *me*, fouls the books you keep so beautifully. Is your privilege to punish him, no?"

"Not a privilege," Dad said, trying to hand the gun back. Kreso had already turned away.

"Everybody here has blood on hands," he said, pointing to his henchmen. "Him and him, blood on hands. Me, blood on hands. Consider this initiation into—" He seemed to struggle with the word, looking to the Mean-Faces for backup.

The smaller one said, "Club Badass."

Kreso nodded, a laughing hiss. "Yesss, yessss. Club Badasss."

Dad still held the gun like someone who needed to read the instructions, as if it were an exotic power tool. "I brought the other stuff you asked for, no problem. But you should call Bricks for this sort of thing. He's the—"

"Bricks has other business. I called you. Now, *do it*."

The boy's head whipped between Kreso and my dad, like watching a tennis match he'd bet everything on.

"Naw, man. Come on. You don't have t—" The kid jerked to the side, threw up on the big henchman's shoes.

Though my eyes were teary, blurring things, I couldn't blink. Hot liquid splashed the back of my throat—inspired by the boy's retching— but I choked it back down, opting for quiet whimpering, a kind unseen since I was little-little and believed something in the closet wanted to eat me.

Dad's arm went rigid; the gun rose level with the kid's forehead. The boy flinched, screamed. I knew the next part and waited for it.

It didn't come.

Dropping his arm, putting three long strides between him and the boy's execution party, Dad said, firmly, "No. This is not what I do."

Kreso's mouth ticked like he was growing extra teeth. The Mean-Faces tensed and reached for their own concealed weapons.

Dad flipped the gun over, gripped it by the barrel, and pushed it toward Kreso. "You do your own dirty work. I'm the numbers guy."

A moment passed. Kreso seemed torn, indecisive. *Who* exactly needed to die tonight? Finally, he took the gun back, and his goons relaxed.

He said, "You are lucky none of these idiots are proficient in math."

In a motion as casual as a shrug, Kreso raised the gun and shot the boy in the face.

No boom, more of a cheap firecracker *POP*. The boy slumped sideways, his mouth gaped in an almost scream, leaking.

I couldn't move. Couldn't breathe. I felt tears in me, filling me like a tub, but my body wouldn't react.

Not until the headlights flicked off.

This was a newer SUV, not the one Dad got mad at Mom over. He didn't have to cut the headlights off because they were timed. Now, Kreso would be able to see in. I couldn't let him see me.

I dived/fell into the cargo hold, a worse mistake than if I'd just stayed where I was. They would've been used to the light, would've needed time to adjust before they saw me. But when I panicked, I knocked into the shovel and the pickax and the lye, causing a racket.

"What the hell is that?" one of the goons said.

Dad said, "Hang on."

I heard his footsteps clomping toward the back hatch, and I tried to scramble under the tarp, or my blanket. Everything got tangled, stuck under something or another. I whimpered like the boy I watched die, tears pouring now, in total panic mode.

The latch released and the hatch rose. When Dad looked, saw me, the horror on his face led me to only one conclusion. Both of us were about to die.

The realization ripped something in me, releasing a sob that might've fulfilled my doom prophecy. Dad saw it coming, reached in, and clamped his palm over my mouth. I tasted gun oil.

"Is there problem?" Kreso called.

Heavy footsteps approached.

"No problem," Dad said, releasing me while holding me silent with his stare. He grabbed the flowered blanket I'd brought along and threw it over my head. One eye remained uncovered, and I saw him pull the shovel and pickax into the open, before shoving me deeper in the vehicle and lowering the hatch. "The tools fell over, that's all."

He met the Mean-Faces on the side of the SUV and led them back to the Mercedes. Away from me.

Kreso said, "At least you did something right. Since you forced me to do the hard work this evening, you'll understand if I take my assistants back to the city. I'd planned to let them help you bury him, but you should have plenty of energy since you didn't use any of it acting like a man."

"You're right, Kreso. I'll take care of the body. Go on and have yourself a good night."

A lull, like Kreso expected more resistance, but after a moment, he said, "Good. Bury him deep."

Another tense minute passed while I cried, and sweated, and almost threw up—waiting. The quiet German engine turned over and I heard the fading sounds of the car driving away.

The hatch rose again, hard and fast enough to strain the hinges. "Tony, Jesus Christ. Come here."

I leaped at him, tried to press into him. Then I remembered the *POP* and I pushed away, though there was nowhere to go. "I want Mommy! I want Mommy!"

"Okay, son. Okay. But I have to do something first."

He still held the shovel.

We were in those woods for four hours while Dad dug, then filled. The ride home nearly silent. No music. Little talk. He did say, "I don't know what you saw, but—"

"I didn't see anything." I spoke the wish I had.

He couldn't have been satisfied. I thought he'd ask me about it, make me talk. People always said talking was a good thing. He never brought it up again.

Dad paid Rachelle, then told her never to come back. When Mom arrived from her dinner, she sensed something was wrong, because she kept asking Dad, and me, then Dad again what had happened.

We didn't tell. The start of a family tradition.

The Bordeaux household underwent a decline after that. I didn't play with my Desperation Friends, and no longer answered questions about my dad's job with a grin. There was nothing to smile about. *POP!*

Dad and Mom fought more, liked each other's company less. Dad got several calls from the boss. I never knew what they were about, but I wondered if Dad was still the numbers guy. Or had he become something else?

Bricks came around less. The last time I saw him, he got into a fight with Dad, told him, "If you've got half of the big brain you say you have, you won't bring that up again. Not around me. Loyalty is what keeps us alive in this business. Don't forget it."

Dad didn't forget it. He ignored it. A couple of weeks later, federal agents roused us from our beds, telling us we were new people. I could never buy it, though.

If I was new, I wouldn't hear that same old *POP* in my dreams.

CHAPTER 41

THE VEHICLE BUCKED, ITS SUSPENSION GROANING like old people getting out of chairs, as we swung onto a rutted road bordered by tall trees. Light-headed from Zach's punch and the overwhelming scent of exhaust, I nearly vomited. A thought flashed through my mind—*Do it! The more DNA you leave, the better.* That's when I realized I might die.

A dark SUV, like this one, ran Dustin off the road. What if it wasn't about Whispertown or the mayor? Zach had been insane drunk that night. He could've caused the accident because Dustin, Carrey, and Lorenz embarrassed him.

I'd embarrassed him, too. So much that snatching me off the street in broad daylight became reasonable. What else fit Zach's twisted reasoning?

We hit a vicious pothole, bouncing me against the floor. Starbursts exploded before my eyes. I yelped.

Russ said, "I think he's waking up."

"Good," said Zach. "You still got that bat?"

Wood slapped palm. "You know it."

Adrenaline sharpened my thinking. The skyline opened up, dense foliage replaced by dark clouds and half-erected building frames. I knew where we were.

Zach braked hard and killed the engine. The doors opened and the SUV rocked as everyone but me spilled out. Next, the hatch would rise and they'd do whatever they planned to do. I tried to recall a timely tip, some piece of wisdom from Bricks, or even Dad, that would reveal the exact move, or behavior, or attitude to get me through this. I had nothing.

Russ's specialty must've been opening the tailgate, because he did that again. Dee and Dum dragged me out as gently as they'd put me in, then marched me over to a patch of red dirt in the center of the Burke Municipal Campus, where Zach waited. He smashed the business end of a Louisville Slugger into the ground over and over, like driving a fence post. Around us, construction equipment remained untouched, and buildings unbuilt. Like my previous visit, without the pretense of a subtle threat.

The sick grin on Zach's face projected what I already knew. No help was coming.

No Eli stepping in with his camera and big brain. No Dustin and his Dead Boy Cavalry. No Dad to hide me from the bad men. Zach liked four-to-one odds, in his favor. Only . . . he'd miscalculated.

He'd made it so I couldn't be Nick Pearson, the kid who played lacrosse, overachieved in science, and enjoyed hip music. Not entirely. I had to be the other guy, too. The son of a criminal, raised by thieves and schemers, tutored by killers.

My heartbeat slowed. My breathing, too.

I was Nick Pearson and Tony Bordeaux.

For the first time, I realized that the odds were in *my* favor.

"Long time coming, Pearson," Zach said, taking short test swings with the bat. "Long time."

Before things started—and regardless of how they finished—I needed to know something. "Are you going after Dustin next?"

He lowered the business end of the bat. "The hell you talking about?"

"You got Carrey and Lorenz on Saturday. Me today. You gonna kill Dustin next? It's a simple question."

He bounced uncertain looks off each of his minions, all of them shuffling, loose and confused. Dum let me go, he was so spooked. I didn't run, though. Running wasn't part of today's plan.

Zach said, "Whatever, dick. Don't try to spin your bad mojo on us. Ever since you got here, people been dying. Our phones were blowing up all morning about Reya's car freakin' *exploding*. Then, there you were, riding your bike like it's all good. Nuh-uh. No way. I don't know what kind of sicko hoodoo curse you got, but I'mma make you eat your teeth."

Eat my teeth? Is that even—never mind. These guys weren't killers. Just because they were all dumb, didn't mean they could play dumb. Their confusion at the mention of Lorenz and Carrey was genuine. More so than if I'd asked them to spell *genuine*. There was still the matter of nailing the mayor and Miguel, the guys topping the Bad Stuff in Stepton pyramid. This first.

"Before I devour my teeth," I said. "I suggest that you break both of my hands, too."

"Huh?" Zach looked like he needed to consult his script.

"You should break my hands," I repeated. "With no teeth, and broken hands, that will make it difficult to communicate for a couple of days at least. You'll have a chance to run."

Russ laughed. "Someone's a funny guy, now."

Zach, perpetually proving his toughness, nudged my shoulder with the bat. "How can you still talk smack when you know I'm about to cripple your ass?"

"I would not advise crippling, and I didn't mean you'd be running from me. I'm talking about the cops, Zach. You'll want to get a head start."

Now everyone laughed. Dee said, "He's going to tell on us."

"Snitch bitch," said Dum in a singsong tease you'd hear at a day care.

I said, "I won't have a choice. They'll want to know what happened throughout the course of my kidnapping."

Laughs faded. They were back to confused. Where I wanted them.

"See, kidnapping is a Class A felony with a minimum sentence of a year. Unless, of course, you're kidnapping a minor—which I am—then we're talking five years. That's *minimum*, guys. Even for the accomplices." The legal talk was some BS. A mix of stuff I'd heard from Dad, Bricks, and a bunch of cop shows.

Of course, they wouldn't know that.

Dee released my arm, wiping his hand on his jeans like I'd soiled him. "You ain't kidnapped."

"I ain't? I didn't come here of my own accord." Got that from an old *Law & Order* episode.

He scrunched his face.

I said, "It means I didn't come here willingly. Don't worry. Your attorney will explain words like that to you before your arraignment. Provided he's not court appointed. The court-appointed guys are too overworked to explain things; they're just going to tell you to take a deal for less time. Maybe as little as a year instead of the five."

I saw them doing the simple math in their heads—one year is better than five, right? I gave them some more data to crunch. "Of course, we're only talking about the kidnapping charge. There's still the aggravated assault, the reckless driving, and attempted murder—"

"Attempted murder?!" Zach said, not noticing I'd taken a step closer to him.

"—throw in any anti-bullying laws this state has on the books and"—I paused, made a show of looking at each and every one of their faces, then smacking my forehead—"wow, all of you guys are white."

Such an abrupt statement of the obvious perplexed them more. I took another step toward Zach. "Four white guys jump a black guy, drag him off in a truck. In the South. That's a hate crime, fellas. A federal offense. By the time this is over you might be looking at thirty, forty years each."

Russ, a quake in his voice, said, "You're lying. You're trying to play us."

"You got a cell on you? Look up anything you want, though I wonder about the reception out in this secluded area you kidnappers took me to."

"Shut up," said Dee.

"Before we shut you up," said Dum.

Not in this century. "Zach might do okay in federal prison. He's big, strong. After a couple of knife-fight wins, he'll get some respect. But you two, I feel bad for. They're not going to put you in the same facility. You've had each other's back since conception. No more of that. If you thought arguing over the top bunk was epic before . . ."

They stepped closer to each other until their shoulders brushed. Two reflections trying to merge. If their mom was here, they would've asked to move back into the womb.

I turned my attention to Russ, while inching closer to Zach. "And you, I don't know what to say. You've got to spend an hour a day getting your hair to look like that. The inmates are really going to appreciate you. *There she is, Miss America.*"

I literally saw him gulp, the lump slipping slowly down his throat. I could've pushed, adding something about how he should get used to that swallowing motion, but I distracted them long enough. Now for part two.

"Or," I said, "you could shut me up for good. Kill me. Do it the right way, and you go on with your lives with the darkest secret you'll ever have. You four are tight, none of you would break and rat on the others. Would you?"

Zach opened his mouth, probably to deliver some corny, unconvincing threat to sway things back his way. Too late.

Ripping the bat from his hand, I shoved his chin high with the heel of my palm. The body goes where the head does. Forcing his skull back at such an extreme angle caused him to fall, a puff of dust rising where he landed. I swung the bat, hard, embedding it in the earth next to his ear.

I felt something turn on in my chest and head and stomach. A red engine with pistons pumping in a shudder, spewing black exhaust. "Ever since I got here, people been dyin'. That's what you said, right? You wanna be next?"

"Guys," he said, in an almost shriek.

I pointed the bat at the twins. "Don't move." They didn't. No need to deliver the message to Russ. He was creeping back to the ride.

To Zach, I said, "There's no win for you here. You douche bags don't have the brains or juice to put me down and get away with it. Anything less than that lands you in jail for the rest of your lives."

His face went cherry, his breaths huffs and puffs, but he still tried to save face. I told him the rest, my secret desires. "Thanks to this brilliant plan of yours, I can do whatever I want and get away with it."

I saw the doubt in his eyes. I smashed the bat into the ground next to his head again and replaced that doubt with tears. "Yes. Yes, I can. Because now it's self-defense. *You* brought me here. *You* planned to jump me and beat me with a bat. I happened to wrestle it away from you and"—I swung the bat by his head again—"fought for my life."

I raised the bat, high this time, like an ax.

Zach threw his forearm over his eyes, pulled his knees to his stomach, full fetal.

I hadn't lied to him. Everything about the potential charges, and their lives in prison, and me having a free pass to hurt them had shades of truth, knowledge passed down from the overheard conversations of Dad and friends. There was another truth, a scarier one.

I wanted to hurt him, do *more* than hurt. I could get away with it, too. Maybe with WitSec's help. Self-defense, remember. My arms quivered, my hands ratcheting the handle.

Slowly, I lowered the bat. Then tossed it into the guts of a partial building, where it rattled against the frame. "Go!" I said. "I'm not hurt. If you leave now, it's just a prank. Not worth mentioning."

Russ was already in the SUV, a getaway driver in the wrong seat. Dee and Dum scrambled. Zach wasn't as quick; he took his time getting his feet under him, turning in an awkward way that did nothing to hide the wet spot at his crotch. He saw me seeing, shot me one final, hateful glare before crouching by a puddle and smearing handfuls of mud on his jeans to disguise the piss stain.

Zach climbed into the vehicle. One of the twins asked about a strange smell before the SUV fishtailed, spitting thick mud from the back tires. They spun in place before rolling away. Not so much as a wink of brake lights until they turned onto the main drag and sped toward town. Where I needed to be.

How the hell was I getting back?

I could've humped the four miles, but I felt achy and stiff from crashing my bike. Calling Dad wasn't an option, and I didn't want to explain to Mom how I got here. I dug in my pocket for my phone and felt jagged plastic. When Zach ran me off the road I'd heard a crunch and I knew where it came from.

I groaned and emptied my pocket, thinking about how a broken phone meant I'd *definitely* be walking back to town. But my phone was fine.

Eli's flash drive wasn't.

Broken, clean down the middle.

"Mother—" My profanity echoed across the construction site.

Get back to town, Nick. Maybe someone can fix it.

I shot a text to the only person I could think of while giving myself a flash-drive-repair pep talk I didn't believe.

> **Me:** Any chance ur not n school AND mobile 2day? I need a ride ASAP.
>
> **Dustin:** I'm on my way

CHAPTER 42

A YELLOW STREAK FLASHED THROUGH THE tree line. Dustin's Xterra turned into the construction site and came toward me, shooting big sheets of dirt behind. He jerked the wheel like a stunt driver, sliding into a sideways stop.

"Dude, what's going on?" he said, his head through his window like a turtle's from the shell, his unnerving blood-bruised cornea lighter now, like a case of pinkeye.

I took the passenger seat, tapping a text to Reya before I settled in.

> **Me:** Is ur mom okay?

I told Dustin, "Go. I'll explain on the way."

"No, Nick. Your seat belt first. They save lives. Trust me, I know."

I did a double take. His jaw clenched and he had a death grip on the wheel, the fresh white cast on his arm devoid of "get well" signatures.

"Lorenz and Carrey?"

"They didn't like to wear them." He shuddered.

"No problem." I'd gone to Dustin because he was my only option. Never considered what being behind the wheel again must be like for him. Uneasy now, I secured the belt.

"Thank you," he said, his tension decreasing noticeably. We were in motion when I got a response.

> **Reya:** She woke up N the ambulance. Where r u? Where did u
> go? Y did u go?

Dustin said, "Yo, people are saying Reya's car *exploded*. I been getting texts, tweets, FB messages, even a MySpace alert about it. I didn't know I had a MySpace account. Everything's been blowing up—" He reconsidered his choice of words. "I mean, everyone's on this, man."

"It's true," I said, deciding which of Reya's questions I should answer honestly. Or at all.

> **Me:** I'm w/ Dustin, ridin back 2 town

Dustin said, "What did you two do?"

"We got too close." Another text came.

> **Reya:** Can u come get me from hospital? Fast?

Not planning to see her so soon—how was I going to explain the flash drive?—I thumbed a text to stall. Hers came first.

> **Reya:** Miguel is here & I don't like the way he's lookn @ me

"Dustin. Hospital. Now!"

By the time we reached Stepton General, I'd filled Dustin in on everything Reya and I discovered together. Talking about Whispertown—WitSec—aloud felt blasphemous, but there was no way to avoid it. He took it as well as I could've expected.

"My dad let a bunch of psychos pull an Occupy Stepton?"

"Not psychos. Unruly witnesses and their families."

"What's the difference? Psycho and Psycho Junior."

My insides churned, fighting the urge to call him everything from ignorant to asshole.

Reya waited for us at the main entrance, hopping from foot to foot and hugging herself despite the day's warmth, a dark soot smudge on her cheek looking like a bruise. She saw us coming and climbed into the back before Dustin was at a full stop.

She stuck her head between our seats. "What are we waiting for?"

Me and Dustin spoke at the same time. "Seat belt."

When we were back on the road, Reya said, "How much does he know?"

"I told him about the files. What's going on with Miguel?"

"He beat the ambulance to the hospital," she said. "He's all like, 'I heard what happened.'"

"From who?" I said.

Dustin said the other thing I'd been thinking. "That's the fastest grapevine I ever heard of, like 4G speeds."

"I know," Reya said. "I mean, I didn't at first, I was worried about my mother. But when she was awake and talking, I started to relax. So did he. All that concern turned to 'you kids are going to be the death of my poor sister,' then he's blaming me, like I blew up my own car. It was weird, and creepy. Nick, I kept thinking about 'family concerns.'"

"What?" Dustin said.

"It's from the videos I told you about," I said. "Eli was worried about breaking the Whispertown story because of 'family concerns.' He had to have been talking about Miguel."

Dustin agreed. "It makes sense. I know that sleazebag—no offense, Reya—"

"That's nicer than what I call him," she said.

"—is tied up with my dad. And Whispertown is *his* top secret project. Who else could it be?"

No one else. Yet . . . it didn't feel right. If Miguel was making a million bucks a day off all the mayor's cover-ups and lies, was that enough to fake his own nephew's suicide, then go after his niece? I still didn't know how Dustin's accident fit in, if it was a part of this at all.

Reya said, "Take me home, Dustin. I need to get Eli's flash drive."

"No!" I said, kicking myself for sounding so adamant.

"Why not?" Reya said. "That's our proof."

Yeah, Nick, why not? "Because the cops are there." The lie came smoothly, as smooth as a sax player riffing. Practice makes perfect. "That's why I left. We can't trust the police. They might have the flash drive already."

Dustin weighed in. "You might have a point. If my dad's involved at all, they won't make a move against him. He's like their god."

Reya punched the seat, cursed in Spanish. "What do we do then?"

I didn't have an answer. I pulled my seat belt, running my hand up and down the tough nylon. My nerves, getting the best of me.

Dustin said, "Regroup at my place. The cops don't mess with me either. I've had patrolmen stop by Dust Offs to grab a beer and scope some high school ass— Sorry, Reya."

She waved it off.

"You guys will be safe there," Dustin finished.

"What about your dad?" I asked.

"Considering everything that's happened, he's probably running damage control. We should be fine."

It was a good plan. The best we had at the moment. I said, "Okay, your place."

The next turn put us on course for North End, where we'd try for answers. I still didn't realize I had them already.

CHAPTER 43

WE SPENT THE NEXT HOUR TALKING in circles while we ate leftover pizza in Dustin's room. We each had a different idea of what should happen next. Dustin, convinced Miguel was behind his accident and Reya's car bombing, felt it was time to get some big government agency involved.

"Like the FBI, or the U.S. Marshals since this is related to Witness Protection," he said.

I cringed, thinking of Bertram arriving in a nondescript car, asking, "On a scale of one to ten, how guilty do you think Miguel Rios is?"

Reya, mostly concerned about bringing Eli's killer to justice, in spite of the attempt on her life, went smaller. "We need to get the flash drive. That's our leverage. We should wait until night and sneak in my house."

"We should think of a contingency plan. In case the flash drive is gone," I said, already knowing it was.

That went on for a while, us saying the same things in different ways, never budging or offering improvements on anybody else's idea. I liked it that way. Being unproductive gave me more time to think.

There had to be something that linked all the death and chaos and made sense of it. The why?

Money? Fear of imprisonment?

We were on our sixth my-idea-is-better-than-yours match when a thunderous door slam shook us all. "Dustin! Are you in here!?"

The mayor was home.

Dustin's expression became a mix of fear and uncertainty. "Be cool, be cool," he said, mostly to himself. He touched his cheeks and forehead like he was molding a mask of composure. He was putting on a brave face. Literally.

Reya whispered to me, "What do we do?"

Dustin answered, "Stay here, be quiet, and let me handle him. He likes to pop in, but never stays for long, not this early in the day. Be cool."

I grabbed his arm as he was leaving. "Are you sure? We'll come with. Strength in numbers."

"No. Absolutely not. You'll just make it worse."

I let him go. It was his dad, he was better equipped. "You scream if anything goes down."

He nodded, disappeared into the hall.

Reya stood in the center of the room, afraid to move, like one step in any direction might trigger another bomb. "Nick, we can't stay here and do nothing."

We could. That's what Dustin told us to do, but I didn't think it was smart. "We can't trust the local cops," I said, reluctantly admitting we were in over our heads, "but maybe the state police are an option."

I crossed to Dustin's desk, hesitated a moment as a memory of Carrey sitting in the chair came back to me. Pushing the thought aside, I sat, catching angry, unintelligible notes of Dustin and the mayor's conversation.

Reya's paralysis broke. She moved closer to the door. "It's getting intense down there."

Flipping up the screen on Dustin's laptop, I saw a new email notification flash in the lower right-hand corner. A message from FuegoGirl@prworld. com with a subject line reading: *IGNORE THIS . . .*

I did. I opened the browser and searched for *Virginia State Police*. The website came up quickly. I clicked on it and was overwhelmed by the poor web design. Info, photos, and links bordered more stuff, like properties in a square around the Monopoly board. I could not find a phone number.

As I scanned, *IGNORE THIS . . .* popped in the corner three—four—more times. Dustin's "conversation" with his dad grew in volume.

"Hurry, Nick," Reya said, her phone drawn, ready to dial.

In the time she urged me along, two more messages from FuegoGirl appeared. In spite of the circumstances and the Virginia State Police's frustrating website, my natural sarcasm broke through, and I thought, *FireGirl should change her name to SPAMGirl.*

I froze.

Fuego was one of the few Spanish words (besides profanity) that I knew. It meant *fire*. That was important. Not the word itself, but that it was Spanish. *Why* was it important? The notice flashed two more times. *IGNORE THIS . . .* , daring me to do the exact opposite.

I opened Dustin's in-box.

Dozens, possibly hundreds, of emails, all from FuegoGirl, all with the same taunting subject.

I opened one at random . . . nearly fell off the chair.

The message from the subject continued. *IGNORE THIS SINCE YOU'RE SO GOOD AT IGNORING ME . . .*

An embedded picture filled the rest of the window. A picture of a newborn boy in a snug blue knit cap and a mummy-tight blanket. There was no signature identifying FuegoGirl or a name for the child. Neither was necessary. I recognized Ricardo Elijah Rios instantly.

Dustin would, too.

They had the same eyes.

CHAPTER 44

I STARED AT THE EXTREME CLOSE-UP of the baby, my vision blurring because I couldn't blink. Pilar's newborn son was Dustin's newborn son. The resemblance was undeniable—I'd seen the kid's green eyes myself at the hospital. I was so focused on sneaking to Dustin's room, I didn't pick up on the shared trait.

Two nagging thoughts, sitting at the edge of my consciousness like massive, immovable stones, suddenly slammed together, fused into something new and grotesque.

Family concerns.

Seat belts.

Me and Reya thought Miguel was the family Eli spoke of in his video—a theory Dustin happily encouraged—but what if it was his favorite cousin Pilar, whose back he always had? What if the purpose of Eli calling Dustin to the J-Room was to discuss the newest branch on the Rios/Burke family tree? How would a conversation like that go? It might get ugly, depending.

Thinking of Dustin that way—the possibilities that I still couldn't wrap my head around completely—jarred something from earlier, something I maybe forced myself not to remember because of the implications.

Dustin said the seat belt saved his life the night of the accident, and that Carrey and Lorenz didn't like to wear them. Thing was, neither did Dustin. I'd seen him driving his Xterra on two occasions before today. At the park, the day after I found Eli. And at school the day the mayor dropped me off. He wasn't wearing *his* seat belt either time.

Why start on some random late-night drive? It'd been a fortunate coincidence, considering what happened. Only, I don't believe in coincidences.

I blinked, restarted time. "Reya, you need to see this."

She turned to me, but a mighty crash of splintering wood and shattering glass sounded downstairs, drawing her attention back to the doorway.

Dustin yelled, "Dad, no! Get back! Get back!"

"You," said the mayor, grunting, in a struggle, "stop that this ins—"

The abrupt silence set off alarms in my head. Dustin's screams drowned them. "Oh God. Help me, guys. Please!"

I said, "Reya, don't."

She was already gone, sprinting to the aid of the boy I suspected of killing her brother, and then some.

Her talents were wasted on the cheerleading squad. Reya should've run track. I couldn't catch her on the stairs, or in the corridor leading to the mayor's office.

"Reya!" I hissed, already knowing it was hopeless. She turned into the room where Dustin continued his crying lure. I paused outside the doorway. If my suspicions about him were even close to right, turning this corner was a stupid, potentially deadly, decision.

What else was I going to do? Reya was in there. I stepped in, told myself, *Think of it as our second date.*

She stood beyond the threshold staring at the carpet—and the corpse—before her, her hand pressed to her mouth. Mayor Burke lay prone, a halo of blood pooling from an ugly dent in the side of his skull. A foot away, his boxing trophy. The heavy metal glove stained with blood, a few black and gray hairs plastered to it.

Dustin sat on the floor by the gun cabinet with his head low, making weepy sounds with no tears. The cabinet itself was smashed, bowed in like somehow had been hurled at it. A couple of the rifles had fallen free, scattered among the debris like NRA pick-up sticks.

I grabbed Reya's hand, squeezed it. Hard. She looked at me, and I cut my eyes toward the door, tugging her arm at the same time. *Let's go. Now.* She shook her head, missing my meaning.

Dustin spoke up. "He lost it, attacked me."

Reya pulled free of my grasp, went to him. "Nick, help me get him up."

Dustin caught my eye in a moment of hesitation. I thought I saw him twitch, but he resumed his dry crying, while Reya gripped one of his arms. "Nick," she said again.

He didn't know I knew about the baby, or suspected anything about Eli or the accident. This might be okay if I played it off. It had to be.

I joined Reya and helped that bastard to his feet.

Dustin lurched, his legs unsteady. Supposedly. He brushed glass shards and splinters from his clothing and smeared blood from a few scrapes along his unbroken arm.

"What happened?" I asked, needing to hear him talk, explain. See if he still sounded like the guy I'd believed was becoming a friend. Or did he sound like the new guy? The murderer.

"He just snapped, I had to." Dustin widened his eyes to sell the shock and remorse, still no tears. "He was screaming about Reya's uncle, and her car blowing up. It was crazy. I think he had some sort of mental break and was, like, confessing to everything we talked about."

The mayor gave up Miguel and the car bomb. How convenient. The only thing missing was a shiny bow.

Dustin kept going. "Then he had this look, like he didn't recognize his own son. He goes, 'Now I have to shut you up, too, just like that reporter kid.'"

"He admitted it?" Reya, horror transforming to contempt, stared at the bleeding body like she wanted to kick it.

Dustin nodded, sticking to the ridiculous story.

Knowing what I knew, and seeing through his overacting, a part of me still wanted to believe him. His was the easiest, least frightening version of everything that had gone wrong since I arrived in Stepton. I *would* believe it. He'd think so, anyway. Until I could get Reya out of there.

"Should we call someone?" I left the decision with Dustin, wanting him to feel in control. It was safer that way.

"I guess. I'm not sure who to—"

The mayor moaned.

No, not now.

Mayor Burke turned his head against the carpet, smearing his cheek in his own blood. Struggling, he forced an arm and a knee under himself, pressing his body off the floor. He almost made it to a crawling position before collapsing, and moaning again. "Dus-tin. Help me, son."

Dustin's Shock Face disappeared, overcome by a coldness that narrowed his eyes and pressed his lips into a pencil line, the look of someone with an unpleasant chore ahead of them.

"We gotta call an ambulance," Reya said, pulling her cell from her back pocket. "He's going to answer for what he did to my brother."

Dustin stepped away, glass crunching under his sneakers by the gun cabinet. He picked up a semiautomatic Remington rifle and aimed at Reya. "Don't dial."

"What?" She stared down the barrel like someone who didn't get the joke, her hand hovering over the keypad. I could only watch, too much distance between me and Dustin to risk a move.

Me and Reya weren't his primary concern. He kept the gun on her, but in an awkward one-hand grasp that had the buttstock protruding past his elbow. That kind of grip wouldn't do for aiming, but he didn't need good aim in a room this size. Still, I kept his improper handling in mind.

"Dus-tin," Mayor Burke said again, pleading for his son's help.

Dustin crouched by his father, stroked the man's back with his cast arm. "It's okay, Dad."

He picked up the bloodied boxing trophy, raised it high, upended it so the glove pointed down. I took one step and the rifle barrel swung my way, freezing me. "Don't, Nick."

"Why?" I said, perplexed and scared of what was coming.

Calm, with that single bloodstained eye on me, he said, "Didn't I tell you the other night? At the party?"

I shook my head, not recalling a conversation about his hidden homicidal tendencies. He reminded me.

"I *do*"—he dropped the glove on his father's head, a squelching crunch, silencing him permanently—"what I *can*."

CHAPTER 45

REYA LOOKED AWAY AS DUSTIN DROPPED the glove on his father's misshapen skull again. I didn't. I watched him kill his dad the same way I watched Kreso Maric put a bullet in a kid's skull, knowing the world was a different, darker place now.

Only question: Would me and Reya be in it for long?

Dustin let the trophy fall from his fingertips, stood, and angled himself so he had line of sight on both of us, easy targets. "Throw your cells into the corner. Now."

We both complied, tossing our phones, the plastic casings smacking the wall, then thudding on the carpet. There was no play other than to follow his instructions and hope for an outcome we could live with.

Reya spoke first, her voice broken by sobs. "I don't understand, Dustin. What are you doing?"

He faced her, but his rifle swept between us like a turret, forcing us into alternating cringes each time we stared down the barrel. He sighed, said, "I'm improvising."

Not unlike my improv routine with Zach at the municipal campus. Maybe what worked once would work again. I said, "If you're going to do this, you might want to—"

"Shut up before I shoot your girlfriend in the stomach," he said, emotionless. "I'm trying to think."

My mouth snapped shut. He wasn't some idiot bully. I didn't know what he was. Seconds ticked by and the rifle swung from me to Reya, Reya to me.

Sweat drizzled down my back and arms; my hands and legs shook. At any second, he could pull the trigger. End our lives when he decided. Or could he?

Unlike at the municipal campus, some Bricks wisdom came to me. Maybe it was because of the gun. Firearms always reminded me of my godfather.

Your generation, Tony, they're punks. Don't fight with their hands like we used to. In my day, you didn't have to worry about no gun until you were in the game. Now, kindergarteners are bringin' them to school. . . .

The lecture was a long one—Bricks loved trumpeting the virtues of his generation over all those that came after—but two bits held weight.

Facing a Firearm Tip #1: A kid pulls on you, you gotta make a decision. The smart move is do what he says. Hand over your wallet, kiss his shoes, whatever. It's better to be humiliated than dead. Most guys want something other than your life. But the other guys, the ones who like to see the light in your eyes go dim, you give them everything except what they want. You get me?

When the gun swung back to me, I said, "It's probably not loaded."

Dustin tilted his head, an educated man up for a debate. "Oh, really?"

"Nick?" Reya said, terror evident.

I ignored her. "You pulled it right from the gun cabinet. Who stores their guns loaded?"

"A reasonable deduction." He aimed the gun at the wall to my left, fired a round that seemed as loud as a grenade. Reya screamed. I barely heard her because my ears were ringing and I was concentrating really hard on not crapping in my pants.

"Dad kept all the guns loaded," Dustin said. "He had to, dealing with a nut like Reya's uncle."

He was talking. Not shooting. Talking was good. *Let's focus on that.* "Did Miguel really cause your car accident to get back at your dad or did you make that up?"

Grinning now, he said, "Some things I made up, some things I didn't. Like those 'inspired by true events' stories. Now, the accident was . . . not. It was intentional. Worked better than I ever imagined, really."

"You caused that car wreck?" Reya blurted. "Lorenz and Carrey were your friends. Since elementary school."

He turned the gun on her again. "They were nosy. Lorenz was, anyway. Though, if I'm being honest, I have to take some of the blame."

"Some?" I said, drawing the gun back to me.

"I wanted a souvenir of my first time, like when I was ten and I lost my virginity to my nanny. I kept a lock of her hair."

I couldn't count how many ways that statement was screwed up, but he'd lost me. "You killed your best friends because they found a lock of hair?"

He shook his head. "My bad. I need to work on my syntax." He swung the gun to Reya. "Your brother told me that once when he proofed one of my lit papers."

"Dustin?" I said.

He aimed at me. "When I said souvenir, I meant the laptop I took from Eli the night I cut his wrists and watched his blood pump like a red water fountain."

Reya sucked in a sharp, whistling breath.

"Lorenz found it in my closet after you two left. I played it off like it wasn't really Eli's, but some of his blood had splashed on it. I could tell him and Carrey didn't buy my story. I had to do something. If the crash hadn't killed them, it would've given me time to get rid of that computer, then blame anything they said on head trauma. Fortunately, things went my way."

"*Te mataré,*" she spat.

"That sounded like a threat," Dustin said, aiming at her, a game now. "I mean, I really don't know what you said, but it *sounded* threatening. Love the accent." Back to me. "She talk like that when you're banging her, Nick?"

"Did Pilar talk like that when you banged her?"

Dustin shuddered, like I'd splashed him with cold water.

"You and *Pilar*?" Reya said, catching on.

Whatever fun Dustin was having playing eenie-meenie-miney-moe with the gun seemed to fade. "Eli couldn't have told you that," he said. "I would've been able to tell that day in the park. That's the only reason I bothered to talk to a nobody like you, to see if that asshole had blabbed."

"If you knew he didn't tell me, why take it this far? You didn't have to tell me anything about your dad. You led us to him." My eyes bounced around the room, looking for some kind of advantage.

"I don't expect either of you to understand this, but killing Eli, it—it created a kind of freedom. Dad didn't see it that way. Once you found the body, he sent some guys to dirty up the scene before anyone could collect any real evidence. Then he grounded me. He tried to take away my freedom. After that, it made sense to frame him."

Of course it did. In Dustin's warped mind. "This was never about Whispertown?"

"Pay attention, Nick. Some things are true, some are made up. Whispertown is very real, and that's part of what Eli wanted to talk to me about. He knew my dad was falsifying records; he also knew that Pilar claimed I knocked her up. I didn't want that slutbag ruining my life, and Dad didn't want to share a grandkid with the local Thug God. Dad approached Miguel with a deal, the cops ignore some of Miguel's 'victimless operations'—which helps Dad's little experiment anyway—and Miguel handles whatever whore child his daughter squeezed into the world, leaving us out of it.

"I did think—hoped—he'd make her get an abortion. Guess it's a Catholic thing. He can sell smack to second graders but maintains a pro-life stance. I didn't overthink it."

Reya collapsed into the mayor's desk chair, the weight of it all crushing.

"You killed Eli to keep your secret," I said.

"I killed him to keep *all* the secrets. He offered me a deal that night. If I copped to Pilar's pregnancy and 'did the right thing,' he'd make Whispertown disappear. Destroy all the files he had, and let my dad conduct business as usual. If I denied the pregnancy, he'd expose Whispertown and ruin everything. I mean, yeah, my name was on the line, but the idea of a bunch of grade A lunatics running around free . . . so many fun possibilities.

"Too bad you won't get to see what comes next. . . ." He swung the gun toward me, his finger curling around the trigger.

CHAPTER 46

FACING A FIREARM TIP #2: *The only dangerous part is the barrel. Control the barrel, control the gunman.*

A rifle has a long barrel. It's meant to kill at a distance. Dustin's swing act reminded me of a metronome, the thing that sits on a piano and keeps time when you're learning to play. Mom insisted on lessons when I was young, wanting to expose me to "culture." I never caught on, but my teacher was fond of saying "find the time between the swings."

I did. Dustin was confident, had gotten used to swinging that gun in a rhythm, more intimidation than action. On that final swing, the one where he might've killed me, I was in motion the second he cleared Reya.

He panicked when I moved, squeezing off a round that would've stopped my heart—had I been where he thought I was. Only the barrel of a gun is dangerous, and that long rifle barrel can be unwieldy for a kid with a broken arm. I went low, under the bullet. He couldn't adjust fast enough. By the time he did, I had a grip on the barrel, directing it away from me and Reya. He squeezed two more rounds, each damaging the wall and nothing else.

I gave him my best punch, right on the chin.

He laughed and slugged me with his cast arm. It felt like a crowbar.

I went down sideways, snatching the rifle from his poor grip, but unable to hang on to it myself. It spun across the carpet.

He moved toward it. I couldn't let that happen. If he got it back, or worse, reached a loaded handgun—much shorter barrel, much harder to control—we were done.

I scrambled on my knees to cut him off, punching him hard in the thigh. His leg buckled slightly, but he managed to swing with his good hand, catching me behind the ear. His punches felt like he was swinging dumbbells.

Can't stay down, Nick. Stay down and you die.

Snagging his belt, I yanked myself up, throwing him off balance. He went for a power hook that I saw coming, and ducked before he took my head off. I positioned myself between him and the guns, raised my hands.

His smile widened as he went to the balls of his feet, brought his cast hand to his ear and his good hand under his eye, forming fists. "A lot of people thought my dad was abusive," he said, faking a jab and a cross. "He was just a hands-on kind of teacher."

The next jab busted my lip.

Two more punches, a hook and an uppercut. I blocked the hook, which was probably his intent, because all of his power was in the uppercut, his cast arm landing squarely in the pit of my stomach, taking me back to one knee.

He geared up for an overhand strike that would likely knock me unconscious. I'd sleep through him blowing my head off if I let him win this fight. He was a trained boxer. His skill at the sport topped mine in every way. But boxers have one universal weakness.

Rules.

I grabbed a handful of broken glass, slicing my palm and not caring, flicked it in his face as he swung. He screamed, and the punch clipped my shoulder. I drove that same shoulder into his midsection, ran him backward, tripping him on his father's dead body. We both went down on a bloodstain, me on top, and I proceeded to beat him with every bit of rage I'd spared Zach Lynch from.

Fists, knees, elbows. He fought, too, but I was beyond pain. For each of his blows, I gave back two. I watched his face darken, and puff, and leak as my hands smashed, smashed, smashed. When one of his teeth flew sideways from his mouth, I paused, finally feeling the throbbing from my split knuckles. The blood on his face was as much mine as his.

The crazy bastard was still conscious, though.

"That's enough, Nick," said Reya. "It's my turn."

I followed her voice. She inspected Dustin's discarded rifle like an expert, turning it this way and that, checking the receiver and ejector ports, staring down the sight.

She said, "Move. I'll finish it."

I didn't move. "Reya, he's done. Let's call someone and they can take him away."

"We can't trust the cops, remember? That's not one of his 'maybe it's real, maybe it's not' stories. You said that. Move!"

Dustin spat up a clump of blood. "Move, Nick. Let me get a go with her."

I punched him unconscious. *I'm trying to save your life, jerk.* "Reya, put that gun down."

"He killed my brother, his friends, tried to kill us. I'm ending that *pendejo*. And don't try to give me some 'I'm better than that' bull. I'm not better than avenging my brother."

I wasn't going to give her that speech. For one, it *was* bull. Stuff they say in movies so the hero won't kill the main bad guy, even though he probably killed a hundred henchmen getting to the villain. The military and the police killed bad guys all the time. Hell, one of the people I loved most in the world killed bad guys for money. Dustin Burke deserved to go.

Reya didn't deserve what came after.

I'd seen what happened when people had blood on their hands. Bricks took pills to sleep, never had a girlfriend for more than a few weeks. My dad turned mean and bitter, basically flushed his family down the toilet. Dustin, he got hungry for more blood, saw it all like some play he was directing.

Offing Dustin in Eli's name might not be a negative for Reya. Maybe she'd grow up to have a good life, healthy relationships, peace. I wasn't willing to bet on it though, even if the collateral was a piece of crap like Dustin Burke.

I stood up, kept myself between her and him.

Twin trails of tears slid down her cheeks. "Please move, Nick."

"I can't do that." I closed the distance.

She aimed. At me. "*Maldita sea!* Move!"

I grabbed the barrel, as I had with Dustin, but gently. She let the gun go. I tossed it aside and embraced her, let her cry.

We still had a problem. We couldn't trust the cops, but we had to call someone.

One person came to mind.

I walked Reya to the corner, retrieved our phones, and made the call. "Dad, I've got trouble."

I explained as much as I could as fast as I could, never taking my eyes off Dustin. He stayed as still as his father. When I was done, Dad got quiet. I was afraid I'd dropped the call.

FAKE ID | 269

"Hello?" I said.

"I'm here." He didn't sound like it. He seemed distracted.

"Did you hear what I told you?" Paper rustled, like when we were on the conference call and Bertram shuffled through his files. "Where are you?"

"I'm at home, son."

"I don't want Mom to know what happened, okay?"

"She won't," he said, still vacant, not engaged. Like I hadn't told him I was in a room with a corpse and a killer.

"Dad, I need you."

"I heard you," he snapped. He backpedaled. "Hang tight. I'm going to take care of this."

"You're coming?"

"Answer when the doorbell rings. No matter what." He hung up.

What was that?

It was an hour before we knew. The doorbell rang, and I answered it, like I'd been told. I'd expected Dad, maybe some of his Whispertown buddies who knew how to take care of things like this. Not the people waiting on the other side of the door.

It was Sheriff Hill and the Stepton Police Department.

He said, "Nick Pearson, you have the right to remain silent . . ."

CHAPTER 47

TWO AMBULANCES ARRIVED ON THE SCENE. Hill allowed me to receive first aid for my cuts and bruises—while handcuffed. They didn't arrest Reya. They should have, because she gave them an earful about my detainment. I'm almost certain she threw a punch at one of the officers, but they let her slide, given the circumstances.

She cooled when they rolled Dustin to the second ambulance on a stretcher. It was gratifying to see handcuffs securing him, too. The motion awakened him, and he gave me and Reya a finger wave before being loaded on the transport. A second, covered gurney came next. The mayor.

The EMTs transporting the Burkes were the same ones who took Eli from the school. It seemed like something I should feel good about. Poetic justice. The universe balancing things. All I felt were aches and the cuffs biting into my wrists.

The ambulance and its half-dead cargo cruised away from the Burke estate, destination unknown. Once I was adequately patched up, the SPD loaded me and Reya into separate patrol cars and shuttled us to the station.

Seems the universe wasn't done with us yet.

I lost sight of Reya's car on the way. When we arrived, Hill handled me himself, rushed me past the booking desk directly into our favorite interrogation room.

Mostly I said nothing, exercising my right to remain silent. I was plenty scared, though. He still hadn't told me what I'd been arrested for. Reya was the only person I trusted who knew I was here. And vice versa. If this police department was as dirty as I thought it was, we could be in more danger than we were with Dustin.

"I'm sure I get a phone call this time, Sheriff."

I thought he'd deny it, I expected him to. He said, "Relax, Pearson."

He left and returned with a cordless phone, uncuffed me.

I dialed Mom. No way to keep her out of it now. I wanted to hear her voice. I did, on her voice mail. I left a frantic message about my arrest, Reya, being at the police department, and I ran down all the name tags and badge numbers I'd memorized while getting alcohol rubbed on my cuts, so there would be people to question if I disappeared. I talked until the digital recorder cut me off.

Head low, I handed the phone back to Hill. He sat across from me.

"Where's Reya?" I asked.

"Down the hall. It's standard procedure until we can get a statement or someone comes to get you. I'd like you tell me everything that happened, in painstaking detail. Now, please."

"I don't have to talk. I know that much."

He looked to the sky for divine assistance. "Kid, you don't know crap.

If you did, you'd realize I didn't book you. No fingerprints, no mug shot, no official record of you being here. I read you the Miranda and slapped on the bracelets for the sake of my new guys. Not everyone knows what's going on here."

I stiffened. "You mean Whispertown?"

"I do. The quicker you can explain how that bloodbath at Richie Burke's house came to be, the sooner I can start cleaning this up, if it can be cleaned."

"Clean it up? Dustin's a killer. I thought you said you didn't sign on to cover up murders."

"I didn't lie to you. Dustin will be dealt with accordingly, but do you want all the work we've done to unravel because that little prick went on a rampage? If we don't do something to smooth this over before it reaches your U.S. Marshal friends, then we might be adding as many as fifty to that boy's current body count. You and all of your WitSec cousins, uncles, and aunts could be at risk."

I shook my head. "Why should I trust you?"

"Because your father trusts me. He called me to come get you. Now talk. We don't have much time."

It could be real, or a trick, or something in between. I didn't know, was too tired to care. This day couldn't get any worse, I thought. Incorrectly, by the way.

I said, "It started on my first day of school, after I bumped into Reya...."

———

Five hours later I was on my fourth bottle of water—death brawls tend to dehydrate—and popping Advil for my throbbing wounds. Hill asked me follow-up questions, double-checking details. He could've been trying to catch me in a lie. For once there were none. I told him everything and hoped I wouldn't regret it.

Two hard knocks on the interrogation room door drew his attention.

"What is it?"

"The boy's parent is here, Sheriff."

He nodded and looked at me. I said, "Where's Reya? I'm not leaving without her."

"Noble, kid. She left two hours ago."

That deflated me, sapping the last bit of energy I had. If she was home, and safe, there was no need to fight anymore. I let Hill walk me to the front, expecting my mom to be there. It was my other parent.

The sheriff released me. "We'll be in touch, James."

Dad shook the sheriff's hand. It was like seeing an owl shake hands with a bat, natural enemies being cordial. Before we left the station, I asked the sheriff, "What are you going to do now?"

He said, "What I can."

Dustin would've enjoyed the way those words chilled me.

In the SUV, Dad didn't ask if I was okay, if I wanted a burger, nothing. That was fine, I didn't want to talk to him anyway. "Where's Mom?"

He didn't answer. I took it as him being vindictive old Dad, mad at me for challenging him, or mad at Mom for defying him.

His silence wasn't about anger. It was about heartbreak.

Soon, I'd feel it, too.

Our house was too dark and still to be occupied. It was past eight, full night. Her car was in the driveway. "Mom?"

Dad moved into the kitchen and flipped the light switch. He returned with a sealed envelope, gave it to me. My name, Tony, was on the front, in Mom's handwriting.

"You probably want to read that in your room," Dad said, which meant *he* wanted to be alone. He returned to the kitchen and clinked ice cubes in a glass, followed them with a healthy dose of bourbon. I took his advice and climbed the stairs. Even knowing the letter was going to be something awful, I couldn't muster any true fear. I'd faced the threat of pain and murder today. My terror reserves were spent. That wasn't necessarily a good thing.

I sat on my bed and tore the envelope, removed the note written on a yellow sheet from a legal pad. I had a premonition.

She left me.

The letter offered details:

> Dear Tony,
>
> I have not abandoned you. I cannot say the same for Nick, or Steven, or Logan, or Tyler. This life of ours isn't living. It's masquerading. A never-ending ball where no one's our friend and we can't step outside for cool air no matter how bad we want to. Safety has cost us everything, and I no longer care to be "protected."
>
> I wanted you with me for this new chapter. I did. But Deputy Marshal Bertram and your dad reminded me that the life I'm choosing now is a dangerous one. Taking you with me would have been selfish. Putting you in harm's way is not what a good mother would do.

I know, I know . . . a good mother wouldn't disappear, either. Maybe that proves my point. You're better off without me. For now.

In the short time you've been Nick Pearson, I've seen you grow more than I have in the last four years. You're making friends, going to parties, you've got that beautiful girlfriend (if I'm premature on that one, be patient, I saw how she looks at you . . .). You can have a real life in Stepton. Provided your father doesn't screw things up. Even if that happens, it's on him. WitSec won't abandon a minor. You'll be safe. Which is my strongest desire.

I still love you and I still love your father. But he's more to blame for this than any of us have been willing to admit. That being said, forgive him. I'm trying to, but you HAVE to, for your own sake. Don't hate him for this.

I'll find ways to keep in touch. One day, when you're done with school, and better able to decide what you want and need, we'll be reunited. Until then, be healthy, and happy, and enjoy the tranquillity of small-town life.

I love you, my baby. Until we meet again.

MOM

I reread it several times, flipping the sheet over, looking for a hidden message. Was this why Dad seemed distracted when I called earlier? Why he left me with Hill for hours?

I exploded from my room, entered the kitchen waving Mom's letter like a declaration of war. "You did this, Dad! Did you go look for her? Maybe she hasn't gotten too far, we can—"

He sat hunched over his untouched drink, crying, tears dripping into the glass. It was as startling as learning the truth about Dustin. Dad looked up at me, unashamed. He left his seat to embrace me. The first hug he'd given me in years.

"I'm so sorry, son. I'm so sorry."

Another first. So many changes today. Not all of them were horrible. Just enough for the good ones not to matter.

CHAPTER 48

IN MY DREAMS, DUSTIN STANDS A hundred feet away with a sniper rifle, sunlight glinting off the massive scope.

"Hard to control the barrel from there, Tony." He pulls the trigger and it sounds like metal scraping concrete.

I woke up choking on my own spit, checking my chest for bullet holes. The metal-on-concrete sound came again. A grumbling engine coughed and died in the driveway. I went to the window, winced from the sun stabbing my sleep-sensitive eyes. I hoped to see Reya, remembering at the last second that she no longer had a car. The vehicle blocking Dad's was a plain gray sedan, a rental or a car someone bought because a car they actually liked wasn't in their budget. The face behind the wheel was hard to place. Until it wasn't.

Bertram.

I grabbed a T-shirt and sweatpants, scrambled downstairs.

Four. That's how many times I'd seen him before today. Always in the dead of night, when he escorted us to a new life in a new state. Never in daylight. Was this how they did it when they revoked protection? Tell you in the morning so you have time to make a run before the sun sets and the wolves pounce.

Dad waited in the foyer with his hand on the doorknob, twisting it before the doorbell finished ringing.

Bertram stepped in, as tall as Dad, but pale with his shaved head and orangish beard. He said, "I think we're going to be skipping the conference call this week."

I didn't move. Neither did Dad.

Bertram stepped between us, entered our kitchen like he was about to whip up breakfast, and folded himself into a chair. "A bottled water would be fine," he said, as if someone had asked.

I expected this to be the starter gun for the pissing contest between him and my father. Dad simply crossed the room and retrieved a cold bottle of Deer Park from the fridge for the U.S. Marshal.

Bertram took three quick sips in succession, then recapped the bottle as if it needed to be rationed. "Where's Donna?"

"Shopping," my dad and I said at the same time.

Bertram eyed us closely. "That was good. Neither of you batted an eye."

He was baiting. Maybe he knew nothing, maybe he knew everything. Didn't matter much either way at this point.

Confirming my thoughts, he said, "We're beyond all that, anyway. Whether or not you're honest with me on this matter is of little importance as of this morning. We're all living in a different world now."

Bertram motioned to the empty chairs at the table. "Please have a seat. There's a lot to discuss."

"Are we out of the Program?" Dad asked.

"Sit. Please."

I moved first. Reluctantly, Dad followed. The sounds of chair legs screeching across the kitchen tile took me back to the day before, the mayor's screams. I shook off the nightmare sound but my hands trembled under the table.

"I've been in touch with Sheriff Hill," Bertram said. "He briefed me on the terrible ordeal you've undergone, Nicholas. I'm glad that you're okay."

Bertram turned his attention to my father. "I'm not sure how much you two know about the Whispertown initiative—though I'm told Nicholas knows plenty, thanks to his late friend—but after all that's transpired, you're going to need some background. I'm about to share some highly privileged information, and the only reason I'm telling you any of this has to do with containment."

"Containment," Dad repeated, emotionless.

"Listen carefully."

Bertram uncapped his bottle and took another sip, then he spoke for an hour straight, briefing us on information we already had. We did as he asked. Listened. Nodded in the right places. Acted shocked and angry over being Uncle Sam's guinea pigs.

"Mayor Burke was entrusted with a secret but made a huge mess of things. He made the mistake of trying be a pioneer—a leader—when his own house was not in order. He's dead because of that.

"His son is a disturbed boy. Hell, he's responsible for, what, four deaths that we know of. Has taken to bomb making." Bertram looked to me. "That little package he placed in your girlfriend's car was pro quality, son. He got the chemicals for it from his dad's construction site. Powerful stuff. You're lucky to be here, you know." I did know.

"There's a hole to be filled. The program Burke pioneered works," Bertram said. "*Whispertown works. The numbers don't lie.*"

I watched Dad carefully. He'd manipulated those numbers himself, knew better than anyone that any benefits from the Whispertown initiative were offset by the negative effects on the community.

Dad wasn't telling.

"What's this got to do with us, Bertram?" I asked.

"The Dustin Burke situation has exposed you to information you wouldn't have been privy to otherwise. That shouldn't have happened."

"So we *are* out of the Program?"

"On the contrary. This is sort of like someone being exposed to a virus, surviving, and being stronger for it. They are able to help the doctors and researchers make *everyone* stronger."

Dad said, "I don't understand."

"It's simple. Your family will be the control group. You know the deal, and we monitor you all the more closely to see how you reside *within* the Program while having full knowledge *of* the Program."

"Which means—" I began.

Bertram cut me off. "You'll be scrutinized more closely than ever before."

"There's something you should know, then, Mr. Bertram." Dad wrung his hands. "My wife did not go shopping. She left me. Abandoned us."

"That is . . . unfortunate." Bertram took another sip. "Normally, we'd consider your cover compromised over this. We might still, depending on what the higher-ups say. I wasn't kidding when I said WitSec was not interested in funding another relocation for you. I can probably push to keep you in, particularly with your new roles in the Whispertown initiative. But Donna's protection is forfeit. Nothing I can do about that." To me, "I'm sorry for your loss."

FAKE ID | 281

Unprotected witnesses don't last long on their own, he'd said so himself. Mom was already dead to him.

More screeching then. My chair sliding back, my hand snapping forward, grabbing Bertram's open bottle and squeezing a geyser into his face. He coughed and sputtered. I was halfway upstairs before he stopped.

An hour later, Bertram scraped his bumper again leaving our driveway, and Dad stood at my door. I made sure the bag I'd packed was safely concealed. I'd wait until nightfall to leave. I had a little money, and I knew tricks for getting more. I guess I'd be forfeiting my protection, too, but screw it. Safe living wasn't all it was cracked up to be. Not in this town.

On my bed, my hands behind my head, I stared at the ceiling. Dad stood silent over me for a long time. I made myself not speak first, no matter how awkward it felt. Keep Quiet champion of the world.

Finally, he asked, "You think I gave her up, don't you?"

"Should I think something else?"

"You heard what he said. We're going to be scrutinized more closely than ever. Unless your mom's 'shopping trip' lasts a year, they would've figured it out eventually."

I sat up. "You didn't have to help."

"Yeah, I did."

"Why?"

"How else was I supposed to convince Bertram that we're cooperating?"

I paused. "Aren't we?"

The corners of his mouth turned up. "After you left, Bertram went on to tell me the vice mayor, Terry Bolling, will take over the Whispertown initiative. He worked with me and Burke on the crime stats. He's going to want to keep this thing going, keep the government money flowing into the community. Same thing with Sheriff Hill. Same with a lot of people in the know."

"How does that help us?"

"Bolling's an idiot. He'll let me do most of the work. I'll have access to all the city systems. I can use their resources to track your mom."

"You'll have access to the cash you were helping Mayor Burke take, too. Right?"

He didn't sound the least bit apologetic. "We're going to need traveling money."

"What?"

"Once we have what we need, once we find your mom, we'll go to her." His stare intensified. "Together."

I sat up, swung my feet to the floor. Stood toe to toe with him, eye to eye. "Why should I believe you?"

"I don't know if you have much reason to. But I'm asking you to try. I'm going to be better, Tony. I hope you stick around to see it." He backed away, left me.

His words lingered. As did Mom's.

Forgive him . . . for your own sake.

I wasn't in the forgiving mood, not toward either of my parents, but I could be patient. Dad might be better. He might step up, track down Mom, get us the cash we needed to live on the run. He might take care of his family, for once. Or not.

I'd follow his lead. For now.

But I'd keep a bag packed. Just in case.

CHAPTER 49

DAD MET ME BY THE DOOR as I tried to leave.

"I'm coming back," I said, with a little snap I might not have gotten away with yesterday. Like I said, a lot had changed.

He stepped aside. "Okay. Try to make it back before six. We should eat together."

A lot.

I needed a new bike. Mine was in a ditch, with the frame bent, thanks to Zach. Good thing Mom left her car keys behind. Dad burst through the door when I started the engine. "Nick!"

"I'll be home by six." And I motored away, unlicensed and unconcerned.

Someone once told me the laws in this town were a little lax. He was right. When in Rome . . .

———

A charred black crater remained on Reya's lawn. The Beetle wreckage had been taken away, and a number of cars hugged the curb, a familiar Jaguar among them. I parked across the street, queasy at the thought of seeing Miguel Rios. He wasn't the one who cut Eli and watched him bleed, but using his daughter as a bargaining chip didn't make him much better.

The Cruz house, once one of the better-kept homes in this part of town, now featured melted, drooping siding and big plywood patches over broken windows. Dustin Burke left his mark all over. I knocked on the door.

Reya's parolee cousin—whose name I still didn't know—answered. "Little homey," he said. "Come in, come in."

A small crowd inside, like the first time I came here, but with different energy. Not happy, exactly, but settled. Everyone carried some sort of cleanup tool, a broom or a dustpan, a mop. In the center of it, Mrs. Cruz was in the same chair she'd been in when I first met her. This time, she was horizontal, her right leg raised in a lavender cast and a gauze strip circling her head. Miguel sat in an adjacent armchair. The two of them spoke quietly until I entered.

"*Hablando del rey de Roma*," said Mrs. Cruz.

I looked to Miguel.

"'Speak of the devil,'" he translated. "We were just talking about you, friend."

Friend? "Nothing bad, I hope."

"I owe you thanks, Nick Pearson. For saving my daughter," Mrs. Cruz said. "Because of you, I did not lose everything."

I stared at my shoes. "How are you, Mrs. Cruz?"

She touched her bandage. "I have a hard skull, Nick. I'll be fine."

Miguel spewed a belly laugh and patted her thigh, the good brother. He left his seat to hug me, pulling me close. I'd showered thirty minutes ago, and I felt like I needed another bath.

He said, "You're a good man, Nick Pearson. A good, good man."

"How's your grandson?"

His loose, friendly embrace tightened. He released me, backed away, his face unreadable. "Hungry. And gassy."

"Eli, right?"

He blanched at the *E* word. "Elijah. His middle name, *sí*." To Mrs. Cruz, he said, "A strong name and an excellent memoriam."

I said, "Little *Eli*'s lucky to have someone like you taking care of him and his mother. If only his namesake could've seen how much you care."

Mrs. Cruz squeezed Miguel's hand. "He would've been proud, *hermano*."

Miguel's welcoming demeanor had chilled. Eli proud of him? We both knew better.

"Nick?" Reya stood in the hall wearing cheerleader sweats, her hair tied in a ponytail. It should've made her look young, but she seemed aged since yesterday morning. Did I look that way, too?

"Come here," she said, leading me to her room.

I wished Mrs. Cruz and Miguel a good day, relieved to be alone with Reya again. She sealed us in her space, where several thick layers of plastic, anchored by staples, covered her boarded-up windows. I spread my arms, wanting her near. She took a seat at her desk like she didn't see me.

Dropping my arms, I said, "You didn't tell your mom about Miguel and the mayor."

"It'll come out eventually. Everything will." Her words felt cryptic. It seemed like the vibe she was going for.

"How are you?"

"Eli's flash drive is gone. Like you thought."

Oh. "The cops took it, huh?"

She swiveled her chair. "See, that's thing. Miguel sent Angelo and some other guys to watch the house. They put up the plywood and stood guard until Mami left the hospital and got me from the station."

"Who's Angelo?" It was all I could think to say.

She tapped her cheek three times, a trail of tears. So that was her cousin's name.

"No cops came here, Nick." She stopped like she'd asked me a question and expected an answer.

I dug myself deeper. "Dustin, maybe? We don't know what he was doing before he picked us up."

A heavy sigh. "How'd you know all that stuff about bump keys and picking locks?"

"TV." I feigned offense. "I told you that."

"What about making a murder look like self-defense?"

"Making a— What are you talking about?" Where'd that come from?

"Zachary called me last night. He told me he tried to talk to you about squashing the beef between you two, and you flipped. He said you were talking about murdering him and you knew how to get away with it."

"Oh my God. Him and his goon squad snatched me off the street. The only thing he tried to squash was my head."

"I knew that part was bull. Me and him have enough history for me to tell when he's lying. He wasn't lying about the murder stuff."

"Is he dead? I played him to get through a bad situation."

"*Only* him?"

"What are you—?"

She punched up the media player on her computer, a freeze-frame from one of Eli's video journal entries. Him in a familiar Superman tee, though

I couldn't remember when I'd seen it on him. "I thought—" I cleared my throat. "I thought you said you couldn't find the flash drive."

"I couldn't. I spent an hour tearing this room apart."

"Then how . . . ?"

"I copied the videos to *my* hard drive. They were the last things I found, and when I saw it was him, talking, I wanted to save them. To hear his voice. I meant to copy everything, but I got sidetracked with the one secured video, then you came over, and . . ."

I knew the rest. Boom goes the Beetle.

The way she looked, I got the sense like she wanted me to say something. Now. I felt a clock ticking, counting down. But she didn't ask the question. "Nick, did you take the flash drive?" I wasn't going to volunteer a confession. I wasn't raised that way. Plus, I was thinking of the wrong question.

The clock expired.

"Fine," she said. "That's how you want it."

"Want what?"

"When I couldn't find the flash drive, I decided to take a crack at that one video." She handed me a spiral notebook filled with our failed password attempts. "Only took me three tries."

The third password in the book was "El M3jor D1a," the name of their father's community paper.

Reya tapped her space bar, resurrecting Eli. "*—don't know what to do. I thought I was wrong before. But now, I'm almost certain that he's one of them. Nick is one of the Witness Protection kids.*"

CHAPTER 50

ELI KEPT GOING, EACH WORD WORSE than a Dustin Burke punch. *"It was weird that he deleted the pictures I took of him—like I wasn't supposed to notice— but okay, nothing definitive. A lot of people don't like having their picture taken. I went to his house, and, I don't know, I thought if he was a criminal's kid, there'd be guns and stolen watches on the table, like* Sons of Anarchy *or something. No guns. Meat loaf. Then Saturday he asks—demands—that I tell him about Whispertown. What's that about, right?"*

I remembered the Superman shirt. It was the Monday after I caught Dad at city hall, when Eli was being a slave driver about the *Yell*. I'd thought inefficiency was his Kryptonite because of that stupid shirt.

"Yesterday, I tailed his dad."

No.

I already knew what he saw. Dad, somewhere, meeting Mayor Burke and confirming Eli's suspicions.

The next thirty seconds were painful, hearing Eli speculate about my true origins and being 100 percent right. My dad was one of the rogues in his stolen reports, I was in town under an assumed alias, the government was protecting us from killers. Columbia University wasn't wrong. He would've been one heck of an investigative reporter.

Watching him, while Reya watched me watching him, I felt like the meat of a banana, every layer of protection peeled away, waiting for the first bite.

Eli continued, tugging off his glasses and rubbing his tired eyes. *"When I started, it was all about 'my big story,' words on a page, my face on camera. Every day it's getting more real. Pilar, her douche bag baby daddy, now Nick. I thought exposing Whispertown was the right thing. Now, I'm not so sure. Not if it hurts people I care about. Nick's not some low-life pimp, or a drug dealer. Maybe the rest of the rogues aren't so bad either. I—I need to think. There's gotta be a way to make this work for everyone. I'm already in at Columbia, it's not like I need a big sto—"*

Reya stopped the video. "Is he right, Nick? Is Nick even your name?"

Lie. A hardwired response so strong, it felt like electricity sizzling my nerves.

No more.

"Yes," I said, "he's right. Nick's not my real name. It's Tony Bordeaux. Or it was until four years ago. . . ."

I told her as much as I could muster in a sitting, only stopping when she interrupted with questions. Everything she asked, I answered. Including the truth about the flash drive.

Honesty is supposed to be the best policy, and I had a weak fantasy of her appreciating the way I fessed up and rewarding me with a kiss and forgiveness. The hardness in her face promised a different form of payment.

"You destroyed evidence of the conspiracy that got my brother killed."

"I was scared, Reya. For four years they told me that if anyone knew about the Program my family might die. I freaked. But, when I took it, I didn't mean for anything to happen to it. If Zach hadn't—"

"My family *did* die," she said. "You heard Dustin, Eli tried to bargain with him to keep all these secrets instead of exposing them. You. *Tony*."

A slap would've been better than her spitting out my real name like rotten food. I reacted. Poorly. "We got Dustin. Those files weren't going to bring Eli back."

Her head jerked like I'd flashed a light, illuminating something she hadn't noticed before. Something grotesque. "'I'm sorry' is a tough concept to grasp, huh?"

"I'm—" Too late for that. Another countdown missed. "Reya."

"Go, Nick. *Tony*?"

"Nick."

"I need time to think."

If not for her tone, I'd have honored her request and left then. But her "I need time to think" had a "I never want to see you again" feel to it. "What are you thinking about?"

"I'm going to finish what Eli started."

She couldn't be serious. "How!? The evidence is gone."

"Not all of it. You're still here. And the other rogues."

Spinning her chair to me, I grabbed her hand, squeezed it gently. "You're mad at me and you should be. But what you're talking about is dangerous. You go snooping around for protected witnesses, someone's going to get hurt."

She pulled away. "I won't look for the witnesses, then. I'll start with their kids and work my way up. I already know one red flag. They're going to seem too good to be true."

I backed off. Pressing my hand to a furnace couldn't have hurt more than what she'd said.

"Don't worry." She softened slightly, mistaking the pain on my face for self-preservation, "You saved us yesterday, and Eli wasn't going to out you. I won't either. The rest of them . . . I can't make any promises."

The rest of us. Like I was a mischievous rescue kitten and the rogues were an untended pack of feral cougars.

She returned to her monitor, to Eli's face. "Leave, please."

"Reya, don't do this."

"Go!"

I left her to her pain, and carried my own away from the Cruz house.

We've barely spoken since.

High winds turned Monitor Lake into swishing spikes. I observed the rough plumes from the car while a sad song played. Actually, it was "In da Club" by 50 Cent, but all the stations sounded sad to me at that moment.

A plastic clamshell from my latest disposable phone lay torn in the passenger seat while I punched in the new number I'd gotten off the web that morning. Bricks had his ear to the street, might have some info on Mom if she was still relying on the kindness of old friends. Our last call was weird, but I was over that and so sorry I'd cut it short. Even if he couldn't point me to Mom, I just wanted to hear his voice.

The ringing stopped, replaced by Bricks breathing hard into the phone, saying nothing.

This Gus's Gyro Shop? That's how the routine went, but I didn't say the words. Call it instinct.

"Who is this?" a voice said, thick with a Slavic accent. "Who is on the line?"

In the background, Bricks said, "Boss, what are you doing with my phone?"

The voice, "I thought that is phone on your hip."

Bricks said, "That's my business phone. You've got my social phone, you know, for women."

"No woman. Silence." Louder, to me, "Hello?"

I said, "Is this Gus's Gyro Shop?"

The man clucked his tongue and the call ended.

I stared at the phone display, entranced, expecting a tanned face framed in dark curls to appear, hissing like Satan in Eden, "I ssseee you."

The thought snapped my trance. I shouldered the car door open, ran to the rough water, and hurled the phone hard enough to wrench my shoulder.

Kreso Maric had that effect on me.

I did go home that night, but left Dad's horrible cooking alone, opting for a Big Mac in my room while willing Bricks to send me a new number. He didn't. For three days I went crazy with worry for him and Mom. Kreso Maric, sticking his head up, after all this time? Nothing good could come of that.

I nearly told Dad. But my confidence in our new Circle of Trust arrangement was a work in progress. I would've broken down and told him everything if day four had come and gone with no word. But I got a private message on my bogus FB account before my self-imposed deadline.

I'm fine. No calls for a while, though. I'll send word when it's safe.

Bricks's account was deactivated before I could respond. It felt like I was reading Mom's letter all over again.

Dad made attempts to talk about my ultimate decision. Stay with him, or leave on my own? I made him no promises. But I think he noticed that my bag remained in Mom's car and I kept the keys on me.

It was the best I could do.

CHAPTER 51

A WEEK PASSED, BUT THINGS STILL weren't quite right at school. Boy Psycho Dustin Burke was the biggest thing that had ever happened in Stepton. There were more than a few whispers about why a bigger deal wasn't being made by the administration.

Or the local news.

Or the *national* news.

I had a feeling the SPD and/or the U.S. Marshals had something to do with that.

Dustin was in Central State Mental Hospital eating applesauce and playing checkers. If Bertram's boys decided to make his stay there permanent to avoid exposure and keep their precious secrets, it wasn't going to sit well with Reya. She wouldn't see that as much justice for her brother's killer. Can't say she'd be wrong.

Reya was still serving her suspension for the Callie fight. On one of the days she missed, I noticed a student guide leading a pair of new kids through the halls. I was glad Reya wasn't around to see them, because I'm sure she'd have been thinking the same thing I was.

Were they part of it? Were they Whispertown rogues?

I'm going to finish what Eli started.

I tried not to think about our last conversation, but she hadn't called or texted since, so that last conversation was the freshest memory I had.

Yeah, I *could've* called her. For what, though? Another fight?

According to Dad, we weren't staying long. We were going to track down Mom. We were going to be a family again. Soon.

When that happened, the other rogues wouldn't be my problem, and Reya Cruz would be in the rearview. Another memory from another school I used to go to. I'd get over her. Move on. I'd done it before.

That's what I told myself.

Since the truth about Dustin was being swept under the rug, the rumor mill went crazy, mixing a colorful assorted bag of made-up goodness. Dustin became this Hannibal Lecter–like serial killer who cut up bodies and fed them to his koi.

Okay, that wasn't *too* far from the truth. . . .

Especially compared to other versions that painted him as a practitioner of the black arts, a chain-saw-wielding inbred with a skin suit, a junior Dr. Frankenstein who was trying to build the perfect best friend, and so on.

I know. Crazy. That's high school for you.

In my favorite version, *I* was the true killer and I'd gotten away with setting Dustin up. Guess who started that one.

Zach Lynch wouldn't look me in the eye and became deaf-mute when we crossed paths in the hall. His crew wasn't much braver. Some rumors are beneficial.

Depending on who else you asked, what day it was, and what was on the lunch menu, you'd get different assessments of me from different people. Zach's popularity translated to credibility for some. The weak-minded saw me as Lucifer with a backpack, and were afraid.

Something else I learned from Bricks: a little fear isn't necessarily a bad thing.

Then, there were the *other* rumors . . .

It took a couple of days before those stories got back to me, because you always hear the bad before the good. When I did hear, they made me more uncomfortable than the worst of the tales.

Some kids were calling me a hero.

It was all nonsense. I tried not to pay too much attention. Though I knew others would.

On the first day of a new week, Vice Principal Hardwick came to personally pull me from fifth period.

"I need Nick Pearson," he said, interrupting class without so much as an "Excuse me, Lowly Teacher."

I gathered my things to dead silence. It was like half the class expected me to stab Hardwick in the neck with a Bic, while the other half waited for him to turn into a lizard monster so I could defend them with my lightsaber.

Damn it, Eli. Now you've got me *casually referencing Star Wars.*

When I stepped into the hall, the class erupted in hushed murmurs, cranking the rumor mill once more.

"What's going on, Mr. Hardwick?"

His face was tight, gave away nothing. "I need you to see something."

"It couldn't wait until the break? What the hell?" I asked, a little pissed that he'd exposed me to further classmate scrutiny.

"Language, Pearson. I was told you'd want to see this as soon as they finished. Exciting."

"See what and they who?" I veered toward the main office, but Mr. Hardwick caught my arm and led me farther down the hall, toward the cramped conference room where I'd had my counseling session.

Two kids in blue wood-shop coveralls were there. One balanced on a stepladder, mounting some plaque over the door. The other stood back like an artist admiring a fresh canvas, nodding his approval.

"What is this?" I asked.

Stepladder Guy finished and descended just as we reached the room. "All done, Mr. Hardwick."

"Good work, fellas."

With their tools gathered, the wood-shop guys went on their way, but not before one of them said, "Way to go, Nick."

Confused wasn't the right word. Neither was *observant*, because I still hadn't looked at the plaque. When I did . . .

THE ELIJAH CRUZ
JOURNALISM ANNEX

Hardwick noticed my shock and grinned. "Step inside."

When was I in here last? Two weeks ago?

Before it had been pantry-sized, a place to put things that didn't get used. I hadn't noticed it was split by a folding room divider, which was peeled back now, giving this new "annex" a spacious feel the old J-Room could only have fantasized about.

Three desks, each with its own shiny new MacBook (bolted down with fiber-steel cables, of course), created an island in the center of the room. Shelves were filled with glossy manuals on iMovie, Photoshop, and Dreamweaver. A small, steel-cage lockup was filled with digital cameras, tripods, microphones, and other devices that seemed like overkill for a high school operation. I spun in place, overwhelmed, and then realized the one device I hadn't seen. "Where's the printer?"

Hardwick said, "The *Rebel Yell* has gone digital. It's going to be a blog. With me having final approval over anything that gets posted, obviously."

"A blog?"

"Sure, that's what you kids are into, right?"

"I guess so." The old-mushroom smell of current events that Eli loved had been replaced by ozone. He would've hated that. I walked the room, still amazed by all they'd done in here. It must've cost a fortune. The MacBooks alone . . .

The bell rang, but me and Hardwick weren't finished. I said, "Why bring *me* here?"

"Why? Because you're our new blog editor in chief."

"What, no—"

"Nonnegotiable, Pearson. You signing on is one of his conditions, and frankly, I don't want to give any of this shit back."

"Language, sir. Whose condition?"

"Miguel Rios, your friend Eli's uncle. He insisted you captain this ship."

Miguel recommended—*insisted*—I take this job? I looked around with new eyes, seeking booby traps.

The bell rang and the people current flowed past the open door. When Hardwick ran from the room without warning, I had a panic moment where I thought something was indeed booby-trapped and about to blow.

Hardwick yelled, "Ms. Cruz, come here a moment, please."

My stomach sank. Reya.

He led her inside. Her neck craned as she read the sign over the door. She didn't notice me at first, even with her new glasses. No kiddie throwbacks with purple frames, but black rimmed, just like her brother's.

She smiled at his name hung for the world to see. When she saw me, her smile went a little crooked. She crossed her arms and scanned the room . . . not in awe like I had, but to avoid me. I was glad. It was hard to look her in the eye, too.

"I hope you're having a good first day back," Mr. Hardwick said. "No more fights. Okay?"

She nodded and tucked her hair behind her ear. "Yes, sir."

Hardwick continued his spiel. "This is our new journalism room, funded by a generous donation from your uncle. Mr. Pearson over here is going to run it."

"Hey, I didn't agree to that. No one asked me anything, and I don't care what Miguel—"

Reya said, "You should, Nick."

The class bell rang again, starting sixth period. I looked her in the eye then. "For real?"

"Yes. Eli would've wanted you to."

This didn't feel like the verbal kickboxing we were into last time. She was being genuine, and kind. That alone was enough to swing me toward a yes. Anything for her to see me as something other than rogue.

Hardwick cheerfully ruined the moment. "I'm sure he could use an assistant, Reya. It'd be a great way for you to honor your brother."

The kindness in her faded a little. "No, this is all Nick. I have other ways to honor my brother."

And there we were . . .

"This is all beautiful, Mr. Hardwick," Reya said, turning her back on me, "but I should get to class. I've got a lot of work to make up. Would you mind writing me a pass since the bell already rang?"

"I'll do you one better and walk you there myself," he said. Then, to me, "Before I forget, Pearson, in or out? I think future editions of the *Rebel Yell* will benefit greatly under your leadership."

That remained unseen. "On one condition," I said.

His eyebrows peaked.

"We're changing the name."

He smirked, tossed me a key chain. "Those will get you into this room, and the equipment lockup. Get familiar with the place, it's going to be your home away from home."

They left, and I gave the annex another once-over. Home away from home, huh? Who would've thought I'd be a Newspaper Nerd? The new Eli.

Hopefully, when I left the job, it would be under better circumstances.

My arms were full when I made it home that night, just in time for dinner. I carried new manuals on blogging that I'd taken from the J-Room, and one other thing. Dad waited and watched. I stacked the books next to a huge bowl of unappealing spaghetti and meatballs, then dropped the other thing—my duffel—on the floor by my chair.

Eyes on my bag, he said, "Does this mean you're staying?"

"For now." I sat and spooned noodles onto my plate, a gesture of goodwill. It was the first time I'd eaten with him, though he'd set a place every night for a week.

"Tony, I want you to know—"

"The plan, Dad. All I want to know is the plan. What's the next step?"

He nodded, slid the bowl aside, and retrieved a tiny notepad from his shirt pocket. As he talked, he jotted things in shorthand. "I'm thinking three to six months to set up bogus accounts and siphon the funds we need. In the meantime, we can tap Hill for help with your mom, see if we get any leads."

"He should try Florida first," I said.

He shot me a crooked look. "Why?"

Just a hunch, really. I remembered finding Mom at the window awhile ago, staring south, thinking about a time when we'd been happy. All I said was, "You know that trip to Disney when I was little? She liked Orlando a lot."

"Right, she loved that place." He scribbled in the pad. "Orlando. As good of a start as any."

We stayed up late, plotting. What we had wasn't a loving relationship, and it may never be, not after all that's happened. We might serve each other's needs on another level. Possibly the only level we could ever truly exist on. Not father and son. Not friends.

Accomplices.

Three to six months to put our escape together. All while staying under WitSec's radar, pretending to be a normal student, and giving Stepton High the news they could use. The Marshals had something different in mind when they created the legend of Nick Pearson. No big.

It's time I started making my own.

ACKNOWLEDGMENTS

FIRST, I'D LIKE TO THANK GOD for the incredible blessing of seeing a lifelong dream come to pass. As for the mortals who played a hand in this, there are quite a few. Forgive me if I miss any of you. It's the head, not the heart, as they say. . . .

Mom, I still don't know if this is what you had in mind when it came to pushing reading over play, but thank you for your particular parenting model. I'll be doing the same when it's my turn to choose the ball or the book.

Adrienne, the role of a writer's wife is often thankless, but you have gone above and beyond so I am thanking you now. You're a bigger part of this than you realize. This could not have happened without you.

Dad, Sonji, Nikki, Tony, Britney, Eboni, Grandma, Mr. and Mrs. Green, and the rest of my extended family . . . your support cannot be measured with words, though I make this paltry attempt. Thank you all.

Jamie Weiss Chilton, my agent, who is my first and best advocate in this industry. Starfleet salutes you.

Eternal gratitude to Phoebe Yeh, my editor, who took a chance on me when so many others weren't willing, Jessica MacLeish, who sends me packages of the best homework I've ever gotten, and the rest of the hardworking folks at HarperCollins Children's Books/Amistad.

Brandon Massey, my mentor and friend. Dark Dreams at Horrorfind '04 is still one of my greatest memories; thanks for making it happen.

Jennifer "Don't Look Down" Bosworth, my West Coast sis who gives great advice and has the most comfortable futon I ever crashed on. Thank you for everything, but mostly for introducing me to Chimay Blue.

Becky and Austin Boyette, thank you for your early feedback and for being incredibly supportive through this whole process.

Thanks to the Harpies (special shout-out to my editorial sibling Ellen Oh) and the rest of the Lucky 13s (particularly Lenore Appelhans, who came through with some timely Spanish corrections in *Fake ID* . . . any mistakes are mine, not hers). Also, my fellow sleuths of @kidlitmysteries, and my friends at Sisters in Crime, Chesapeake (Teresa, Cindy, Maria, Michael, and Lyn).

Aimee L. Salter at Seeking the Write Life, Ken at Heroic Times, Stephanie Kuehn at YA Highway, Cindy Pon and Malinda Lo at Diversity in YA . . . you all inspire me in ways I don't have the room to express here.

Thanks to the other industry veterans who have never turned me away when I needed help or advice: Steven Barnes, Tananarive Due, Terence Taylor, Christopher Golden, Douglas Clegg, Brian Keene, Sheri Reynolds, and Daisy Whitney.

To Willette Hill and the Go On Girl! Book Club, you're the best group of readers I've ever had the opportunity to spend time with. You throw a heck of a party, and any author lucky enough to get invited knows exactly what I'm talking about. I hope to be in your company again soon.

Last but not least, special thanks to some friends who have absolutely nothing to do with this industry, but have joined me for the ride because that's just how they roll: Alton Jamison, Michael Frazier, Anthony McGlone, Erica Williams, Dawn and Rasheed Owens, Mrs. Nydia Arvelo, Andrea Gordon Gardner, Boni and Durant Kreider, Orlandrea Jamiel, Priscilla Artis-Lukoko, John Wiseman, Randall Kern, Nora Marien, Richard Le Master, Rashad Phillips, and many more.

TURN THE PAGE FOR A SNEAK PEEK AT ENDANGERED!

CHAPTER 1

I'VE HAUNTED MY SCHOOL FOR THE last three years.

I'm not a real ghost; this isn't one of *those* stories. At Portside High I'm a Hall Ghost. A person who's there, but isn't.

The front of the class is where I sit because despite ancient slacker lore, teachers pay more attention to the back. Between bells, I keep my head down and my books pressed tight to my chest, brushing by other students a half second before they think to look. If they catch a glimpse of me, it's most likely a blur of dark curls and winter-pale skin flitting in the corner of their eyes. Depending on who they are—or the sins they've committed—they might feel a chill.

Okay. Yes. I *sound* like a real ghost. But I promise I'm alive.

Jocks don't bump into me, and mean girls don't tease me, and teachers don't call on me because I don't want them to. Hiding in plain sight is a skill, one I've honed. My best friend, Ocie, calls me a Jedi ninja, which is maybe a mixed metaphor *and* redundant. But it's also kind of true.

I wasn't always like this. There were days during the first half of

1

freshman year when I couldn't make it from the gym to social studies without running a gauntlet of leers and insults.

Time provided new targets to ridicule, fresh scandal—with some help.

Patience let me slip under the radar, then burrow deeper still. From there, it was easy to engineer my Hall Ghost persona. Now, in the midst of junior year, I've perfected it.

My name is Lauren Daniels. On the rare occasion one of my peers addresses me to my face, they tend to call me "Panda." Not always affectionately. My most popular alias—likely because no one knows it's *my* alias—is *Gray*, the name under which I provide a valuable, valuable public service. I make myself unnoticed by day because I need to be unsuspected by night.

It's what all the cool vigilantes do.

We're all something we don't know we are.

Take my dad, who doesn't know he's romantic because mostly he's not. Sometimes though, like on a random Wednesday or Thursday, he'll bring home a bunch of *Blachindas*—these German pastries filled with pumpkin; here in the States, we'd fill them with apples and call them turnovers. He tells Mom he really likes the taste. Which is true, he does. He skips the part about how difficult it is to get the foreign delicacy. He has to special order a dozen from this Old World bakery in town every time he wants to surprise her, and the extra effort on the part of the chefs isn't cheap.

What he also doesn't say is that she introduced him to the dessert on their first date eighteen years ago, outside of an army base in Stuttgart, Germany. Every time she gives her account of that night—with her eyes glassy, like she's reliving the evening, not just talking about it—I feel I'm there, too. A time traveler spying on the prelude to my own conception. I love it, and them, and I gulp *Blachinda* even though I hate pumpkin just so I can hear more. While she talks, Dad's dark fingers and Mom's pale ones intertwine like yin and yang in the flesh. She blushes while he nods and eats. It's an incredible ritual to witness, Dad wooing Mom instinctively.

My parents are my Happy Place Thought as I lie prone in the bushes, pinecones and night-chilled rocks clawing at my stomach despite my layered clothing. A beetle slowly prances up my forearm toward my shooting hand. I brush it away as gently as I can and reestablish my aim. My target is stationary, in a parked car, one hundred yards away. A quick lens adjustment turns her face from fuzzy to sharp despite the darkness. An easy shot. Which I take.

Keachin Myer's head snaps forward, whiplash quick.

I shoot again.

Her head snaps back this time, she's laughing so hard. Odd, I was under the impression the soulless skank had no sense of humor.

I rub my tired eyes, and switch my Nikon D800 to display mode. I scroll through three days' worth of dull photos stored in the camera. Saturday: Keachin using her gold AmEx to treat her friends at Panera Bread. Sunday: Keachin dropping a hundred dollars to get her Lexus detailed. Today: Keachin—rendered in stark monochrome thanks to the night-vision adaptor fitted between my lens and my camera's body—belly-laughing at whatever joke the current guy trying to get in her pants is telling. Basically, Keachin being what everyone in Portside knows she is. Rich, spoiled, and popular. Nothing the world hasn't already gleaned about this girl. Nothing real.

I intend to fix that. If she ever gives me something good.

Keachin Myer is as clueless about what she is as anyone else. And being unfortunately named is not the part she's unaware of. If you let her tell it, her parents strapped her with such an ugly handle because, well, she couldn't be perfect, right? That sort of conceited admission would come off like a dare from most kids, opening them up to a barrage of teasing akin to machine-gun fire. No one challenges Keachin, though. Because she's beautiful.

That she knows, too.

She's girl tall, with a curve above her hips that seems custom-made for football players to grab and lift and spin her while she squeals and fake-pounds their chests. I swear, it happens at least three times a week. Her eyes are *blue* blue. Her hair is long and shines like black glass. She's got boobs that more than a few girls in the school may be describing to a cosmetic surgeon one day. *I need something slightly bigger than a C, but really round and perky, like, well—have you ever seen Keachin Myer?*

Here's the part that Keachin doesn't know about herself: she's a Raging Bitch Monster.

I'm sure she suspects it, but not in the way, say, a meth-head might suspect that smoking chemicals brewed in a dirty bucket isn't the best move, thus triggering thoughts of a lifestyle change. Keachin, as best I can tell, does not have such moments of clarity. To her and her pack, bitchiness seems to be something more altruistic. An act of kindness because, otherwise, peons might not know their place.

I've watched her do it for years. Not the way I watch my dad and his pastries. There's nothing about Keachin's judgy tirades that I like. I'm an observer by nature. I needed to know if she required more of my attention.

For a long time I thought not. Sometimes my peers are douche-nozzles. Period. There aren't enough hours in the day for me to nip that bud. But, there's mean, then there's what happened to Nina Appleton.

My fingers are shaking, and not from the cold. What Keachin did to that girl . . .

Breathe, Panda, breathe.

I suck in frigid air, so cold it feels like ice chips cartwheeling down my throat and into my lungs. I fight the shivers. Something rustles a nearby grove of trees, and I'm no longer breathing or shivering. I'm stuck mid-exhale, listening, or trying to. My suddenly elevated heart rate causes blood to roar in my ears. Of all my senses, unimpeded hearing is the one I want most in this moment because my eyes are useless under the moonless sky. Unlike my namesake, I don't have an enhanced sense of smell. I need my ears to confirm/deny what I fear is true.

That I'm not the only watcher in the dark tonight.

A twig snaps and I choke down a yelp. Screw this. I point my camera in the general direction of the commotion. The whole forest flares neon white and gray in the LCD display. I pan left to right over X-ray-like images of inanimate trees, and brush, and long dead leaves. Nothing capable of making any noise without assistance from the wind, or, um, an ax murderer.

My heart keeps pounding, I keep panning, and when I detect movement to my extreme left, I freeze.

There. Staring at me. A raccoon.

It scopes me like the trespasser I am, a silver animal shine in his eyes. I toss one of the pebbles that's been making my evening uncomfortable in his general direction. He jerks a foot to his right, though he was never in danger of being hit, then slinks off into the night, rustling more forest debris on his way.

I reposition, adjusting my lens for another clear view of Keachin in the car. The scene change is apparent.

She's no longer laughing her head off, or facing the proper direction. She's turned toward the rear of the car, propped on her knees and hunched, her head lightly bumping the vehicle's ceiling. The passenger seat she occupied is reclined so it hovers inches over the backseat. Also, the guy who drove Keachin to this secluded spot, his face in shadow, is in the seat with her. *Under* her. Directing her slow up and down motion with hands on hips, which has the car rocking to their rhythm, the geeky *My Other Car Is an X-wing* bumper sticker rising and falling by degrees. . . .

As a reflex, I reach for my shutter release to take the picture. My finger jabs the button with half the pressure required to trigger a shot. I pause, waiting for the perfect moment.

The guy's having a good time, he's thrashing his head in ecstasy, first to his left, toward the steering wheel. Then right, toward me. His face is visible in my display now.

Oh. My. God.

I recognize him. Anyone who goes to Portside High would.

He's been teaching there for years.

CHAPTER 2

NINA APPLETON, THE GIRL KEACHIN HUMILIATED, is not my friend. I don't have many of those.

I like her, though. Before last week, I would've said everyone in school liked her, too.

Nina has cerebral palsy and walks with the aid of forearm crutches. That's not what's most memorable about her or the reason she's so well liked. She's not the school's pity mascot for disabilities or anything like that. People like Nina because she's funny as hell.

We had algebra together once, and Mr. Ambrose worked this problem on the whiteboard. It was all this exponential, carry the such and such, divide it by whatever stuff. In the end, the answer was "69," and you could just about hear him curse under his breath as he finished writing it.

He spun around, saw the grins on all our faces, then stared Nina down.

"Go ahead," he said, anticipating the dirty joke he'd set up, "I walked right into it."

Nina's eyes bounced over the room—her audience—then she threw her hands up, exasperated. "I got nothing."

It was enough. Perfect timing. Expert inflection. Playing against the tension and buildup. The class roared. Even Ambrose smiled, appreciating how classy she'd been in the moment.

Class Clown three times running, she was quoted in the last yearbook as wanting to be the first disabled regular on *Saturday Night Live*. Personally, I think it's foolish to bet against her. As long as her spirit's not broken. An atrocity Keachin may have already committed.

That atrocity must be repaid.

Funny kids have a way of pissing off humorless people. When Nina, perhaps thinking herself brave, interrupted Keachin's reaming of a lowly freshman girl to say she saw Keachin's new red leather jacket on sale at Goodwill as part of a Santa outfit, it put her on the Fashion Tyrant's radar in the worst way.

I didn't see what happened in the bathroom after that, but I heard. Everyone heard.

Nina's crutches got "misplaced," and she was forced to crawl across the filthy floor, crying for help. No one heard her until class change, over an hour later. The vice principal had to carry her to the nurse's office while everyone watched.

When the administration questioned Nina about the assault (make no mistake, that's what it was—not a joke, or some "kids being kids" BS), Nina kept quiet in some misguided attempt to honor the code of the streets. Snitches end up in ditches, or something.

I don't blame her for that. I've been there.

But now I'm *here*, doing what Nina can't do for herself. I depress the shutter release, capturing Keachin's tryst with Coach Eric Bottin, gym teacher and fearless leader of our district champion football team.

I take more photos, fighting the unease of watching such a personal, and possibly illegal, *performance*. Of all the times I've done this—of all the secrets I've exposed—this is easily the most mind-blowing.

Get every detail, Panda.

Increasing my aperture, ramping down my shutter speed, and a bunch of other tiny in-the-moment adjustments are the difference between crisp images and blurry abstractions in such low light. I make all these changes across the mission control–style menus in my camera without looking. Like Petra Dobrev—a celebrity in the wildlife photography community and my idol—says you should.

"When you're shooting a pride in Africa," Petra says in her instructional photography DVD, *Lensing Wild Things*, "you want your eyes on those hungry lionesses, not your switches and buttons."

Then again, Petra also says, "If you're determined to shoot hungry lionesses, I recommend a camera trap. The plastic and metal are much less appetizing than flesh and bone."

A camera trap shoots without a photographer being in the vicinity. Great if you know where your prey will be ahead of time. My work rarely has that sort of predictability, so I have to know my camera the way a blind man knows Braille. I use it the same way I use my lungs. Inhale, adjust exposure. Exhale, shoot.

The car's bouncing motion increases with such verve, I hear the suspension squeaking. There's a final groan from the shock absorbers, and it's done; a panting Keachin hurls her sweaty self into the driver's seat as if Coach Bottin is suddenly too hot to touch. He twists and shifts oddly. After a second, I realize it's the motion I use when I tug on my jeans lying down.

Maybe they're too tired to perform whatever limber maneuver got them into opposite seats, because they open their respective doors and circle to the rear of the car, where Keachin adjusts her skirt and gives him a brief peck on the lips before reentering the vehicle for Coach Bottin to drive her home. I've got shots of it all. The hungry lioness never knows I'm there.

There's another piece to Petra's advice, though. A piece I forget. Or ignore because I'm giddy over the debauchery gold that's now stored on my SD card.

"When you're watching a beast, ensure no other beast is watching you. Lest you're caught unaware. The roles of 'hunter' and 'prey' can reverse with a breath and a pounce."

Coach Bottin and Keachin drive away, and I gather my equipment to make the hike back to my own car. Never realizing that I'm not alone, and I'm not talking about a raccoon.

We're all something we don't know we are. In that moment, I have no idea that I've gone from watcher . . . to watched.

CHAPTER 3

IT'S 10:37 P.M. WHEN I GET home, nearly an hour past my weekday curfew, and there's mud on my steering wheel.

I'm in my beat-up Chevy, parked in the driveway behind Mom's Honda and Dad's truck. I have four missed calls from my parents, and every light is on in our house, like they're looking for me behind the furniture. I peel off my dirty gloves, shimmy free of my dark zippered hoodie. Hitting the switch on the dome light, I check my face in my visor mirror for smudges, sweat, and/or blood. When you're sneaking through the woods, hopped up on adrenaline, you might not feel a stray branch or briar scrape you. With my complexion, the slightest scratch looks like I've been mauled.

I'm claw-mark free, so I take the time to mentally rehearse my story while I pop my trunk to stow some of my more nefarious tools. My rolled-up shooter's blanket goes into the duffel bag with my climbing gloves, grappling hook, night-vision goggles, lock picks, a couple of wigs, and a few other knickknacks relating to my, er, hobby.

I push all that to the corner of the trunk and gently dress the bag in a bunch of car junk—jumper cables, a rusty jack, half-full bottles of tire cleaner.

I slip my Nikon case into my school backpack. That goes inside with me. Always. Before I start the show, I remove the battery from my cell, drop it in my hip pocket.

When I enter the house, hobbled by my heavy bag, they descend on me immediately. Parental hyenas.

"*Wo warst du, Lauren?*" Mom says. I can tell she's irritated because she's speaking German. *Lauren, where have you been?*

"*Bei Ocie, lernen.*" *At Ocie's, studying.* I answer back in German because it seems to calm her. She likes the bond.

"Try again," Dad says. "Ocie's mom said you finished studying over three hours ago." He sounds every bit the army drill sergeant he used to be. Sometimes I let him believe his intimidation voice still works on me. Like now.

"Yes, that's true." I reach into my bag and produce a kettlebell-heavy copy of *The Complete Shakespeare*, purchased yesterday. "We're doing *Macbeth* in Lit Studies, but the school's copies are all scuzzy. I went to the bookstore to grab my own. When I got there, pumpkin spice lattes got the best of me and I lost track of time in the photography section. Sorry."

Mom switches to English, but her accent comes through, she's still half-irritated. "There is no point for you to have a phone if you do not intend to answer."

"Battery died and I forgot my charger." I hold up my dark, dead cell. "See?"

My parents maintain their wide-legged, crossed-arm stances, and exchange looks. Mom softens first, relieved I'm home and not stuck in some serial killer's basement. Dad maintains the attitude, but I know how to soothe him. I produce another book, also purchased yesterday. "Saw it in the bio section and thought of you."

One corner of his mouth ticks, though he recovers quickly. He suppresses his grin as I hand over the biography on the late, great Sam Cooke. Dad's got a whole playlist dedicated to Cooke's songs, having proclaimed the singer/songwriter a genius many times. I suspect Mr. Cooke's music has some significance to my parents grand back-in-the-day romance. Unlike the *Blachindas*, I haven't heard any backstory here and I don't want to.

Mom glances at the book and they exchange looks again, this time with the *ewwww* factor cranked up. If I have a new sibling nine months from today, it will only be a mild shock. I sneak upstairs to my room while they're distracted. To finish my work.

Nudging the door shut severs a column of hallway light, leaving me in darkness, where I'm most comfortable. I unpack my camera and power it up. The hi-def display flares, casting me in blue light before tonight's photos appear. Cycling through them, mentally flagging the best shots, I'm short of breath.

"This is real," I say, the depravity stuttering before me like a flip book.

Pushing a button on my desk lamp illuminates the soft marble eyes of two dozen panda bears. Or rather their glossy photos, plastered on the wall over my desk in a neat grid. I take my chair, plug my camera into my MacBook, and view the images in a larger aspect, each mouse click causing my pulse to snap. I've got more than forty usable shots, but I only need a few to tell the story. The imaginations of my many loyal followers will fill in any blanks.

Minimal touch-ups are needed. A slight hue adjustment makes the skin tones more natural—wouldn't want Keachin's flawless makeup to go unnoticed. Then, some shifts in the levels to decrease the shadows. Almost done. One final touch, a caption.

Keachin Myer takes phys ed way too seriously.

I publish the pictures to *Gray Scales*, my anonymous photoblog. The site's done up in all the shades of gray, except for the photos I reveal. I even have the blindfolded justice lady with the sword and the scales as my logo. When I post the Keachin/Coach photos, it triggers an alert on the cell phones, tablets, laptops, and PCs of my subscribers. The whole school.

All my various social media are arranged in separate windows on my desktop. Twitter, Facebook, Tumblr, and, of course, the comments on *Gray Scales*. I watch them refresh for the next hour as the scandal goes wide and the world sees what Keachin Myer really is.

When I pop the battery back into my cell, it immediately buzzes with an incoming text. I already know who it's from.

> **Ocie**: Oh Sugar Honey Iced Tea. Gray strikes again. Have u seen?
>
> **Me**: I don't pay attention to that trash. It's like high school soaps.
>
> **Ocie**: Today's episode is TV-MA. You've got 2 check the site. Keachin Myer and Coach Bottin. Emphs on AND
>
> **Me**: No way. I don't believe it.
>
> **Ocie**: Totes. It's like porn. Or prom.

The texts go on, Ocie having a gossip aneurism, me playing dumb. I'm still watching my monitor so I see the email the moment it comes in.

The sender's address is unfamiliar, **SecretAdm1r3r**. I might've written it off as penis-growth spam and doomed it to my junk folder if not for the subject.

A PANDA in her natural habitat.

I want to believe it's innocent, some marketing thing triggered by all the wildlife sites I visit. But the caps lock on "PANDA" makes me uneasy before I open my in-box. Part of me knows.

I preview the message, dropping my phone when I see the embedded photo.

It's me, skulking through the woods at the scene of Keachin's tryst. Another message arrives, same subject, but this one is a wide shot of me taking pictures of Coach Bottin's car. A third message/photo comes through, this one of me by my car as I lose my footing and plant both gloved hands in a huge mud puddle to keep from falling on my camera.

Me. Me. Me.

The pictures even come with a caption: *How do you get the color Gray? Throw a Panda in the blender and turn it on.*

Even though the sender's grasp of color theory is suspect, I get the point.

I'm busted.

CHAPTER 4

WHEN I STARTED THIS WHOLE GRAY business, the second person I exposed was Darius Ranson, a Portside baseball star who'd developed a pregame ritual known as "Target Practice." It went like this: Darius and his storm troopers snatch some frail/shy/defenseless underclassman and drive him to Kart Krazy, a run-down arcade and go-kart track. Also on the premises, batting cages.

The owner was a huge baseball fan who gives—*gave*—any Portside Pirate player the run of the place, which was all but deserted on weekdays. Darius and his teammates used one batting cage exclusively, having removed most of the safety netting to meet their needs. In that cage, they tied up their victim somewhere *behind* the pitching machine. If Portside's next-day opponent had a weak left fielder, the underclassman got positioned to the left. If the right field was vulnerable, he was placed to the right. Then, Darius and the rest would take turns popping line drives over the kid's head. If he was lucky.

Stupid. Illegal. Dangerous. All words applied. Inevitably, something went wrong. A concussion-and-broken-nose wrong. Claiming the injury happened innocently—intimidating the battered kid to back up a ridiculous story—Darius snaked out of any consequences and resumed Target Practice with updated safety regulations. New targets got an umpire's mask.

I did my thing, taking pictures of a Target Practice session from two hundred yards away with a telephoto lens. Had to climb a tree for those shots. Among my pictures were a few of Darius making a shady exchange with Kart Krazy's owner. Cash for a crumpled paper bag. It got me thinking about our star shortstop, and how he excelled beyond so much of the competition in the district. A couple of days later, I snuck into the team's locker room during a Saturday practice and picked Darius's lock. That's how I discovered his steroid stash.

A few quick snaps with my cell phone and I had a complete collage. *Gray Scales* was new then, so it took days instead of hours, but word spread.

Kart Krazy was shut down, the owner arrested for dealing dope and endangering minors. Strict drug-testing rules were implemented for all Portside High athletes. Darius got kicked off the team, then expelled thanks to zero tolerance. Harsh, maybe. But so was bouncing baseballs off other humans for fun.

Busting him was a flagship moment for my crusade. What I did made a difference.

I think of Darius as I click through the candid photos of me spying on Keachin and Coach Bottin. On to the next I go, not seeing myself, but the unsuspecting faces I've dragged into the light of day over the last three years, exposing their twisted moments.

Darius threatened to kill "the guy" who outed him. Surely the dozen others who've suffered his fate have similar vendettas. This is so, so bad.

There's always been a buzz around the school. Who is Gray? Whenever a new scandal debuts on the site, along come new theories. An angry friend or jilted ex. It *has* to be someone close to the exposed. Everyone watches too many cop shows.

It's never personal. Not after that first time. That's how I don't get caught.

Until now.

How could I *not* notice someone else with a camera out there? How many of *my* targets think the same thing?

I hit REPLY on the first email, type, and send a single-line message: *Who are you? What do you want?*

The mystery photographer won't reply. That's what I expect. But I'm wrong. I get a response almost immediately.

;)

That's all. An emoticon. I resist the urge to demand answers, realizing the stranger's response is an accurate one. He's enjoying my anxiety. Winky face.

Ocie keeps texting past midnight, but I don't have it in me to respond. I sit up all night, scared, barely noticing the Sam Cooke music coming through the walls from my parents' room. I wait for the secret photographer's pictures to go live somewhere, outing me as I've done to so many others. At dawn I'm still waiting. It never happens.

And that scares me more.

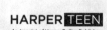